I0589249

"Theatre Wagon" is a prequel to the stage disaster novel
"And Burnt The Topless Towers"

The author, Cliff Dix, has worked in the entertainment industry
for over fifty years. His autobiographical reminiscences are
published in "Up The Fire Escape And Through The Kitchens"

To Ann, for her patient reading, with thanks.

THEATRE WAGON

All characters and events in this book are fictitious, and any resemblance to any person living or dead is purely co-incidental.

Chapter 1

John was not the slightest bit surprised.

He was irritated, in fact he was quite angry.

But he was not the slightest bit surprised.

She had acquired a bad reputation for late arrival. In fact she was known for it, and the rest of the company routinely waited for her arrival like courtiers dancing attendance on a great lady. Which was probably exactly what she liked, he thought.

The windscreen was misting over from the cold February morning air outside and the breath of three actors and a stage manager inside. It wasn't actually freezing this morning, but he turned the heater up to full and adjusted the direction of the blower so the warmer air cleared the screen. The condensation dispersed reluctantly from the bottom, starting with a couple of small arcs near the vents, and gradually, slowly, spreading upwards to let him see out completely. Still no sign of her.

Behind him the cast were silent, but for the rustle of the turning page of a tabloid newspaper.

He began to play his mental game again. It was a very simple game really. All you had to do was think of names for her. Well perhaps not names, epithets. Originally he'd amused himself by thinking of what he might call her to her face once this tour ended, but now he was trying to compile a full description of her and her behaviour, and in the past couple of days he'd decided on doing this alphabetically. His glee this morning at realising that 'B' stood for 'bitch' was enormous. He mused over further 'B's, a search that would occupy his idle moments for the rest of the day.

He looked at his watch. She was now a quarter of an hour late. Despite the habit he had formed of calling the company earlier than should have been necessary to reach the first venue of the day it was now going to be a real rush. It annoyed him. The rest of the company managed, daily, to be on time and ready. Her digs were easy walking distance from the company office that they routinely left from. He convinced himself that this was the studied lateness of self-importance.

Windscreen clear, he turned the heat down again. The fan motor whine reduced. He shrugged and slipped the van into gear to roll gently forward to the gate of the yard, stopping with the front bumper just outside the boundary. He could see straight along the street in the direction she would have to come from. There was no sign of her.

"Are we off then?" asked a voice from behind.

"Can't, till she arrives."

"It's a pity we can't manage without her royal highness."

"Yes," he agreed, "it might do her good to find she'd been left behind."

As he spoke he saw her come round the corner fifty yards away along the street. She gave no sign of haste, though he knew she'd seen the van ready, engine running, half out of the gateway. She came towards them with a conscious disdain and a flaunting swing of her hips, evident despite her winter coat.

A shopkeeper, in a sports jacket with leather patches on the elbows, came out of his doorway, carrying an 'A' board, which he set up on the pavement. She walked past him, and he stopped, leaning on the sign, looking after her as she went along in a frank study of her bottom. Luckily he didn't whistle at her. John knew that would have put her in a self-righteous temper for the rest of the day. He thought it strange that she could make such blatant use of her curves to get her own way, yet be so seemingly aggravated by anyone's admiration.

He was distracted, momentarily, by a young, pushchair pushing, mother, leading her children to school along the road that the yard opened onto, who scowled at him in the cab of the van, and made great play of having to steer her buggy around the front of the vehicle where it slightly blocked the path. By the time he looked back his missing actress was crossing the road towards them. She arrived at the van, and one of the cast slid the side door open so she could climb in. Barely waiting for her to seat herself he said;

"Belt up!"

and dropped the clutch viciously to swing out of the gateway and left into the morning traffic.

She sat down with a bump and scrabbled with the seatbelt. The actress in the passenger seat beside him looked at him disapprovingly, but he was concentrating on threading the van through the morning rush.

"Left!" the girl in the front seat said, "You need to go left here."

"I know."

'Heaven help us, he thought, we've been to all these damned schools before with one show or another. I should be trusted to know where the local ones are.' But obedient to the advice he worked the vehicle into the nearside lane. He had swung very wide out of the gates, and had gained several vehicle lengths in the outside lane by doing this. The manoeuvre was not popular with someone in the queue, and a sharp blast of a horn told them so.

The cause of their lateness had seated herself properly now, flicking her blonde hair into place and straightening the top of her coat, and was looking haughtily out of the van's side window. It was the only rear one you could actually see out of. Despite the fixed seating in the rear half of the company van, and the side windows, most of the vehicle was crammed tight with the scenery and props for the show. In places this equipment had had to be laid alongside the seats, between them and the windows, in order to make it all fit in. The comfort of the cast had been ignored in order to allow the show to tour in one vehicle. There was no conversation in the back this morning.

Scenery, he thought, was a bit of an exaggeration. The minimal scenic oddments that they were using gave no more than a suggestion of location. The production budget of a theatre in education show was not geared to spectacle or style. In any case the company's style was, like so many small scale touring shows, built on the premise that the actors were the core, the raison-de-être, of the piece. That was a conceit which only really worked if the actors were of exceptionally high quality. It was just an excuse for low budgets he felt. He missed the presentational aspects of what he thought of as 'real theatre'. He doubted the much-used excuse that giving the pupils a taste of performance would lead them to become avid theatre-goers. Frankly he doubted that the presentation of this piece would enlighten them much about the set text that it was based on either. Could any pupil's exam result really be improved by a cheap performance of part of the plot of a set book?

He indicated, and, lucky with the traffic lights, swung the wheel to set them running out of the town into the leafier suburbs.

"Fork right up here, John."

He shouldn't be annoyed. The girl in the front seat was trying to help. He reminded himself that she'd only joined the company at the start of this show. She hadn't trailed through these same dreary, smelly echoey school halls with several shows. To be fair to her though he wondered whether she really liked theatre in education touring. He wondered if anyone did. Had her ambitions at drama school really been for low budget performances of worthy pieces in front of disinterested classes of teenagers in halls where an actor's likely stage direction might read 'enter from by the fire extinguisher'? Had she aspired to a real stage in a real theatre, with all the associated attractions? Or was she, perhaps, just grateful for a few weeks of regular paid employment before slinking back to the world of casual labour; of washing up in back street cafés or serving behind noisy bars in a succession of pubs. Perhaps not, he thought. Though helpful and eager to please she was the most withdrawn member of the company, or of any company he had dealt with.

He thought of the job as a stop gap, which had dragged on till now he was on his third tour, and third school text adaptation with the company. From the outset he had told himself it would only be for a few weeks. His own career had always previously been in real theatre venues, working on shows that lived or died by the box office. In that world the entertainment of the public was king, not satisfying the curriculum demands of the next set of exams. His audiences had been attending because they wanted to, not through compulsion. His audiences had expected, and, generally, received entertainment. His audiences had gone to the theatres he had worked to have fun. He mused, wistfully, that his previous work had also offered spectacle through its content. 'Fun', not the pompous, and to him, the boredom of the sort of texts chosen by exam boards. This would be the last, he promised himself.

Today would be the dull round of a couple of schools, this one for the morning, another just like it for the afternoon.

"..and left at the next junction."

They would arrive, he knew, to antipathetic staff, only one of whom had booked them. A vague possibility of a couple of boys from among the pupils to help with the get-in. Always boys, he mused, never girls. These helpers would be conspicuously missing when it came to the get-out and loading, he predicted, whisked away to their next class.

There it was, just ahead. A new, or newish, school, blocky in appearance with its flat metal framed windows set almost flush with the exterior brickwork so that the whole edifice had a featureless, slab sided look. The architect had tried to relieve this appearance by adding rectangular panels, the size of, and between, the ground and first floor windows. These were flat, and painted in a range of pastel colours with no apparent logic to the sequence. They gave the building a slight air of being a painter's shade card, from which the builders had yet to make a choice. As he turned up the main driveway, past the sign that informed visitors of the headmaster's name and the office telephone number, he could see the concrete lintel above the main entrance steps, embossed with the school's name in a spindly Roman typeface: The Thomas Lincoln School.

He was aware of the cast behind him shifting in their seats. There was the click of a seat belt being undone and the rustle of a newspaper being folded.

He was forced to jockey around a couple of school buses, which had dropped their passengers and were idling before moving off, and to slow for the tail end pupils arriving for the day, to make his way to a space more or less adjacent to the side doors of the school hall. The late arriving pupils mostly ignored the van. The hall was to the right of the main doors. He'd been to this school before and knew its layout.

Once he had stopped the van the cast piled out of the side sliding door, dragging bags and cases with them, and headed for the building. His front seat passenger paused a moment longer. It struck him how very young she seemed.

"Shall we help off-loading?"

His mood mellowed a bit. At least one of the cast wasn't treating him as a servant today.

"You go with the others and get into costume," he smiled at her, and relieved to have avoided the off-loading, and, perhaps pleased that his temper seemed to have improved, the young actress smiled at him and jumped out of the front door of the van, following the rest of the company into the hall.

He set about the task of dragging the odds and ends of furniture and props, that served as the bulk of the setting, out of the vehicle and through the side doors. He made numerous trips back and forth. During his absence at the van fetching one of the loads one of the actors had come and acquired the costume rail. He assumed it had found its way to what would pass as a dressing room here. The hall was indistinguishable from a thousand other school halls across the land. An over polished wooden floor with sports court markings painted onto it was surrounded by tall brick walls punctuated by floor to ceiling metal framed windows, some of which were double doors, with long patterned curtains, mainly in shades of rust brown, hanging beside. Most of these curtains, even in this fairly new school, had come away from their track at one or another end and now hung badly as a result. One end of the hall boasted a small balcony area over the corridor that fed the main entrance doors, which were positioned just below the front of the balcony. At the opposite end a platform stage, with stairs either side, was hidden from view by maroon house tabs about four or five feet away from the stage edge. He knew that behind these would be a clutter of tables and abandoned rostrum blocks. A vague odour of cabbage hung in the air. He ignored the stage and proceeded to set up the 'show' on the floor of the hall.

He glanced up towards the roof, more in hope than expectation, and decided not to attempt to light the performance. The ragged curtains would never have provided a blackout against daylight even when new, and access to focus the rather mean selection of small lanterns, which, despite being fairly new, showed a distressingly thick layer of dust, would need to be from either a scaffolding tower, or at least an exceptionally tall ladder. Neither was in evidence so he gave up the idea, as he was forced to do so often in school halls.

He laid out the furniture and the bits of scenic backing with the upstage edge against the hall's stage platform. Then he dragged some of the stacking chairs around the space to enclose the performance area on the other three sides in what is known as 'thrust' format. Personally he disliked any layout but endstage, but the company had originally rehearsed the show for thrust owing to the director's preferences, and although they would accept whatever layout he decided on, because nominally it was his decision at each venue, he took the line of least resistance whenever he could. It just wasn't worth the discussion that sometimes followed when he had made an endstage decision.

He went in search of the company. They were in a store room off the corridor that ran across the rear of the stage. It was a cold, breeze-block constructed room, with narrow slit windows near the ceiling. Most of the space was occupied by sports equipment, but the actors were making the best of it. The girls had retreated behind a couple of wooden vaulting horses and a tangle of crates loaded with unwieldy items like balls and rackets. They had already donned their costumes, although the boys in the company were milling around a small table in a semi-dressed state. Trousers were conspicuously missing in their cases, and the focus of attention was on the kettle and mugs, balanced on the table, which had just that moment boiled, distracting the actors from changing. The company carried a wooden case with kettle, mugs and tea, coffee and sugar. Only John took sugar, but, as the drinks kit was all his, the provision was there. In theory the cast chipped in a few coins to keep the stock replenished. In practice John added teabags and coffee to the normal weekly shopping for his flat.

He glanced at his watch. Yes, just about time for them to have a cup of coffee before the scheduled start time.

"Seen any sign of the school staff?" he queried, shuffling the paperwork he held in his hand.

The cast shook their heads, and one of them held up the coffee jar and looked at him with a 'do you want one?' type gesture.

"No thanks. I'd better go and chase up the local staff."

"One came by and said they'd be back after registration." said one of the actors.

"Do you know who it was?"

"No. A youngish woman. She wasn't very friendly."

He made his way out of the assembly hall into the main entrance and along the coridoor to reception. The glass was closed across the window, and the secretaries were visible at their desks inside. He stood at the window. The secretaries ignored him, though, as they sat facing the window, they could not have failed to see him. Resignedly he gave the bell a slight ping. One secretary looked up and straight down at some paperwork, the other continued to ignore him, though she was nearest, being within a yard of the window. It annoyed him. He waited, then gave a longer press of the bell and the woman who had initially ignored him came to the window, opened it and said, "Yes?" uninvitingly.

"I'm with the TIE team in the hall. We need to tell er..." he hesitated and glanced down at the crumpled booking sheet on the top of the pile of papers he held, "Miss Robinson that we are ready."

"Along that corridor, second door on the right," informed the receptionist, and stopped further conversation by sliding the glass shut. John considered ringing the bell again to say a sarcastic 'thank you' when she came back, but thought better of it. He set off along the wide, echoing corridor.

He, and the company, had been to this school before. And he vaguely remembered Miss Robinson. This present cast probably didn't, because not all of them would have been in the last show he'd brought here. John Mason's intentions to return to professional shows were firm, and re-enforced by this sort of reception, but the director of 'Theatre Wagon', as the company was styled, had pressed him to staying for a second, and now a third show. All book adaptations, and all with tiny casts, doubling parts to present books that happened to be on the syllabus at that moment, these were not his choice of show. But repeat visits to schools had some advantages. It was convenient to have an idea of where you were driving to without constantly referring to a street map while at the wheel. In this case, knowing the building layout had meant that he had been able to set up without reference to the staff.

John mused about his favoured entertainment shows. He liked an audience that had both chosen to attend and would leave with a happy glow, preferably whistling some hit from the show. He yearned to return to the magic of houselights fading down to glowing, warm, welcoming tabs that flew out to reveal a stunning scene that would draw a spontaneous round of applause from a willing public. Willingness was very unlikely with press-ganged pupils, unless they saw it as an escape from the classroom. Only a very small minority of any class of pupils would actually chose to read the classics, which are mostly dated period pieces with little relevance to the lives or interests of a secondary school pupil in the mid 1980s, he thought. It was impossible that press-ganged pupils would experience the 'suspension of disbelief' that draws an audience into a staged and happy show in a theatre while they were perched on hard seats in a bleak hall with precious little staging to disguise the surroundings.

He swore to himself once again as he walked down that corridor that no matter how the director pressed him, this would be the last tour with Theatre Wagon. The internal friction the unloved actress caused daily within the company made his decision even more determined.

He reached the second door. Although the school was less than ten years old the paintwork was chipped and one of the lower metal panels was badly dented. The early gloss of this building had worn off and the pupils were clearly treating it with careless contempt. He knocked, and, knowing that teachers rarely heard a door knock above the hubbub of a class; opened it and stuck his head inside. It was not as he'd expected. The pupils, who were about fifteen, were seated at desks in formal rows with cowed expressions. Miss Robinson stood at the front of the class. Clearly, he heard the tail end of her sentence as he looked in, mid-way through giving her charges a fierce and threatening lecture about how to behave at the coming performance in the hall, which seemed to him to be calculated to discourage them from any element of enjoyment.

She was quite young, in her mid-twenties he thought, but dressed in a plain grey suit with her rather dull brown hair tied back. Her face was humourless, and her mouth, which she now shut rather sharply as she faced him, turned down sourly when at rest. There was clear annoyance in her posture and expression.

"Ah, Miss Robinson?" he said as she looked at him, "John Mason from the TIE team. We're ready in the hall."

She eyed him up and down with something like disdain. It made him feel a bit uncomfortable and rather aware of a scruffiness caused by getting the scenery into the building and setting it up. Perhaps he should have taken a moment in the dressing room to comb his hair. By comparison to most of the cast his usual dress was fairly respectable. He wondered if he was letting his standards slip.

"I will collect the other classes and we will be there shortly. Be so good as to wait." she said.

'Be so good'? he thought. Who talks like that these days? But he answered "Thank you. See you shortly" before withdrawing. He shouldn't have done it really, but as he left he looked at the class, who were naturally all looking his way, and winked. A few of the girls giggled. Miss Robinson, who couldn't see the wink from her position, raised her voice at the class.

"That's quite enough of that."

He went back to the cast. Coffee cups were empty, and costumes had been donned. He told them that the classes were on their way, and moments later the hall doors could be heard to crash open. The scraping, banging and chattering of several dozen pupils echoed around the room as they dragged stacking chairs into position around the performance area he had marked out. Teacher's voices could be heard above the din, scolding, instructing and remonstrating. No group of school children ever seemed to be able to resist the opportunity to shout and chatter at high volume. No school architect seemed to be able to build any hall that was not an echo chamber that would exaggerate and amplify the noise of a class.

'What a way to start a performance.' he thought.

He began rounding up his little flock of performers into the appropriate order for them to enter, checking occasionally with particular actors that they had props they needed. This should have been entirely the individual actors' responsibility, but he'd found that they were regularly unable to look after themselves and his professional pride went against his natural instinct to try to teach them a lesson by letting them fall as a result of their own failings.

Once the cast was gathered in the doorway of the storeroom he went out into the hall and over to the teachers who were standing around behind their, mostly now seated, charges. One held out his hand in greeting. John shook it.

"Tony Seymore, Head of Drama," said the handshaker.

"John Mason. I'm the stage manager." He had found long ago

18

that the term 'company manager' easily confused people outside the profession. "Say when you want us to start."

"I'll just say a few words to them and then hand over to you." John's expression was glum as he stood and waited while Tony Seymore gave a dull, predictable talk to the pupils, covering a precis of the book plot and an exhortation to behave while the performance was under way. Looking round he could see Miss Robinson seated against a wall with a clear view of the pupils, but hardly one of the 'show', scowling with dislike at the proceedings. The third teacher in the room was unfamiliar to him, but was also clearly disinterested, and had even settled with a pile of marking on his lap meaning to use the time to do paperwork.

The hall itself was lit by its floor to ceiling windows on one side. On the other a row of roller shutters, closed now, would, he was sure, be the serving hatches for dinner. He glanced at his watch. If they didn't start soon they would run into the dinner time. Eventually the teacher wound up his talk and nodded to John, who looked over to the cast and waved 'go' to them. With commendable energy they launched into the performance.

Chapter 2

John settled himself on an uncomfortable stacking chair by the side wall. Realistically he had nothing to do while the actors performed on occasions like this where they couldn't use lighting. The show was blocked so the cast themselves did any of the minor scene changes, which really only meant re-positioning a few pieces of furniture, as the action progressed. None the less he forced himself to watch, and to make a few notes in the diary sized pad he was carrying. He noted 'time up', and added a brief description of the school, and of the staff attitudes. These notes went back to the company's office, and were supposed to influence what requests might be made if there was another booking from that school. In fact the company simply filed the show reports. Whatever criticism a company manager out on the road might issue there was no way that the TIE office would ever turn down a booking from any school, even if some of them probably deserved to be excluded. John understood the financial reasons for this, and how rejections might affect grants, but still felt that some form of protest could be sent when it was warranted.

When he had started with them he had made a point of digging past show reports out of the system to see what he could expect at different schools. He had soon discovered that previous casts had been very lax about giving any useful information, and that fore-knowledge made no great difference anyway. He'd played this school with a previous production, although on that occasion it had been an afternoon performance, and the get-out, he remembered, had been fraught due to pupils gathering in the hall ready for buses.

As he daydreamed, and the actors went through their lines and moves in front of what was clearly a not too interested audience, he became aware of noises on the other side of the wall he sat against. He had been right about the shutters. Obviously this wall backed on to the kitchens. He tried hard not to become too annoyed at the disturbance, as it was impossible for him to do anything about it. In any case the teachers ignored it, either marking papers, frowning at the proceedings or watching with seeming rapt attention according to their moods.

The teachers, and pupils, were all seemingly able to ignore the occasional bursts of bell-ringing from electric bells which had been positioned immediately outside the glass double doors between the hall and the main coridors outside.

He sighed. This was not 'theatre'. This was, as it always was with theatre in education, he thought, glorified child-minding. Noticeably the children being minded were also somewhat bored by the long show. Under the threatening gaze of Miss Robinson they remained as quiet as you could reasonably expect. The whisperings and scuffles were occasional and scattered. But he could tell that they were mostly not really interested. One or two were possibly following the story, but then as the text was on their syllabus they should have been able to track even the convoluted plot of the classic novel almost despite the abridged nature of this adaptation.

He watched his actors. 'Bloody-minded', he decided, adding to 'B' in his alphabetical string of epithets about her. She played the lead, of course. Sweeping around the performance area like a diva. It was rather out of keeping for the character she was playing. He'd not bothered to read the novel. He, like the bulk of the pupils, had no interest in classical literature, but he'd gathered enough of the original plot from being with the show to form that opinion. They were reaching the fire scene. Soon the actors, without the benefit of any effects, would run about wildly, waving long strips of red and orange cloth in an attempt to convince the audience that the house was burning down. The clatters from the kitchens were more noticeable now as the early lunchtime approached, and John was grateful, on behalf of his actors, that the kitchen noise coincided with the loud fire scene.

For all his dislike of the girl's behaviour and his antipathy toward the business of theatre in education he didn't feel that the actors should really have to work against such interruption of their performances. Sadly, from that point of view, the reunion of the now blinded Rochester and Jane, the emotional culmination of the piece, was played to the redoubled efforts of the caterers to provide a percussion backing track.

The cast took their bow to this and somewhat muted applause and were barely off the 'stage' before the shutters were flung up and furniture shifting commenced.

Hastily John gathered the scattered furniture and props and shoved them into the corridor near where the cast were changing back into street clothes. No one offered to help, and the sensation was, he felt, like that experienced by a small field rodent trying to escape the oncoming combine harvester, as tables and chairs were positioned all around him for the coming meal. He plodded back and forth to the van, hot from the labour despite the chill air outside, restacking the show in the vehicle.

They were just about to leave the building, the cast grumbling slightly at the rather average reception for their efforts, at the failure of the school to provide them with lunch and at John's gentle chivvying that was needed to speed them to the next school for the afternoon show, when Miss Robinson appeared.

"Thank you," she said, in a tone that implied she didn't really mean it. "It was.." she paused, searching for a word, "interesting."

The cast made grateful noises, missing the implied criticism.

"I don't approve of cutting pieces from a text, or modifying it to suit what you want to do, as opposed to what the author meant."

John thought he'd better come to the rescue.

"Well it's a good job there were cuts, or the dinner ladies would

still be waiting to start. It's a very long book you know."
"And for good reason. We can't be expected to give the pupils a feel for the style, the depth, of a classic novel by cutting bits out."

It could become a bitter dispute, thought John, if I really cared. But it wouldn't be good public relations. He was just about to do one of those 'I'm sorry you feel that way' speeches when Tony Seymore arrived.

"I wanted to thank you before you left," his glance and gesture encompassed the whole cast and John, "and say how much I think it helped the pupils. I would have been here sooner, but I had to dismiss my class. I think what you did was great. Half our pupils won't even have read the book, so it will have been a great help to them."

"I have made sure my class have read it." said his colleague, "I'm not sure that the version we've just seen will have educated any of your pupils who've not read it. It's a set text. They must read it. Their exam results will depend on it."

Tony Seymore looked at her, bit his tongue, and held out his hand for handshakes all round. Any further conversation was curtailed anyway by the jangle of electric bells, louder, even overpowering, here in the corridor, and the cast, mouthing 'thank you' made their way out to the van.

John climbed into the driver's seat again. The cast shuffled about. By some sort of unwritten agreement they generally rotated the seating, so each had a turn at the front seat, and at the unobscured window seat in the back. John looked to his left. The actor playing Rochester had the front seat for this trip. He started the engine and set off toward the school gates.

Adam Alexander played the male lead. He adjusted the angle of the back of the passenger seat to suit himself as they passed along the driveway.

"I think that woman was probably right," he commented as the van passed the gates out onto the suburban streets, "we don't have enough time to show the kids all the depth of the text, I mean, when do we show the difference between the moneyed class and the workers?"

John leant forward and looked to his left across Adam, whose face was half obscured as ever by his long, rather lank, dark hair, as they negotiated a junction.

"I didn't think there was much class distinction in the thing, unless you count the orphanage," he said, straightening up on the road they'd turned into.

"My point exactly. We should be teaching the pupils about the inequalities of that era, and the class struggle."

"If we are supposed to be teaching them, heaven help us, I thought we were supposed to be pushing them towards reading the set text for their exams." John never liked the use of theatre for political ends, and even if this was not what he would call 'theatre' he certainly disliked the use of school for those ends. Besides, he thought, it's bad enough for the poor kids that they are condemned to study these 'worthy' bits of outdated fiction just to pass exams.

It was hard to tell if the rest of the company were following this exchange of views. Crammed in the back of the vehicle they were, as usual, either staring at the passing streets, or reading newspapers and magazines, or, as it was lunchtime, eating packed lunches. John could hear crisp packets being opened, but no conversation. He made a mental note that he would need to sweep the back of the van out when he got a chance. Idly he wondered when they would next be at a school where he could leave the cast to it, like this morning, and take the opportunity of an empty vehicle to do this. He ran his mind over what he could remember of the itinerary. Yes tomorrow afternoon was a probable one.

Adam wanted to continue the chance to put forward his views. He was always keen to try for a convert. Realistically he knew from the chats he and the company had had with John during this run that he was probably dealing with a lost cause. He didn't see much prospect of converting their company manager to 'proper' opinions. He differed from John in his political slant, in his attitude to theatre in education, indeed in his view of theatre in general. His views had been moulded by three years at a drama school which had been staffed by former actors with strong political leanings. Already youthfully biased that way, Adam had taken every opportunity during his time there to absorb his tutors' views and discuss the inequalities of the world with them and other like-minded students. Shows that had been staged at this drama school were utterly slanted to his views, and he revelled in the propagandist background they had given him.

John steered the van through the remaining outskirts and they joined a main road that would take them right through the city centre. That route led them along a road past the Imperial Theatre, one of the country's great venues. John looked at it wistfully as they crawled past in a queue. He could not resist a comment:

"Real theatre."

Adam rose instantly to the bait. "They don't do proper shows. There's no message."

"No, you're right, there's no message, just real entertainment."

"Pah!" Adam made a noise of disgust, "Mindless musicals and variety."

John pitied him.

Despite the lunchtime traffic they were able to make a fast run to the neighbouring town where, with a combination of half remembered route and a folded town map, they came to the next school on time. This was a different school altogether. Superficially it was old and slightly run down, but a couple of new buildings sprouted from its site. One was, naturally, John thought, a sports hall; but one, unusually, was a small theatre. He'd been to this venue before too. It was a studio theatre, which seemed to John a shame, when it could equally well have been built as a 'proper' endstage theatre with all the advantages that would have offered. None the less he welcomed the possibility that he would be able to get the show staged in a manner that presented it as a performance, rather than a shambles of mumming on a flat floor.

They went in through the gates, and were met on the driveway by a teacher and three pupils. Smart, in expensive uniforms, the pupils stood alongside the driveway with a master in an almost caricature sports jacket with leather patches on the elbows. He slowed the van, and one of the pupils came to the driver's window saying "Follow us please."

John was already swinging the van in the right direction, but he allowed them to lead to the theatre. Once there the pupils helped off-loading the van, guiding the cast to the basic but clean dressing rooms and assisting John in setting up. For a few minutes it was almost like returning to 'real' theatre. The cast were delighted to have dressing tables and mirrors. John was pleased to be able to set the show in what he saw as a proper staging, even if that was an open stage with no proscenium, and once done he looked into the lighting situation. The master had vanished, leaving the three boys to attend to the show.

"Come and show me the lighting," he said to the schoolboys, and followed them as they led the way up the rake of the auditorium seating to a door in the back wall. The seats were upholstered in black and mounted on a charcoal grey carpeted tiered unit that could be moved into different configurations. He took a cursory glance up at the lighting gear suspended over the stage area and the auditorium. Inside the control room became crowded with bodies and loud with staccato explanations. John ignored most of these, allowing the boys to turn on the power, and demonstrate the desk to him. He didn't need the desk explained. His background was such that no school was going to have lighting control equipment that he couldn't drive. He barely looked at this one. It was typical of recent school installations, with manual and memory control of a couple of dozen dimmers. The front edge of the desk had been adorned with a selection of sticky labels with notes and numbers, scribbled on in a variety of both handwriting and pens.

John reached in his pocket, took out a reel of white tape, and stuck this straight over the existing labels. He got a black pen from his top pocket, sat down at the desk and said,
"Right, let's see what we've got."

Once again there was a quick jabber of largely unnecessary information. He chose to ignore it and began a routine flash through the channels, writing a cryptic note on his tape beside each one. There would be no time to refocus and colour any of the lanterns, but he could make a stab at lighting the show. Watched by the boys he plotted a few states into empty memories of the desk.

Time was running out. He ran back down to the stage and re-positioned a bit of the set to match where the lighting was, then went to the dressing rooms to make sure that the cast were ready. He was only just in time, as he could hear their audience coming in over the show relay speakers.

'Luxury,' he thought. Show relay and calls to the dressing rooms. It was hardly necessary for this show, as the tiny cast meant that no-one was off-stage long enough to make use of a dressing room to wait for their next entrance.

He passed back through the stage and auditorium to the control room. Pupils were filing into seats, harangued and ordered by teachers. He recognised the one that had met them by the gates as they arrived. They met at the back of the auditorium by the control room door. The door was painted in black gloss. The walls were painted in black emulsion. The building had that oppressive, if practical, studio theatre feel that had become the fashion ever since the start of the seventies and was now established wherever theatre was staged under the banner of being one of 'the arts'.

"I think we're pretty much ready. Have you got to do any introduction?" he asked.

"No, no, you carry on. All the pupils are in now, so as soon as they are sat down you can start."

He thanked the master, relieved to find the show would be allowed to stand on its own two feet without a teacher's preamble, and went back into the control room. There was a backstage calls system over the lighting desk.

"Ladies and gentlemen this is your beginners' call." he announced down the mic.

He sat down behind the desk.

"You lads stopping up here?" he queried.

They nodded. He guessed that they were pleased to be an elite that didn't have to passively watch the show. For the first time he had a moment to form an opinion of them. Two were so alike they might have been brothers, though maybe it was the uniform that tended to give that impression. The other was rather serious, skinny, and had numerous ink stains on his right hand fingers.

"I'm Brian, this is Andrew."

He noticed that somehow the third boy with the ink stains wasn't included in the introductions.

"Want to do the houselights?" he asked Inky.

"Yeh!" enthused the youngster. John had the impression that he'd not been allowed this, or been given any other minor privilege, before.

There was a slight murmer of dissent from the other two boys, but John has cast the die now.

"I'm John", he told them, "All ready? OK, Standby houselights." he looked behind him at the others, "Stay around in case I need you to tell me where things are," he said, as a sop to their self importance.

Inky reached over John's shoulder to a rotary switch on the wall by the window.

"Houselights go," John said, quietly.

The boy turned the knob. It wasn't the smoothest fade ever. To start with he'd failed to angle his grip on the control, so he ran out of turn on his wrist before reaching the end of the potentiometer's travel. In addition the fader was designed so at the end of the fade the houselights were still just perceptibly on, and the switch had then to also be pressed to actually turn the lights off. John made no comment, faded the preset lighting state on the stage area down to a blackout, waited for a beat to allow the cast to enter, and faded up what he had decided on for the opening scene. The cast began the performance.

"He hasn't done houselights before," one of the boys said, in a loud whisper.

"Don't worry," John whispered back, writing the time up on his pad, "He has now."

'Inky' loitered uncertainly near the window.

From John's point of view it was just another standard performance. It had the slight gloss of being given a bit of a lift from some lighting and being staged in a properly blacked out, and, from the point of view of school bells and kitchen noise, sound proofed space. So far as the performance by the cast went it was unexceptional. He noticed, despite that, that Brian and Andrew were watching the leading lady closely through the control room window. If they only knew what she was like, he thought to himself. He watched her too, but thinking once again of suitable epithets, and wondering at the unsuitable stage presence she displayed despite her character.

He followed the play with half-hearted attention, knowing it so well that even busking lighting as he was he could operate on a sort of autopilot. He was idly playing with a little row of fuses that were lying on the window-ledge, balancing them each on end, when the control room door opened and a master came in without any niceties, striding into the tiny space and confronting the three boys.

"What are you three doing in here?" the master barked, with little regard for the usual lowering of voice required by a performance.

"Keep it down a bit!" John said softly, before any of the school boys could speak. "..and they're helping me."

The intruder looked at him with the expression usually reserved for something nasty on a shoe, gave a loud humph, and left, making sure to slam the door as loudly as possible.

"Who's he?" John enquired mildly.

Once again there was an overlapping, but he was pleased to notice, soft, gabble of voices, from which he extracted the information that the visitor had been the gym master.

There were no further disturbances, and the play ploughed its way to the fire scene, where he was able to provide some flickering from the lighting rig to accompany the cast's running about, and the waving of the ribbons. He noticed that the ends of these ribbons were gradually fraying as the run of the show progressed, and made a note of this in the show report, intending to see if the company's part time wardrobe mistress could run a hem across the end of each sometime.

He gave them a tight area of lighting for the denouement, and brought a full state up for them to take bows. The applause was a bit better than it had been for the morning performance. They trooped off stage and he said:

"Houselights up."

'Inky' reversed his previous fade, though predictably he started turning the knob before pressing it in to switch the dimmer into the circuit so the houselights snapped on at about half and then faded up to full. Brian and Andrew grunted a 'typical' which John felt would do nothing for 'Inky's' confidence, so he commented:

"One day I'm going to find who these idiots are that put rotary push on/push off faders on houselights and encourage them to stick their fingers in a live socket." as he noted the time down.
The boys laughed, and somehow their internal tensions were broken by this and there was some chatter. As they'd been talking the classes had mostly left the auditorium and they walked down to the stage where the boys helped him with the strike and get-out.

Chapter 3

The cast said their goodbyes to a couple of members of staff and joined John at the van, where the three boys were still hanging around in the winter afternoon twilight, clearly trying to make their escape from teacher supervision last as long as possible. In any case the school day was winding down. He'd parked the van as near as possible to where they'd performed, and now the way out and off the school premises was almost completely blocked by the row of school buses waiting for the pupils. John urged his performers into the van. One arrived at the van carrying the box of tea things. He took it from her and thanked her. Then he thanked the boys once again, and, as he got in to the driver's seat he could hear bells inside the buildings announcing the end of classes for that day. Doors burst open from every visible wall of the surrounding buildings, and pupils of all ages swarmed out. He started the van, and eased gently forward through the throng, squeezing between the back of one bus and the front of another, onto the driveway out of the school.

On the way back to the company's offices he and the cast discussed the day and the afternoon performance. They had plenty of time to do so as they made the stop-start trek in the chilly, damp, gloomy, early school-run rush hour. He followed the tail-lights ahead of him.

Unsurprisingly, to John, Adam was putting forward the view that the morning show had been better because a bland school hall was less elitist in his opinion than a school that had a dedicated performance space. The cast generally didn't agree with this extreme view, but they were not slow to quibble about whether the afternoon staging had been ideal. Minor criticisms about positioning were aired. The leading lady chipped in with her gripe, that in one particular scene she hadn't felt that she was well lit in the position she'd been blocked to be.

John started to point out that they'd had no time to focus the rig,

and he'd had to busk lighting states with what happened to be
there, a situation that was familiar to all of them and hardly
needed reiterating. Adam, once again in the front passenger
seat, craned round to look at her when she made her complaint.
He interrupted John.

"I was in the dark half the time, Penelope, but that's what
happens when you insist on trying to have lighting and staging
on no budget instead of relying on the performers to create a
scene in the imagination of the audience. Of course you
wouldn't know about limited finances would you?"

She bristled, but unusually bit her lip and failed to snap back at
him. The others pitched in to the discussion, and the
conversation left the realms of whether the performance had
been good, bad or indifferent and became a wide ranging
expression of entrenched opinions on class, money and
eventually unions and worker's rights. John drove on. He'd
heard these discussions too often before in too many situations,
with too many cast and crews. He could predict the present
cast's positions from the familiarity that the close confines of a
small scale tour provide.

There was Adam, of course. Left wing and anti-establishment to
the limit. Despising legitimate theatre, and believing that the
purpose of performance was to educate the audience, preferably
with what he felt to be correct political views. His slant had
been honed during those years at the slightly known drama
school, where teachers, almost all with the same outlooks he
was now displaying, had led him and his contemporaries
through a selection of the political, agit-prop and art-house
shows. Adam was no fan of Penelope. He was grudgingly aware
of her talent, but he had discovered early on that she came from
a moneyed background, and that, to him, was a sin that there
could never be any forgiveness for.

Quietest among the company was Nicole who had brought the
tea box out to the van. She was reduced in this show to playing

a succession of minor roles supporting Penelope's 'star' part. She rarely expressed opinions, being surprisingly nervous for an actress. She, of all of them, came from the poorest working class background, and, had the rest but known it, had fought the hardest to get into a drama school. She was not very talented, and her recognition of this seemed to make her even more reticent. Theatre in education was probably the height of her realistic ambitions. John understood her failings, and rather liked her. She was pretty in an average sort of way, and whenever she was in the room you had the feeling that she was looking about like the shy person at a party, to see if she could find some washing up to take out to the kitchen so she could hide away. Her slim form bordered on 'petite' and her straight hair, too dark to be blonde and too light to be brown, hung to her shoulders. John was fairly certain that any longish period of 'resting' between acting jobs would see her leave the profession.

Hugh felt that the whole situation, the company, the show, the venues, was beneath him. With no formal training, and as a child of just nine years old, he'd had a small part in a television drama. This had run through three series and had kept him in the public eye off and on for nearly four years. But when it ended he'd found himself back in his secondary modern school, in the Midlands, full time, where his peers found every opportunity to mock and bully him. He had been delighted to get occasional work in commercials, but even these backfired on him in the classrooms, where advertising slogans and the whistled theme from the series could be, and were, used as sneering attacks.

From this experience Hugh developed a thick skin, and made a living over time in a succession of menial jobs, before some recent frustration at this situation led him to buy a copy of 'The Stage' and apply for, and get, a part with this company. It was perhaps his lowest performance experience, and he made no secret of comparing it to his long past television career.

As John turned the van in through the gates of the yard where the company's office was the discussion was still raging, but it died with the switching off of the ignition, and turned into a noisy scramble for bags and coats.

"Eight-thirty tomorrow morning please!" John shouted over the melee, "And I do mean eight-thirty." he added, looking pointedly at Penelope.

"Might be a bit early for the idle rich." Adam said bitchily.

She didn't offer any reply, and certainly no apology, simply climbing out of the van, tilting her head slightly up in that snooty way he had come to hate, and walking off without saying goodbye to anyone. The rest of the cast exchanged 'Goodbye' and 'see you tomorrow' with each other and with John and made off into the dreary evening streets which were shiny with moisture under the streetlights.

John locked the van and went into the office. The secretary was just putting on her coat ready to leave.

"He says he wants to have a word, John," she said, and passed over some papers.

John turned over the pages of tomorrow's venue details and times he had just received.

"How the hell are we supposed to get from St Clement's School to the Broxford High School in that time?" he queried, mildly annoyed at an itinerary which he could see implied a race right across the city between the end of the morning performance and the start of the afternoon one. Another missed lunch, he thought.

"I don't make the bookings, I just type them up," Alison replied a bit defensively.

"I know, I know. But surely someone in this office has got the common sense not to keep doing this to us."

"You'd better take it up with him." the secretary said huffily. "I've got to go and get my kids' tea ready," and she left.

John went through into the inner office, privately sorry to have upset Alison. There was a small, but rather pretentious plate on it saying 'Nick Thornhill. Director'. It crossed John's mind, as he pushed against it to open the door, that he'd heard it said that Nick couldn't direct traffic.

"Hello Nick," he said almost before he was though the door, "Did you want something?"

The director's desk was piled with paperwork, mostly dog-eared copies of classic books and some scripts, and he lounged behind it on a swivel chair looking glum and depressed.

"Come in John, sit down. I want your opinion."

This was a bit unusual. John couldn't recall a direct request for an opinion since he'd started working at 'Theatre Wagon', though he had never been backward in expressing them, and he settled himself on a seat. To his right the uncurtained window was dark and smeared with the drizzling rain that was settling over the city for the night. The headlights of cars approaching the junction swept across every so often, and the office grew gloomy again when they had passed, but Nick gave no sign of wanting to turn a light on. Instead he launched into an explanation of what was troubling him.

"We've only got another five weeks of the schools tour to go. How did today go, by the way?" and without waiting for an answer he went on, "I've got an idea that we could revamp it as a small, or better, a mid-scale tour to play in arts centres and village halls, maybe even theatres. We've got to have something to start selling, and adapting this would be easier than starting from scratch. What do you think?"

John debated about his answer. He had no interest in the show, but he could sympathise with Nick's problem. The show had only really sold to schools through being based on a book on the syllabus. He knew that Nick had struggled to give any real direction to the cast. The actors had done most of the editing of the long and complicated period novel themselves, devised the conceit on which production hinged, and basically rehearsed themselves to performance. It was a technique common to devised drama, but Nick had taken laissez-faire to an extreme degree. John's own opinion was that Nick had burned out, had run out of ideas, if indeed he had ever had any worthy of note. The previous shows John had toured for them had been directed by visiting guest directors. They'd not been brilliant, but at least the cast hadn't had to make it up as they went along. The idea of a slight revamp and a subsequent small scale tour must have great appeal for the director, allowing the company to be seen to be continuing to present performances with a minimum of creative work for him.

He considered it from a selfish point of view. He had no work in prospect once the school tour ended and although he had no doubt that, in time, something would turn up, the idea of getting another season without hunting the vacancies pages of 'The Stage' had some appeal despite his determination to escape this company. It struck him that even village halls, and certainly arts centres and small theatres, might be preferable to a schools tour. Then he thought about the leading lady.

"Would you use the same cast? Penelope and the rest?"

"Oh yes," Nick was hoping for the least work possible, "if the current cast wanted to do it I'd be pleased. I think we might try a bigger cast, you know, add an actor to cut the doubling on the minor parts a bit. It would be OK if we budget it in now before we start selling, and it would add a bit to the prestige."

John felt himself slump slightly. 'Prestige'! Really? Anyway he'd been looking forward to being free from the actress' selfishness. He dithered. Was easy security worth the daily grind and misery of working with her? He thought of nervous little Nicole, out on the road in a succession of theatres with the bullying likes of Penelope and the politically opinionated bombast of Adam. He thought of Hugh with his dwindling recollections of TV appearances as his only consolation, and despite his detestation of the whole set up he found himself being railroaded into this commitment. Although protecting lame ducks was not much of an incentive for sticking with it.

Nick was droning on, justifying his plans and expanding and exaggerating the theatrical potential.

'He'll have us in the West End in his mind before long' thought John. He let his thoughts wander back to his grammar school roots, and how his involvement with the school plays had sparked an interest, not in performing, but in the mechanics and technicalities of theatre. It was an interest that had led him through a succession of medium sized provincial theatres, where he'd been everything from stage hand to electrician, to bigger and bigger venues. His short marriage to a dancer from the chorus of a show he had worked on had culminated, eventually, while they were both working on a major musical, in vicious shouting matches that had included the destruction of almost all the wedding present crockery through it being hurled violently at him, till he had walked out, subsequently paying the price when the dancer's solicitors had managed to drain him and his bank account of any small savings he had built up over the years of long theatre hours. Back in the theatre world, where he had risen to the level within the small circle of workers in the industry to be moderately well known and respected, even sought out by producers for particular shows, he continued to work on major shows. Then one of those unaccountable lulls in employment that actors call 'resting' had led him to take this theatre in education job to keep the roof of the rather worn flat he rented over his head. Now he sat with his hands in his pockets, fiddling with some forgotten fuse he had found there, and being wheedled, cajoled, and ultimately threatened, for he had no immediate work prospect otherwise, into this extension of a TIE style contract. Whatever Nick said, no matter how he talked it up, this further tour was still really just theatre in education. The drab gloom of the office matched his mood and reaction, but eventually he found himself saying yes, and leaving the company's building to go back to his lonely flat, saddened and somewhat dejected.

Nick locked up the offices, and went home to his wife pleased with the outcome of the discussion. He considered it a victory, as he told her that evening, that he could now set the office staff to selling a tour of a show that would only need minimal work.

Chapter 4

Penelope looked at the envelope that the landlady had slid under the door of her room during the day. She knew exactly where it had come from by both the handwriting and the smudged postmark. Her digs offered bed, breakfast and evening meal, and that was what she paid for, so she knew that she should go downstairs almost immediately for the meal. She hesitated. To open the letter now would delay her, and might well put her in a bad mood. On the other hand she wondered if she could suppress her curiosity to sit through a meal with the two other lodgers in the house. They were both some sort of salesman, and arrived every Sunday night, stopping for the week, and vanishing back to their wives and children at weekends. The Saturday and Sunday meals were a luxury for her, even if the morning to night solitude of school performance free days was tedious. At least for those meals she had the dining room to herself, except when Mrs Bray, her landlady, chose to loiter around when delivering or collecting Penelope's plate to hold forth on some mundane topic, usually the weather. Mr Bray was invariably invisible in the kitchen, but his wife would occasionally feel it her duty to offer casual conversation to her guests. Penelope could just tolerate the woman's chatter if it didn't go on too long, but the salesmen were another matter.

She gave a slight shudder of disgust that was not just snobbishness as she thought of them. They were almost identical in age, manner and dress, falling into a shabby suit, collar and tie mould, coupled to beery breath from business socialising, both with strong accents from somewhere in the North-west, and both making no secret of their admiration of Penelope's appearance.

Reluctantly she put the letter on the old fashioned dressing table that provided the only flat surface in the rented room. Looked disapprovingly at the bed, the wardrobe and the single soft chair, drew the flowery curtains, and went downstairs to eat.

"Ee, we was beginning to think thee had stood us up!" she was greeted.

"That's reet. And we can't have the glamour missing from our meal," added the other.

She gave that haughty half toss of the head that she used so often when she felt that someone was beneath her and sat down in her place. It was curious how, from the day she had arrived in these digs, her position at the head of the table had been established and acknowledged almost before two words had been spoken.

Now too many words were being spoken. Mrs Bray's comings and goings with the flower patterned dishes failed to interrupt the flow of chatter about the day's travelling, and sales made or lost.

"...and the receptionist was a cracking bit of stuff I tell you. Not a patch on our Penelope here mind," here a knowing leer, "but a real cracker none-the-less...."

She ate silently, failing to rise to the occasional innuendo, or blatant come-ons. And she deftly fielded the outright invitation to come 'down the pub' with the pair. She was musing on the possible content of her letter. These particular communications only came occasionally now, mostly at holidays or special occasions. She supposed she should count Cynthia, the letter's author, a friend, Cynthia Hynes-Smyth. Even in the expensive private school that they had both attended Cynthia had managed to create the impression that she was above the rest of the students, but somehow, possibly due to Penelope's father's money boosting her social standing to a similar level, the two had forged a sort of alliance which had lasted after school was over.

Now, with Mrs Bray's slightly chewy steak and kidney pie dispatched, it was cheap meat Penelope decided, and the incongruous tinned pears and ideal milk 'afters' finished, and the salesmen departed to the pub, she picked up the envelope again in her room and opened it. For a while she didn't take the letter out of the envelope, but sat, holding it and staring at the roses and ribbons pattern on the wallpaper until the floral shapes blurred and began to form weird faces in her imagination. There were two flowers in particular which each seemed to look like the MGM lion in mid roar. Once you had seen this it was impossible to look at the wallpaper again without seeing them. She shook off the illusion, and began to read.

It was as spiteful as she had feared.

For Cynthia had soured as the years had gone by, and her disapproval of Penelope's career dripped from every sneering word on the page.

'Dearest Penny', it started. Penelope hated being called Penny, and Cynthia knew that.
'I do hope that you are well and happy in your little show.'
The 'little' was an unnecessary swipe.
'As you know Alan has become very successful in the city, as a result we regularly hold big dinner parties here at 'The Gables' for important and influential friends.
'At the one we held last Saturday we had several people from the arts field. I was talking to Edward, the director of the next show for the Royal, and he told me that he would be staging 'Othello' there. The lead is being played by Robert Anderson, but 'Edward', (showing off that they are on Christian name terms,) *was telling me that he has yet to cast Desdemona.*
Of course I could have suggested that he talk to you, as an internal recommendation is always a good way of opening a door, but I knew that you were appearing in your TIE show so you wouldn't be interested, even though it seems rehearsals for 'Othello' start just after your current run finishes.
'I hope that you have arranged some form of work for when your show ends.'

Penelope groaned. The names that were being dropped were exactly those that could have helped her career, and she was under no illusions that Cynthia was quite correct in saying that a word in the right ear could have swung a part, even possibly a leading part, for her. Penelope had been born and bred to the advantages of nepotism even though her father's approach to her throughout her life had been to try to force her into the family business to work her way up the hard way.

He had given up the attempt eventually and used his money to oil the drama school path she had chosen. The money was no hardship to him. The disappointment at her rejection of the family business was. Neither mother nor father could comprehend the attraction of the stage. Father talked of the financial insecurity, mother worried about 'immoral' tales that she gathered from the tabloid press.

Penelope herself couldn't quite recall what had drawn her to the profession, but had distinct memories of the wheedling and begging that had gained her grudging permission to undertake stage school training. Sighing she turned back to Cynthia's letter.

'Do tell me what your next show is,' it went on, *'as we are all waiting to see your name in lights if you can manage it.'*

Penelope was torn between fury at the sneer and self-pity at the hidden truth behind it, for she knew in her heart that this small scale, low budget, theatre in education touring was not what she had aspired to. It frightened her to think that she might become mired in an unending succession of shows of this scale. Somehow she had to move up to bigger than TIE. A grain of realism told her that she needed more than just some luck to climb to the level in the profession that would make her truly happy.

'Of course, if you can't make a go of it we will all understand and a warm and sympathetic welcome home awaits you.'

She could imagine the 'warm and sympathetic welcome home'. An endless round of the more pretentious houses, packed with an 'in' crowd which whispered behind her back that she had failed and was now returned with her tail between her legs to live off Daddy. She loudly sniffed back a tear that was starting to form, screwed the letter into a loose ball and hurled it viciously across the room. It hit the wall and slid down, to wedge very unsatisfyingly half down the back of the dressing table.

She looked at her watch, squinted at its tiny face and found the time on her travelling alarm clock beside the bed instead. She had received the watch as an eighteenth birthday present, but the delicate and expensive thing had no numbers on the dial and was almost impossible to read. She wore it because she felt she should, and because its obvious prestige played to her wish to be a bit superior with her acquaintances. She toyed with, and dismissed, a wild idea of walking to the nearest pub to join the travelling salesmen. They would, she knew, be more than happy to ply her with drinks for the rest of the evening, but she donned her coat and, leaving her digs, turned in the opposite direction and made a brief visit to the local general store, returning armed with a magazine and a bottle of gin which, unless she were to ask for funds from father, she could ill afford. She headed for a solitary evening consuming the gin surrounded by roses and ribbons looking like MGM lions.

On the other side of the town John stared at the four walls of his one bedroom flat and mulled over the prospect of a vamped up version of the schools tour show. With neither interest in the show's subject matter or original classic text, nor any great sympathy with the presentational style or some of the cast, especially 'her', he thought, the future didn't look welcoming. He was under no illusions. 'She' would doubtless be offered an extension to her current contract, and so far as he knew she had no other plans in the pipeline. Grudgingly he admitted to himself that she played the part competently enough. At least on a bigger scale tour might mean he could escape her presence.

He gulped down the glass of whisky he held, and refilled it.

He thought about Nicole again. In a mindless, hazy way he vaguely fantasised, wondering if she might make the weeks of the tour more bearable. He realised he'd thought about her this way a few times lately. He shook himself out of the reverie and went back to considering the show.

How big would the scale be, he wondered. It seemed hugely unlikely that the little production company would stretch itself to book its show into what he would call 'proper' theatres, but it might claw its way up to a few arts centres and some minor provincial mixed policy venues, away from the pipe clad walls of school halls. He might be able to run to hotel digs, but not a flat like this.. as he guessed that the show would be unlikely to play more than a few days at any theatre.. but if he was arranging the company's accommodation he could, at least, make sure he didn't have to share the breakfast table with them by booking himself into different B&Bs from the actors. That, and travelling in separate vehicles might make it tolerable. Yes, he sighed, he would do it; he could always back out if something more to his liking was offered before the show went into re-rehearsal.

Chapter 5

The talk in the van on the way to the first performance a few days later was all about the bigger scale tour. The cast had been told of the plans and asked to consider whether they wished to stay on. Initially it amused John to eavesdrop the different predictable views that were being propounded in the back of the vehicle.

Turning toward the rear from his seat beside the driver again on this particular journey it was Adam who had started the morning discussion.

"We need to be sure that the re-write gets a proper message across," he was saying.

John had no doubt that 'proper' meant left wing to Adam. The other occupants of the van were by now so used to the endless and monotonous repetition of his views that they failed to rise to the bait, and the babble of voices that followed his pronouncement was concerned with the possible length of the run, the type of venues and how much the touring allowance would be.

Hugh said, "If it's going to be a proper show I suppose there'll be posters and things. Do you reckon we'll get our names on the billing?"

"Who's going to know your name anyway?" sniped Adam, "We should all be equal, the star system makes some actors more important than others."

"At least audiences have heard of me. They've seen my name on the credits. I used to be in...."

"All equal. Some companies don't even publish the actors' names in the programmes. We don't want prima-donnas in this cast," Adam butted in, oblivious to the irony of his making this pronouncement.

"I want to know what we'll get paid in allowances if we've got to travel," Penelope said,

"You'll get the agreed Equity rate. That's why it's vital to have a union. Everyone gets the same minimum, even people with money. Though why rich kids like you should need to worry I don't know."

"And it will be the minimum with this lot," muttered Hugh in response to Adam's comment.

Penelope snapped at Adam, "I've told you before, my finances are none of your business."

"Oh. Sensitive," he taunted, "A guilty conscience at your moneyed advantages? The trouble with people like you is you are in everything for what you can get out of it...."

"I think that's enough don't you?" John shouted across them from the driving seat. He had little inclination to defend her, (today's epithet was 'exasperating' following his alphabetical sequence), but some sort of company unity had to be preserved, and the cast were not going to find it too easy to portray their characters in a few minutes time if they started off at each others' throats, It was, surprisingly he thought, the first time that the simmering animosity had visibly surfaced. Even more surprising to John it had not really come up though any fault of hers. He anticipated a sullen silence following his intervention, but unexpectedly it was Nicole who stopped this by saying:

"I think it would be nice to be in real theatres."

"Quite right," John told her. "But sadly, just for now we are at yet another school." and he turned the van into the gates of their destination, immediately becoming involved in a traffic jam of buses and parents' cars leaving, having dropped off their passengers.

"You don't like performing in schools do you."

"No, not at all. Do you?" John answered Hugh's query.

"It's not the same as film and television. In TV it's much more controlled and we have people to do all the menial tasks."

"Whereas all you have for the 'menial tasks' today is me."

The quip went un-noticed by most of the company, though John thought that Hugh was biting back a retort.

As they maneouvered he added to the cast, "We're going to be very pushed for time between the morning and afternoon shows again, so please don't dawdle after this performance."

The inadequate gap that he had criticised to Alison a few nights previously had proven to be a major headache, and the resulting late start at the second school had made the show run beyond the end of the last lesson of the day. He had little expectation of help with off-loading or loading, but he hoped the cast would speed up both the pace of the show itself and their packing up and getting back in the van at the end of the first performance. He was going to be disappointed on both counts today.

There were delays starting the performance at the first school. A succession of mislaid props and quibbles from the cast about positioning added to a rather lethargic staff, who seemed in no hurry to herd their pupils into the typically bleak echoing hall and made for a late start. He noted it on his pad. He'd hoped that the cast could make up the lost time by accelerating their delivery of the show, but the reverse happened.

The two leads were barely on speaking terms following the spat in the van, a situation that made their characters' love a bit risible, and they both did their best to annoy each other by constant upstaging and stealing the limelight. John made critical notes about this strange relationship between 'Rochester' and 'Jane' in his log, though it is doubtful if any of the noisy and inattentive audience would have noticed.

From his point of view the unplanned pauses and looks with which the two peppered their performance simply extended the running time on a day when he had specifically asked for it to be as tight as possible.

The hasty repacking of the van for the move to the next school was made even more miserable by drizzling rain that threatened to become sleet before they reached their next booking. No help was offered by any of the cast except Nicole, and he could hear them still bickering as he came and went with the loads finally cramming the box with the tea things onto the remaining space inside the back doors. Repeated practice with the loading had resulted in everything having a place in the packing of the van. The load was untidy with haste this time, and it shifted noisily as he wove the vehicle through the city traffic.

As he drove John decided to read the cast the riot act.

He said, "That was a rather disgraceful display this morning."

"You hadn't put the set together properly." Adam accused him.

"I'm not talking about props positioning... which is your responsibility anyway as you well know, I'm discussing you lot taking your petty differences on stage with you and using the performance to score points off each other."

"She's a spoilt rich brat..." "I don't see why I should have to put up with his insults." Penelope and Adam shouted above each other.

"Quiet! At least you're both aware who I'm talking about. Now even if you can't be friends you can make sure the audience doesn't suffer this afternoon. I've put a note in the show report, and I don't want to have to do the same again."

"I don't care what you report to your masters. There's a principle here. We're all equal, and that's exactly what it's all about. She thinks she's above us. And you shouldn't be running telling tales to who you see as your 'boss' anyway."

"We're not all 'equal', and while we're out on the road I happen to be in charge. I also happen to be responsible for reporting back to the office anything that affects the show. Your behaviour..." he paused significantly...."your behaviour, both of you, affected the show. I didn't expect that of 'professionals', so prove me wrong this afternoon."

"You're a lackey of the company. A company that deliberately wrote out the workers struggle against the bosses from the adaptation."

John decided to bite his tongue about being a lackey, though it did frequently feel like it, but argued back on the issue of political slant despite not having read the book himself.

"You were part of the adaptation.... I seem to remember you complaining that you had to help write the script, and there isn't any workers revolutionary propaganda in the book." He kept his metaphorical fingers crossed as he made this statement, as he wasn't sure of the truth of that pronouncement, but it remained unchallenged. "The point is that we can't have the show mucked about with so you can settle scores," he paused, "with each other."

There was a sullen silence from behind him. Stopping at traffic lights he looked briefly over his shoulder. He couldn't see Adam very well, but the glance showed him Penelope scowling, and Nicole sitting staring forward with tears running down her face. He felt sorry for the girl. She looked so helpless. He wanted to reassure her that it was all right, that it wasn't her fault, that she shouldn't be upset. Instead he said,

"Let's leave it at that. We're nearly there, and we're running late, so please all muck in and let's do a good performance."

Hugh, rather unexpectedly, said "Here here." as they turned into yet another school gateway.

Chapter 6

The cast were subdued as the off-loading started. Just for once they came forward and assisted, though there was clear resentment at his reading them the riot act, and their contribution to the get in was in some cases very minimal. Penelope only picked up a very small item, Adam seized a chair and strode off with it. Hugh mucked in with a good grace.

Nicole arrived last at the rear doors of the van. John stopped what he was doing. He dug in his pocket and found a clean handkerchief and gently wiped the wet streaks running down the girl's face.

""Hey, don't worry. It's not your fault."

They were shielded from view from the school building by one of the open back doors of the van. He put his arm round her and gave her a light peck on the cheek. She looked up at him pitifully, gulped back a sob and made off into the building with a box of props. Hugh arrived back at the van for another load.

"She gets upset a bit easily doesn't she?" he said.

"I think she might have had some justification this time, don't you? See what you can do to get them all to pull together and stop their bickering will you."

"Worried about the show or your girlfriend?"

"Nicole isn't my girlfriend, but yes, her, and the show. You've got a bit of seniority from your past career; try to appeal to their professionalism or something."

"When I was in TV we had people to deal with the cast's requirements...."

John gave a short laugh, "We've hardly got people to move the props about. Don't get delusions of grandeur, we're all scraping about at a low part of this food chain."

"How right you are," said Hugh with a wry grin, and hefting another bit of furniture from the van he disappeared into the school.

Off-loading finished and John shut and locked the back door and went to lay out the set on the floor of another school hall.

The show reports made their way back to the office later, and did result in the cast being called in to be given a mild talking to on the next day when chance gave them only one school to perform in. They were a bit put out by this, as they'd been looking forward to a free afternoon even though the weather was dull and overcast and being told off ate into their rare free time. Even this early, just after lunch, many cars had lights on John noticed, as once again he found himself looking out of the window of Nick's room.

Penelope, Hugh and Nicole were wisely holding their tongues while Nick gave a feeble rambling lecture about trying not to let personal feelings affect the performance. John and Hugh were standing. The girls had the only spare chairs, and Adam had taken up a position leaning against the filing cabinet in a way that seemed to dominate the room. The metal drawers creaked now as he shifted his weight and interrupted Nick to say:

"OK, so Penelope and I don't exactly hit it off. She's a little rich kid paying at being an actress. But the important thing is to make sure the new version of the show sends out the right message to the audience...."

"Adam we're not discussing the new production, we've got to get through the rest of the bookings for the schools tour. What do we need to do to stop you two fighting?"

Penelope butted in, "We'd not have disagreements if he stopped going on about my private financial situation."

Nick seized on the opening, "Well that solves it then. Carry on as before, but private finances are off the agenda. Everyone happy with that? Good. Have a better couple of shows tomorrow, I expect it will all have blown over by then." and he got up, came round his desk and opened the door to usher them out.

"Eight-fifteen tomorrow!" John shouted after them as they left. He turned to Nick when they had all gone. "It doesn't really solve the problem you know, the two of them are at daggers drawn."

"I'm sure you can keep a lid on it," said Nick, "There aren't many weeks of the tour left."

"And then?"

"Well," Nick hesitated, "If it's really impossible we'll have to replace one or the other of them. We can hold off the new contracts for a little while."

"She is very difficult to work with, you know."

"She's a good actress though. But I'll think about it."

John left, hoping that it would be Penelope whose contract was not renewed. He admitted to himself that she was the victim, in this case, of Adam's unremitting political and personal attacks, he admitted to himself that she was attractive, but it was she who got on least well with the rest. It was she who despite, or perhaps because of, her tantalizing curves that John found most annoying.

His view did not change over the following days.

'Grumpy' seemed to be a suitable epithet when, having waited for her as usual, the van set off next morning. The cast were clearly trying to behave normally but there was still a frosty atmosphere that was nothing to do with the early morning air. Adam was unusually silent, failing even before Penelope's arrival to comment on their waiting for her yet again. She boarded the vehicle with her customary air of disdain, omitting to acknowledge John's slightly sarcastic "Good morning" and spending the journey looking out of the window. She'd got a window seat again he noted.

The school get-in routine went on as normal. John was not unduly bothered to discover that yesterday's piecemeal help from the cast with unloading, and, after the performance, loading the van had fallen by the wayside. It hadn't lasted long, he mused. At least by a return to the status-quo-ante the company had unwittingly removed a problem he'd experienced for that one day of helpfulness, that of never knowing what had and hadn't been loaded after a performance. Doing all the manual labour himself did have the virtue of reducing the necessity for an 'idiot check', (hunting around for mislaid and forgotten items) to a bare minimum cursory glance about the hall on leaving.

The day brought them to two unremarkable schools, and the performances were very standard, though he assiduously noted the details for the show reports.

On one of the journeys between schools the cast's conversation turned to their existing digs, and what arrangements they might have to make if they were in the new tour cast. John listened to what they were saying, interested in hearing the sort of accommodation each had ended up in. Hugh's digs sounded as though they were run along the lines of an old people's home, and the inmates, from his detailled and somewhat colourful description, seemed to spend most of their time in front of the television in the lounge.

Penelope, dragged into the discussion for once, was scathing of the North Country travelling salesmen who occupied other rooms in her B&B.

Adam had, John was not surprised to hear, taken up residence in what seemed from his description to be some sort of commune, or at least a very loosely organised house share.

Nicole was a bit reticent about her digs. When pressed she admitted that the food was awful and that the landlady was a tyrant. "But I think she really means well," the girl excused her.

Eventually someone asked about John's accommodation and he answered briefly that he had a rented a flat in the city.

Generally though the cast were quieter now, and that remained the situation for the rest of that week. Newspapers were read more thoroughly, as a means of avoiding conversation, and the cast were less talkative as they travelled. The periodic comments about things seen through the limited windows of the van seemed fewer and further between. Even the largely unnecessary navigational directions that had sometimes been offered to him as a driver had dried up except when Nicole was seated up front, but there were no more outright arguments. John was glad to turn into the yard in the damp darkness of Friday afternoon and switch off the van's engine for the last time till Monday morning.

"Eight o'clock start Monday please. Have a good weekend all of you," he said, as they scrambled out, dragging bags after them and, the two men at least, discussing meeting in a pub for a drink during the weekend. He suspected that neither really wanted to spend social time with the other, but that they both considered a planned meeting better than drinking alone.

He pulled a cloth from the glove locker and walked round to the flat front on the van, wiping the road grime off the wet windscreen to be ready for the early start on Monday. Coming back to the driver's door to return the cloth he was surprised to find Nicole beside the vehicle standing in the drizzling rain.

"I thought you'd gone home." he said.

"I don't really like my digs, so I'm not in a hurry." she confessed. Her hair had gone lank and mousy in the rain he noticed. Her cheap coat didn't look very waterproof. She was a picture of a miserable abandoned waif.

"No, I gathered your landlady wasn't much good." He took pity on her, "Well don't stand here in the rain. Come into the offices, I've got to drop the show reports in."

She tamely followed him inside. As they went in they passed Alison leaving. There was a slight shuffling past each other in the tiny lobby which pressed John and Nicole damply together into a corner by a filing cabinet.

"Just dump them on my desk," Alison instructed. "Goodnight you two." she looked at them speculatively and meaningfully.

The door slammed shut behind her.

"You don't think she thought...." Nicole started, and stopped before she had to voice the conjecture.

John separated himself from the filing cabinet, flicked the wetness off its side with a hand and started trying to dry and smooth out the damp and slightly crumpled show reports as he placed them on Alison's desk.

"Yes, I expect so," he said, completely unconcerned but feeling an unexpected excitement at the implication. He began turning over papers till he located the show details for Monday, folded them and slipped them into his jacket pocket. He looked round the office, turned off the light and led the girl back outside, releasing the Yale lock catch and slamming the door behind them.

"Have you eaten today?" he asked.

"Not since breakfast, but I suppose there'll be something at my digs later."

"Food any good there?"

"No, it's horrible."

"Come on then," he said, and led the way across the road and along the street opposite. They walked past a shop, dodging an 'A' board that half blocked the pavement, and John turned down a side street and into a small, slightly gloomy and very steamy and greasy café. The place was almost deserted, the only occupants being two overall clad men at a table near the counter. He motioned the girl into a seat next to the window and sat on the opposite side of the table.

"What would you like?"

"I don't mind. I'll have whatever you're having," she said, avoiding a decision.

He went to the counter. The woman in a slightly grimy apron lifted her eyes from the tabloid newspaper spread on the shelf below the high front of the corrugated hardboard faced servery and said 'Hello John.'

Back at the table while they waited he wiped the steam off the glass, leaning across the table close to Nicole to do so. She still seemed uneasy, and was looking round at the pale green gloss painted walls with their curling posters advertising boxing matches, and the piece of soft-board screwed to the wall and smothered in visiting cards for taxis and trades from plumbers to transport firms. On the inside of the window that John had wiped a self-adhesive plastic sign peeled at its corners inviting passers-by to pay by Luncheon Voucher.

"I suppose you come here a lot?" Nicole ventured.

"Once in a while," he replied truthfully. "Where do you go?"

"I don't really. I mean I don't like being sat in these places on my own." A pause, "They knew your name."

"Some places, usually the family run ones like this, seem to make a point of it. A bit like a local pub. Which is the local pub for your digs?"

"I don't go to the pub."

"You're not teetotal or something are you?" he managed to sound quite shocked at the thought. "I don't think we can live this sort of life without the occasional bit of relaxation. When I used to be at....," he paused, "no, it makes me sound like Hugh if I say that."

"Poor Hugh," she said with a burst of charity, "he really missed out on a TV career didn't he?"

"Well, child actors' careers.... oh, thank you.." he broke off as the waitress arrived with two mugs of tea, ".... child actors' careers are pretty short by definition, and I guess that lots of them don't get picked up quickly as adults. I mean, let's face it, if you're used to seeing Bert Blenkinsopp running about in shorts with a few other kids and a scruffy dog solving banal minor crime mysteries on your Saturday morning tele it's a bit of a leap to accepting him as a serious police detective in a panda car pursuing a murderer on a Friday evening isn't it?"

At last she smiled, and he thought how it transformed her, if only for a moment. "Wasn't he in some adverts?" she asked.

"Yes, I think he kept popping up with that vivid pink frothy drink. What was it called..?"

She giggled. "It didn't work as an advertising campaign then did it? I mean, if neither of us can remember the name of the drink."

"Sic transit gloria." She looked at him uncomrehendingly. "Loosely translates as 'thus passes glory'. Benefit, or disadvantage of a grammar school education," he explained.

"Oh. Did you go to a grammar? I think that must have been so nice. They're so much better behaved when we play them than the other schools."

"I agree about the behaviour, but you wouldn't want to go to one. Well, unless you were obsessed by sport and liked cold showers and being ordered about as if you were in the army."

He stopped. The hatch from the kitchen opened and he turned at the noise. Three plates were handed through to the woman behind the counter, who brought them to their table. First came big plates of sausage, egg chips and beans, then she returned with a smaller plate of buttered sliced white bread and some knives and forks.

"Here you are John. And your young lady, of course." and she studied Nicole shrewdly, awaiting an introduction, and receiving none she returned to the tabloid paper. John had considered introductions, and wasn't sure that Nicole was comfortable enough yet. He'd seen how she shrank away from the meeting and greeting involved in talking to teachers at schools they played. Odd for an actress he thought.

"I don't know if I can eat all this," said Nicole.

"Eat it up. It will do you good. I don't think you eat enough." John said, helping himself to bread and butter and liberally shaking salt around.

Eating stopped the conversation for a while, during which the workmen rose and went out into the dark wet street. The cold draught from the door opening and then shutting behind them blew across the table and swept a paper napkin onto the floor. John leant sideways and picked it up. Rising back above the level of the table-top he saw Nicole watching him, a forkful of food poised halfway to her mouth. She grinned again.

"You have to clear up after everyone don't you."

"All the time," he joked, thinking of the endless task of clearing up after his little gang of actors.

He wiped his plate with the last piece of bread. He was pleased to see that she had eaten most of her meal. Somehow he had expected her to pick at it, but she had shown a pretty healthy appetite.

"You were hungry."

"The food at my digs is awful, and the other lodgers are awful. Actually the landlady..."

"Is awful," he finished for her. She giggled. It was good to hear her amused, he thought, even if just these brief moments of levity.

"I think she means well, but she overcooks everything, and she wants to order you about and drag you into conversation all the time."

"They all do. You only open your home up to a stream of strangers as lodgers if you are desperate for cash or for company, or both I imagine."

"Well anyway I don't like to mix with the others. They're so old." She wrinkled her nose as if being old was something distasteful and shaming.

I'm old, he thought, but said "I don't think you really like mixing with other people at all, do you?"

"I thought that I'd get confidence with the drama course I went on, 'cos I'd been really shy at school, but everyone was so loud and boisterous, and, oh I don't know, full of themselves I suppose and I never seemed to get any good parts in the productions. They made me be the ASM on most shows."

"Nothing wrong with stage management, so they tell me. Were you in productions at school, or didn't you get any chance till college?"

"They didn't do school plays where I went. It was a bit rough. And then I had to fight and fight to get into drama college. I had to do two auditions, because they didn't seem to be too sure if they'd take me, and Mum and Dad couldn't help, because they couldn't afford to, and then when I got there it all seemed a waste of time. I had to work in part time jobs all the while, and the other people on my course were all going to see shows every night, but I couldn't afford to, and then none of the agents who came round were interested in me, and I just got one or two bit parts till this job with Theatre Wagon, and..." she stopped, running out of steam and gulping back what might have been a self-pitying sob. "I'm sorry, you don't want to hear all that. What about you. Why are you doing this?"

"You've just had a rough time, that's all. I think you should have more belief in yourself." He didn't really think she had much to believe in. "You're young, and pretty, and it will get easier."

She seemed to be a bit startled by being told she was pretty. Her diffident nature made that a comment she wasn't used to hearing.

"Do you think so?"

"Of course." John searched for a topic to deflect the course of the conversation, and settled on the history of his own career. "I started as a humble stage-hand. It took years to build up to being a senior head of department in big theatres. I did everything from sweeping the stage to painting scenery and driving lighting desks. But it does get easier."

Nicole had really meant did he think she was pretty. Now he had started on his background she was curious. Within Theatre Wagon there was speculation as to whether the rumours of John's previous high flying career were true, and if so why he should now be stage managing a theatre in education show in a Transit van. Her shy interrogation was disturbed by the waitress collecting the plates.

"Will there be anything else?"

John and Nicole looked at each other, he raised an eyebrow, she shook her head.

"No thanks," he said, and followed the woman, with her load of used crockery, across to the counter. Nicole started to make a feeble protest, but he ignored her and paid the bill. He had struggled into his coat, which he had hung on the back of his chair while they ate, and she was picking hers up and he was helping her as she threaded her arms into the damp sleeves when the door to the café opened to a noisy crowd of teenagers.

"Our cue to leave, I think,"

"Yes please," she said.

Outside they hesitated. Their routes home lay in different directions. John had no wish to foist himself on the girl, and she probably couldn't have invited him back to her digs without some disapproval from the landlady. Nicole would have been happy to be invited to John's flat on the excuse of a cup of tea or coffee as a means of avoiding the drab misery of early evening digs, but he didn't do so.

"Thank you for buying me tea," she said.

"You're welcome," and there was a momentary hesitation, as if he might yet ask her to his flat, before he turned away with a brief, "See you Monday." and made off into the drizzle.

She stood watching his retreating back for a few seconds, then hunched her shoulders against the invasive wet and turned sadly in the opposite direction.

In his flat John was cross with himself. Cross that he had abandoned the girl when she was so obviously lonely. Cross with himself for caring. Cross that he had avoided bringing her to his flat. Perhaps they both needed the company he thought.

Back at her digs Nicole sat on her bed and stared miserably at the wall. She could go downstairs and join other residents watching a gameshow on television, or she could read, or...

Chapter 7

The company all had bad weekends. John's guilty feelings stayed with him through Saturday and Sunday, and his caring became distorted into some furtive fantasising about Nicole who kept springing into his mind. He was also still doubtful about having committed to more touring with this show, however expanded and adapted.

Nicole's time was spent in glum contemplation of both her circumstances and the meal she had shared with John on Friday evening. To many it would have just been a casual thing with a work colleague, but to her it seemed a major event that had fallen flat. She felt she'd missed an opportunity to forge a deeper friendship. She considered her future prospects with the show. Her fears made her more and more certain that the show would be recast for the bigger tour and that she would be replaced by another, more charismatic, she even admitted more talented, actress.

Hugh's Sunday afternoon was rather spoilt by the chance television screening of a repeat of one of his child acting appearances. He failed to revel in seeing this, as he was honest enough to acknowledge that it really wasn't very good, and neither was he. What galled him most, however, was that the TV lounge at his digs was fairly full for this program, but that most of the house's residents ignored it and read the paper, and not one of them recognised him. Or if they did they didn't comment. He was never shy about discussing his past successes, but somehow the occupants of the overstuffed chairs and sofa in the B&B seemed to be quite the wrong people to try to impress.

Adam went to a political meeting. He came away frustrated that the guest speaker, a well known name in the party, failed to propose or support action to achieve the changes he saw as desirable. This annoyed him to such an extent that he narrowly avoided outright violence at the working men's club where he stopped for a drink after the meeting and started to pronounce his views as though on a soap-box. Much of his free time was therefore spent weighing the likelihood of being able to convince 'Theatre Wagon' to include his propagandist wishes in the revised production. Deciding that this was not going to happen without a serious revision of the company's aims and objectives he pondered the advantages of joining an existing politically motivated show, or setting up his own company. Slowly he came to the view that there were lots of small production companies that were based on his views and that it was just a case of finding a way into one.

Penelope spent much of the weekend writing letters. Like her fellow cast members she found herself mainly confined to the bedroom of her digs, a space which did little to raise her spirits. She would, she was certain, because Nick had now spoken to her privately and given assurances, be part of the cast of the re-vamped show, and was comforted by the security that this offered her. None the less her mind wandered among 'might-have-been' ideas, prompted by the content of the letter she'd received.

Now she was writing both a reply to Cynthia and a long overdue letter to her parents. The flowered wallpaper was irritating her more and more, and somehow she could imagine that the MGM film lions which she now always saw when she caught sight of the pattern were an indictment of her failing career. No film stardom for her. There had been minor highlights in her career when she'd played in a few provincial repertory companies, and she looked back at those moments fondly. She tried to bolster the importance of the new tour of the show, plying Cynthia with optimistic phrases about the expansion of the play, and with completely invented likely itineraries covering venues which she claimed were considering it. The venues in question would probably have been surprised, as the company office had only just started on the business of selling the show to potential touring houses. She felt no guilt in this subterfuge, which she also perpetrated on her parents in their letter. In the case of Cynthia she saw it as retaliation for the woman's attack on her; for her parents she saw it as an attempt to reassure her mother, and make her father feel that his money had not been entirely wasted.

Had the money been wasted? She was less than sure. Her mood vacillated between over-compensating confidence and uncertainty. It was partly the disguise of these thoughts that appeared to her colleagues to be snooty superiority. However she could recall the timid young girl who had been obliged to try to represent her father in the family business. Could recall how she had shrunk away from the boisterous and sometimes ribald attitudes of the common men who were employed by her father, and whose behaviour to her during the brief period when her father had put her in an office to oversee a minor part of his empire had only been tempered by their knowledge that their jobs depended on behaving just within the limits of propriety. The period had been one during which she dreaded going to work where she was both frightened by the lewd and transparent propositions and disgusted with the men, and with herself for a feeling of curiosity that the remarks aroused. The stage gave her refuge from contact with such roughness, though for all his theatre culture affectation she could see the same working man in Adam, and the recent spat between them was but one manifestation of a slight fear she had of him. In a way the same protection that her father's ownership of the business had afforded her had been carried on at her drama school due to his financing of the place, but that was not present at Theatre Wagon. Nor in her digs she admitted, thinking of the sales reps. She vaguely fantasised in her room about John, feeling him to be safer, and with a longer more successful career, more secure, and privately, reluctantly, sometimes admitting to herself a physical attraction.

Drama school had been a bewildering kaleidoscope of larger than life characters among the student body, and intense, but greying, tutors. The tutors were well aware of the considerable sums that she had brought with her. One had remarked in the staff room, on some occasion when students were being discussed, that Penelope might not be a godsend to the stage, but she was certainly a boon to the bursar.

It may have been this situation that had caused a certain amount of behind the scenes pulling of strings that, unbeknown to Penelope, had eased her from her final year into a minor role in a provincial rep company.

Competent and attractive as she was she had managed to stay in work, for a while, in companies of that sort, moving, as all actors do, from theatre to theatre, from company to company, from show to show, but imperceptibly downwards. She accepted smaller towns and cities and less respected companies. The longed for 'big break' failed to materialise and the end result had been acceptance of this theatre in education job.

There were lots of reasons that she disliked and despised the TIE world. Not least was the loss of the anonymity that stage lighting gave. Not her own anonymity, for like all actresses of whatever ilk she did yearn for applause, but the anonymity of the audience. For with a proper stage and lights the audience vanished into the gloom as the glare and dazzle of the lighting hid them from the performers' view. This was gone in a school hall, where she was painfully aware of the reactions of the audience, whether appreciative or bored. It was worrying to her to realise the crude thoughts of her father's workforce might also be present in the minds of the underage schoolboys she was now performing to. Missing too, she decided, was the warm welcoming feel of a proper auditorium; replaced by the cold harsh utility of a school hall. Even the repertory theatres she'd worked in usually gave an air of comfort to their patrons, despite most of her experience having been in buildings built in the late sixties from rough shuttered concrete during the era when leaving the wood grain of the shuttering as a décor style had been the vogue resulting in walls that would snag threads from your sleeves, or graze a bare arm, if you accidentally brushed against them.

TIE also failed to give her any personal acknowledgement. Even as the most minor player in the provinces she had always seen her name, if not in lights, at least in tiny print on the billing and in a programme. If any recognition was given to the players by a school, and it rarely was, it would be in the form of a mention by a teacher of 'Theatre Wagon' as a whole. She knew that the pupils were not followers of theatre, and couldn't be expected to pay attention to the names of the cast, yet this lumping together of the members of the company under one credit niggled. Adam would be very much in favour if he chose to consider the issue, but Penelope railed against it. Though she despised, and even feared, the frank interest of the teenage boys in any audience she did feel that they should at least know her name. She hoped for a day in the future when, with her name in lights, the members of today's school audiences would see her image on television, or in newspapers and magazines and say 'I remember her in...' even though she knew this to be unlikely.

She shifted her position on the bed. It was almost impossible to write letters using the dressing table as a desk because her knees wouldn't fit conveniently under it, so she had adopted a place leaning against the headboard with the writing pad on her lap. It was not very comfortable, and had the disadvantage that she tended to find frequently that she had slid down the bed to an ever more reclining position.

Remembering Adam had annoyed her slightly. She pondered the other members of the company. Normally she gave them little consideration but on this slow tedious weekend she had little else to do.

Nicole, she decided, was inconsequential. She had not, and would not become a friend. Penelope failed to see that this was mostly due to the defensive stand-off that she herself established with all the cast, and that Nicole lacked the confident push that would have been required to break that barrier down. They were thrown together by the circumstances of being the two females, and so they frequently shared what dressing room accommodation there was, but conversation was limited to the bare necessities of such forced human contact and an awareness on Penelope's part of the other's cheap and worn clothing, which even struggling on a TIE actress's salary Penelope soared above.

Penelope did realise that it was possible that Nicole had more professional drive than she, even if she lacked Penelope's innate talent, for Nicole had gained her drama school place by effort. Penelope was not certain, but sensed that her path had been paved with her father's gold to a greater extent than she had been told at the time. It was possibly the one aspect of her career that gave her cause for major uncertainty and might have dented her outward confidence seriously but for the hard and slightly defensively prudish shell she erected around herself.

She was envious of Hugh's child actor success, but saw his present position, like her own, as a fall from grace. His appearance in television adverts was, she decided, not dissimilar to the shameful period near Christmas last year when, failing to be cast in panto, she had spent part of November and most of December as an elf in Santa's grotto in a major store in the city centre of a northern conurbation.

Two 'Santas' had worked in rotation through the day, but the two elves had been employed for eight hour shifts. She and the other girl had managed short breaks by covering for each other. The work had consisted entirely of marshalling toddlers and their parents in a queue dressed in an indecently short red and green outfit which might have been designed to encourage the dads. The Santas themselves were elderly men who did this job every year and had done so in the same store ever since the grotto was introduced in the seventies. Both were jovial, and both were prone to offering suggestions with a wink to the girls at slacker times when the public were not there.

'Why don't you come and sit on my knee?' could have a very suggestive tone when these men said it.

The experience had not been pleasant. She had disliked the men, she had disliked the silly hat, which squashed her hair, she disliked going back to her digs with glitter in all sorts of inexplicable places. Mostly she disliked the public. Pushy parents, who were usually dismissive of the cheap toy that was issued, and who were not slow to say so. She and her colleague quickly developed a technique of returning to the queue as soon as a customer emerged from the box-like structure of the grotto, so that they were fairly inaccessible to punters who had been through, unless they wanted to line up in the queue again to make a protest.

She thought about Nick Thornhill. She knew nothing of his background. She knew he was married and that he had founded 'Theatre Wagon' about seven or eight years previously. Although he had nominally directed this show, and she assumed he would direct the larger scale version once that went into rehearsal, she understood that he usually hired in a freelance director for any new production. Because 'Theatre Wagon' kept going on a continual round of different shows this practice meant that strange faces were frequently to be found in the offices. She thought she understood Nick. Nick had little flair and few ideas. Unkind rumour said that he had run out of steam and would soon step back from directing entirely and be simply an administrator. It was not in her nature to feel sorry for anyone else, but her feeling about Nick made her attitude come as close to sympathy for him as she was likely to get. What would it be like, she wondered, to be attracted to the world of theatre, make a career in it, and then have to step back to be just an office worker?

John came into her mind. She was acutely aware of his antagonism toward her. There were days when she perversely went out of her way to annoy him as a matter of routine. Her habitual lateness was partly due to that, partly due to an attempt to avoid waiting around with the rest of the cast any longer than absolutely necessary. Sometimes she realised she had annoyed John quite inadvertently. It was not in her nature to consider others in her actions, so that she didn't notice that the rest of the cast were irritated by many of the things she did, such as those occasions when she would make herself a cup of tea in a dressing room but fail to ask if anyone else wanted one. Despite any number of reminders from Nick and from John himself that all the cast were expected to help with loading and off-loading the van her contribution would never be more than carrying her own personal hand bags. She assumed that set, costumes and props would be delivered to where she wanted them and cleared away afterwards as a matter of course. Her family background had bred that assumption into her, the innate job demarcations of the rep theatres she had worked in, and living in digs had meant that she never had to undertake any of the mundane domestic chores that most people spend their lives completing daily.

Aside from the occasions when she deliberately baited John she really didn't see what caused his antagonism toward her. It mystified her if she bothered to think about it because she was convinced from the way he looked at her that he fancied her a bit. This idea annoyed her too, partly due to her approach to all those who came in contact with her, but also because, somewhere in the back of her mind she constantly knew that she was attracted to him.

She determinedly placed him firmly in the same league as all her company colleagues, one who had ended up in this small and insignificant company due to some slow slide down the ladder.

She knew that he had been a senior staff member in several major venues before joining 'Theatre Wagon'. The company gossip, which she eavesdropped while, standoffishly, not contributing to it, was that he had just emerged from a divorce which had left him with no house and little financial security. She wondered what his wife had been like and who had been at fault. John probably, she thought unkindly. But she wondered too what life had been like for them before the break up. A fleeting tinge of jealousy of his wife crossed her mind.

Snorting briefly she turned back to her letter writing, shifting herself more upright on her bed and re-positioning her writing pad. The bed squeaked annoyingly as she did this and she found herself trying to avoid moving. These letters would take a long time to write, she thought.

Chapter 8

Like an innocent man's sentence the schools tour dragged on. School hall after school hall, school dining room after school dining room, and occasionally a drama studio.

The company's mood changed periodically as the final weeks dragged by, from the excitement and promise of security caused by the prospect of the bigger scale tour, to uncertainty for some over who would be cast in the revised production. Some had uncertainty as to whether they actually wanted to be in the new show. Gradually word seeped out that the cast would be expanded, and a rumour spread that they might also have a second member of crew.

These hints and guesses mostly leaked via the company office, which the cast had started finding excuses to call in to before and after the daily round of performances as a means of keeping tabs on the developments. The secretary was usually on the verge of departure, to deal with her child following the school day, when they returned from any performance, but there were odd days when light traffic and a nearby venue got them back in time to ask how things were going with the plans. Alison was willing to leak news, although strictly most of the initial planning should have been fairly confidential. She was less happy at the crowding of her space by the cast who were usually insensitive to her desire to leave work. It was unusual, for normally she hardly ever saw the actors except when they reported for auditions and when a cast meeting was called. Rehearsals took place in other buildings.

John was better informed, due to a succession of meetings, if such a formal description could ever be applied to a conversation with Nick, to discuss the staging, the cast size, budgets, crewing and a hundred and one technical and administrative details. Strictly many of these details were beyond the responsibilities of John's job, but he preferred to check on details, knowing that Nick's organisational skills were rather limited.

Now, with an outline plan in place, though still no revised script or firm casting, selling was under way to venues. Office staff sent out promotional letters, accompanied by the first versions of the new show's leaflet, inviting bookings. These were followed up by phone calls. Where a venue expressed any vague interest Nick became involved for the specific negotiation of terms. There were many major logistical hurdles, not least attempting to fit the tour schedule around the available dates in the calendars of the venues. At one point the whole production's opening date was bought forward by a week to allow a booking.

The presence of the original book on which the show was based on the school curriculums and its classic status gave some impetus to sales to arts and arty venues. A very few medium sized theatres also expressed interest, but John was pleased that even those few would help to leaven what he anticipated as the dullness of the majority.

The show's staging and design remained rather fluid as these bookings dribbled in and contracts were issued and signed by both the theatres and Theatre Wagon. This was mainly because Nick dithered about appointing a designer, and was regularly attempting to alter what basic concepts had been sketched to suit each newly booked location. John was frustrated by this, and also by the growing awareness that the bookings were being accepted with little recognition of the travelling distances involved between the theatres. He foresaw, correctly, that the company would be trekking in an erratic zig-zag pattern across the length and breadth of the country throughout the whole period.

In some frustration, one afternoon, after a particularly trying couple of schools performances during which Penelope had been more than usually demanding, he was discussing the settings with Nick, and Nick was failing to be decisive, John grabbed a pen and some paper from the director's desk and sketched a rough drawing of what he thought was required for a set. Nick immediately accepted this as a finalised design, and thus the company dodged any set design fee. Later Nick would ask John to design the lighting and so make the rigging and plotting part of the routine get-in at each venue, showing yet more economic saving.

John sat in the café with Nicole one early evening. They had drifted into occasionally sharing a table and a meal after the day's work. John was more and more attracted to Nicole, and she, in turn, found these sporadic meals a welcome moment of enjoyment in that otherwise drab life in which she was frequently ignored by her colleagues. Nicole was pressing John for more news about the new tour, still unsure, despite the verbal assurances from Nick, of her continuing contract.

"Well it seems to have settled at thirteen weeks." John replied to her question about the likely length of the tour. "Though there's a few gaps as yet. We want to play the second half of the week and weekends at each venue, but some of them are shoving us into the first half of the week and including schools' matinees so they can have bigger draw shows on Fridays and Saturdays. It means we may have some long weekends off."

"Would we lose money if that happened?"

"No. Your contract means you get paid whatever happens."

"I haven't got a contract."

John mentally kicked himself. "You will have I'm sure," he told the girl, knowing that hers was typed up and in the file ready to be issued and signed as soon as the tour was a viable production.

"I thought we'd be stopping at each theatre for the whole week," she said.

"It would be nice, but I don't think anyone reckons they can sell it for a whole six night run. Better all round to have a few big houses than to play to acres of empty seats."

"But you'll have to keep doing get-ins and get-outs won't you?"

He laughed, stirring his second cup of tea with a slightly bent spoon that he then laid on the table.

"That's pretty normal, you know. You might have noticed I'm used to it."

Nicole blushed and looked down at her empty plate. She took the comment as a criticism of her for not helping more as they moved from school to school.

"I'm sorry. I'll try to do more to help."

John was quite surprised. He hadn't meant anything critical by his comment, especially so far as Nicole was concerned, for she, out of all the cast, helped carrying the props and costumes to and from the van more than anyone.

"You help more than anyone else," he reassured her, "and you've got just as much preparation before a performance, probably more with having to double parts."

She gave him one of those 'little-girl-lost' pathetic looks of hers, not sure whether he was telling the truth or being kind. She hoped he was telling the truth. No she hoped he was being kind. Oh it was no good, she couldn't work out her feelings either way. Part of her wanted to please him and to be seen as a helpful member of the cast, part of her wanted him to take care of her. These irregular tea-time tête-a-têtes were a highlight of her week. Cossetted in the steamy warmth of the café, its worn gloss paintwork slick with a build-up of ancient grease, she experienced a brief period of belonging, of having a friend. She liked her 'friend'. She liked having a friend and thinking of him that way. She wondered if there would be other cafés in the other towns that they would visit on tour. If he was right and she would be on the tour, she qualified her speculation. She hoped that she would be in the cast, partly for financial security, but mainly due to a desire to avoid having to deal with too many new and unknown people. She was just beginning to feel secure in John's company.

"Thirteen weeks," she mused aloud. "If I was on the tour could I stop in lots of short term digs and give up my digs here? Well I'd have to. I don't think I could afford both."

"Well you'll get the touring allowance, which helps."

"How will we travel? Will it be the van?"

"No. The set and so on will go in a rather bigger truck. You'll get some travelling allowance, but I guess they'll expect you to use cars. I'd start buttering someone with a car up so you can share with them."

She looked at him a little coyly. "Can I butter you up?"

"I think I'll be travelling in the truck."

Nicole looked downcast, and was silent for a moment. Outside the street lights had started to come on. Then she said, "I'd rather come in the truck with you."

John had been afraid she might suggest that. He quite liked the idea of company, of her company, for he was certain he would end up driving the vehicle due to Theatre Wagon's low budget ways, but he also knew that the schedule would mean him arriving long before a cast call so as to deal with the get-in and fit-up, plot the lighting, and sort with the numerous details that incoming shows have to attend to before an audience can be let in. For Nicole to travel in the truck would involve her in longer, more tiring hours than she really had to endure if she hitched a lift with some other member of the cast. It seemed more logical to him for her to do that. Surely she would not be cold shouldered by all the company? He made a mental note to gently sound out the cast members who remained with the revamped show and any new ones who joined after the auditions that were looming.

Changing the subject John started asking about her time at drama school. He soon established that she'd had to fight for the place and to pay her way through the course.

"Did you go out to see many shows when you were there? Most acting school students do."

"I had to work most evenings, and theatre tickets were too expensive for me anyway. Though we did get comps sometimes," she confessed, "I saw all the shows we did at the school though," she said hastily, lest he should think she'd shown a lack of interest.

"I expect the school productions were very.." he searched for a polite word for what he meant, "worthy."

"Well if you mean they were either classics or famous modern plays, yes, I guess you are right."

"I bet Adam would have approved of the modern stuff wouldn't he?" John could just imagine the kitchen sink dramas that a school would have chosen, straight from between the covers of 'Plays and Players'.

Nicole smiled faintly. "They did all seem to have downtrodden families struggling to survive, yes. But then I suppose I identified with those characters, even if I never seemed to get to play any of them, because I was having to make each penny count. You don't like Adam do you?"

"I think that there's something very sad about people with his standpoint and political views. Actually I feel sorry for him and all his type, their lives are sadly blighted by their hatred so they live in a permanent state of jealous rage."

He picked up the spoon and traced random damp trails on the formica surface of the table. He felt that the talk was heading in an unfortunate direction. He also knew that if he heard too much about modern political theatre he would start to put forward his own views on how theatre should be for entertainment, and that might be too much for the little actress, introducing, as it would, a prospect of debate.

"We'd better make a move or they'll be charging us rent." He looked across at the counter, where the woman had put down her paper for once and was watching them. Their eyes met and she grinned and winked at John with one of those knowing looks that people use when they think that they are observing a pair of lovers. Becoming aware of something happening behind her Nicole too turned towards the counter, but was too late to see, or failed to read, the conspiracy implicit in the woman's look. Responding to nearly being caught the woman opened the counter flap, which caught a loose edge of the hardboard frontage, causing it to snap back against the timber framework behind with an audible bang, and came bustling about collecting plates and cups.

"Got any plans for the evening then, you two?" she asked.

John and Nicole looked at each other, but neither made any move to take a step to admit their tentative relationship any further than they had and John said, "Oh nothing much I don't think."

The woman, disappointed, realised she wasn't going to learn any more about her customers' association, though her curiosity about how close they were was still unsatisfied, she gave John a hard questioning look and returned to the counter with much clattering of crockery, and another bang from the tortured hardboard. John stood.

"Thanks very much," he raised his voice slightly addressing the woman. "See you again." and he helped Nicole on with her coat and held the door open for her as they left.

Nicole looked at him when they were outside wistfully as he shut the café door, hoping he would make some suggestion for the evening. Cinema, or a drink in the pub perhaps she thought. But tonight was just like others, walking some of the way to her digs together and parting with a cheery 'See you tomorrow.'

John worried about what he possibly could, or should have done or said all the way back to his flat. More than conscious that Nicole was a lonely girl too shy to join in any conversations at her digs without being pulled into a group, and that she was attracted to him. Oh dammit! He was attracted to her. But he wasn't sure that starting a more serious relationship than the occasional greasy-spoon meal was a wise idea. He still smarted from his violent split with his dancer ex-wife, and the financial loss. Had Nicole been a more extrovert, even happy-go-lucky, kind of girl he might have been likely to move into some more serious sort of relationship. But he couldn't see Nicole as a long term partner, and was sensitive to the possibility of her being badly upset if, or more likely when, things didn't work out. This tour was near to its end, the new one would occupy no more than four months even allowing for rehearsals. He was sure that by the end of that time he would have lined up work on some major production, and it was inconceivable that Nicole would ever be taken on by shows of the scale he usually worked. The inevitable separation and certain implication of rejection, both on a personal, and a professional level would be too much for her, he thought.

Better, surely, to stay at arms length than to build up the girl's expectations or hopes and then dash them.

He stamped his feet on the pavement in annoyance and some

frustration as he strode towards his flat.

Nicole trudged sadly to her digs, fumbling in her pocket for the front door and room keys. Why wouldn't he move to see more of her? She really wanted to spend time with him, to share more experiences than a short meal, even, she admitted to herself, to let him love her. Her female instinct told her that he was attracted to her physically, and scared though she was of a sexual relationship she felt that he was kind and caring enough that with him it would be all right.

She let herself in to her digs, and was immediately accosted by the landlady, fussing about, saying that dinner would be ready almost immediately, and how late Nicole was today. The girl thought the title 'dinner' was pretentious for the evening meal, and her stomach rebelled at the idea of trying to eat the landlady's substandard fare on top of the café meal she had just had.

"I'm sorry. I don't think I can manage a meal tonight. I don't feel very well," she lied.

"Oh you poor dear," fussed the older woman, "Is it, you know, a woman's thing. I'll get you some soup and a hot water bottle." and before Nicole could raise more than a protesting 'No honestly Mrs Odet, I'll be all right,' the woman was off toward the kitchen saying commandingly "You go straight up your room, I'll bring it up for you."

Nicole ascended the stairs slowly and reluctantly, opening her room and leaving the door ajar as she went in. She knew better than to try to stop Mrs Odet in full flow. She knew better than to try to stop Mrs Odet from barging authorititively into her room. She sat on her bed, and it seemed only moments before the landlady, all fierce, seemingly motherly, concern and commotion, appeared with a tray with a bowl of tinned tomato soup and a hot water bottle in a flowered cloth cover.

"Now you eat this all up, and get to bed with this bottle. You'll feel much better in the morning," came the instruction, as the bottle was tucked between the sheets of the bed and the tray was balanced on the bedside table.

It was a relief to watch the door close behind the controlling woman. It was a relief to have been given tinned soup, for surely no-one could ruin that. Nicole picked up the spoon and tried the soup. Yes, Mrs Odet could even manage to spoil tinned soup, for she had clearly allowed it to heat in the pan without stirring it and had burnt the bottom layer on the hot metal of the saucepan. She struggled through some of it to show willing, skimming the less burnt part from the top of the bowl, before abandoning the tray and its contents on the dressing table, well away from her bed.

Despite the early hour she gave in to temptation and undressed and got into bed. Strangely she found herself relaxing, cuddling the bottle and enjoying its comfort. Slowly Nicole drifted off into a sleep in which she had vague nebulous dreams of dark stages, packed audiences, endless journeys in the front of vans, and no sign of John at all. She didn't stir when Mrs Odet, sour faced, but quiet, entered and retrieved the tray.

Some distance away, across the city, John slept badly. He too was dreaming. Dreaming of reaching out helplessly towards a pathetic looking Nicole, who was being mysteriously pulled away by some strange flood. He could have caught her, but Penelope was grasping one of his arms and holding him back, just out of reach of Nicole's plaintively outstretched hand. It was a very slow flood. The useless struggle seemed to continue unchangingly for hours, and he fought and tossed and turned most of the night. He woke in the morning with his bedclothes crumpled and feeling not at all refreshed.

Chapter 9

John ran out of letters of the alphabet for insulting epithets for Penelope before the schools tour ended. If it had not been for the problem of finding even coarse or crude words that suited her character for some letters, a problem which resulted in him thinking about certain letters for a couple of days, he would have had to go back to the beginning of the alphabet before they said goodbye to the last school. In the end he never did come up with anything for X or Z, he felt 'zombie' wasn't quite a description of her though he accepted 'vermin' when he thought of it.

The final part of the schools tour was enlivened by Nick holding auditions for the new version. Nick had suggested that candidates could be allowed to come along to school performances to see the play in action, but John had firmly vetoed that, pointing out that not only was it undiplomatic to have candidates watching the performance of people they would be replacing, for Adam had declared his intention of leaving, but that they would also see a very different show from what was intended to replace it.

The cast did see the auditionees in most cases, as they tended to still be waiting for the verdict in the offices when the show returned to base in late afternoon. The cast were curious about who had applied, and about who was to be offered parts. Unusually none of the applicants were acquaintances of the current cast so where they did meet in the crowded spaces around Alison's desk the conversations usually took the form of interrogation. Naturally the auditionees wanted to know about the company and the show. The existing cast wanted to know about the newcomers' backgrounds. Neither set of enquiries gave much insight. The existing cast knew little about the re-write of the show that was furiously taking place in a semi-detached house half a mile away where one of the more regular Theatre Wagon writers lived. The newcomers had usually already submitted whatever CV they had and explained any oddities to Nick. They were not very forthcoming when pressed to do this again as they realised that the cast would have little or no influence on the outcome of their application.

There were a few exclamations of "Oh yes. I've worked there." from both sides over the days, but no overlaps that might have led to renewed friendships. 'Or enmity,' thought John cynically to himself.

The applicants did not realise it, but John might have been the person to impress. Universally they ignored him, and he them. But Nick queried his opinions daily once everyone had left. Repeatedly John impressed on Nick that since he had only seen these people in a non-performance situation he couldn't give any view on their skill or talent. What he did express an opinion on was how each might fit into the company on a social level. As ever Nick was timid in making decisions. He had parted from each of the candidates with a stereotypical 'We'll let you know'. As a result John's views on the social graces of the people who applied carried more weight than would be usual or than it should have done. John was to remember this later as the personal relationships of his charges altered.

The discussion with Nick each evening, short though it was, disrupted the casual post show meal arrangement between John and Nicole. After several days when he found that she had drifted away from the company offices during his informal meeting he caught her as they got out of the van one night. The days were lengthening now as the months passed, and Easter was on the horizon, with the tour due to end with the schools breaking up. It was dry, but a cold wind was whipping through the little courtyard in front of the offices where the van was parked overnight and John eased Nicole into the shelter of the lee of the vehicle.

"Come and have a meal at the café tonight," he said.

He saw her hesitate. Slightly surprised he added, "I'll be as quick as I can with Nick. Look, I tell you what, you go and grab a table an order yourself a cup of tea and I'll join you as soon as I can get away from him."

Nicole nodded slowly.

"Ok," she said, "but please don't be long." And she went out of the yard through the gates and across the road towards the café. She was hesitant about going into the place alone. The other customers had never bothered her when she had been with John, but some of them struck her as being rough. Her real reservation came from her insecurity about John's friendship with her however. Ever since the night when she'd had to lie to Mrs Odet, because she'd been eating a meal with John, she had expected and then hoped that their occasional trysts would continue. Circumstances had meant that they had not. At first she had accepted that John's job as a company manger occupied different working hours to hers as a performer, but as the days turned into weeks she had become disillusioned, and then suspicious. She realised that she knew little, if anything, about his private life. He was said to be alone, but did he have a girlfriend that no-one knew about outside the TIE team? Was that why on several occasions, not least that last time, he had not invited her to spend more than the brief duration of a meal with her?

The wind snapped at her coat. It was not really thick enough for the cold of England in a spring which had not yet fully arrived. Like all her clothes it had been made to last a long time, and had been bought as an economic compromise between a winter coat and one that could be used in summer showers. She was pleased to open the door and enter the steamy warmth of the café. The woman behind the counter looked up from her usual newspaper and said,

"Hello dear. It's been a long time. What have you done with John?"

'What have I done with John?' Nicole wondered, and sadly realised she had never done anything with John apart from sit here and eat.

She said "He's supposed to be following me. May I have a tea while I wait please?"

"Sit down over there, I'll bring you one," said the woman. And the room resounded to the sound of pressurised steam and water forcing its way into the dented steel teapot, the clink of crockery and the bang of a loose bit of hardboard as the counter was opened and her drink brought to her.

"Thank you." Nicole said with genuine gratitude.

"You're welcome."

And the counter hardboard banged again as the woman returned to her paper. Nicole had the feeling that the woman would have said more.

She was half way through the tea when a blast of air from the door heralded John's arrival.

"I'm sorry. Nick would discuss todays auditions," explained John. "Yes please, tea..." He said in answer to the raised eyebrow behind the counter. "Have you ordered?"

Nicole shook her head.

"..and two all day breakfasts please. And I've brought something for you," he said to the waitress. She looked surprised. He pulled a hammer and some nails from his coat pocket, marched to the counter and with a few deft strokes nailed the loose piece of corrugated hardboard back to the counter's frame. Two workmen, seated at a table alongside the wall, turned to watch what John was doing.

"Now she'll be able to creep up on us," joked one when he had finished.

"What makes you think she'd want to creep up on you?" the other asked.

John put the hammer back in his pocket. "It was getting a bit annoying wasn't it," he said.

The woman behind the counter thanked him, and pushed his tea across the counter towards him, saying "On the house."

"Some people will do anything for a free cuppa," quipped the second labourer.

"I notice Mary's had to hand that tea over the counter to you now you've nailed the door up," said his mate.

John laughed and joined Nicole. She smiled sheepishly.

"You really are everyone's good Samaritan aren't you?"

"Oh it's just a nail or two. It didn't take a lot of time and effort."

"No, but you thought of it. It's really nice of you." She decided to press him. "What was Nick saying? Or is it all confidential?"

"Oh, nothing much. I gather he now thinks he's decided on the new people, and the script is pretty much complete, so he's ready to start as soon as the schools tour finishes. Well as soon as the new contracts take effect, which might be a week or so later."

"I still haven't been given a contract."

"Trust me, it's no real secret, you will get one to sign as soon as the office gets round to it." John decided to reassure her. "You'll get a nice rest after the schools, and then into rehearsals."

Vague hope surfaced for Nicole. "Will you get a rest too?"

"No such luck," actually he hated the periods of enforced idleness that came occasionally in the theatre world, "the set construction will be going on, and you can bet your life that Nick will be wanting new props for the new tour, so that means buying trips."

Nicole's disappointment was disguised by the arrival of their food. As the workmen had predicted the absence of the sharp bang caused by opening the counter door meant that the two of them didn't anticipate the woman's approach. Nicole jumped. John laughed, and said, "He was right, you can creep up on us now, Mary."

"Sorry to have startled you if you two were up to anything." said the waitress.

"We weren't...." started Nicole, and then realising that it was said in jest, stopped, and changed to saying, "Thank you." Mary smiled at her indulgently and winked before going back to her newspaper.

John was liberally sprinkling salt and pepper on his egg, and scraping around in an almost empty pot of mustard when he suddenly suggested, "You could come on a props buying trip or two if you liked, if you've got nothing to do."

"I'd like that. Where do we go?"

"It depends what comes up on Nick's list. We sometimes use one of the theatre hire firms, but if he's only looking for bits of furniture we can probably buy suitable stuff cheaper from the local second hand shops."

"Surely furniture of this period would be expensive antiques?"

"Strictly, yes. But we'll do a bit of butchering of some stuff that looks old."

"Will that work?"

"Oh we'll get away with it. There'll be the odd individual in any audience who knows it's wrong, but they'll get a nice superior feeling by spotting any errors."

"I think you are cynical," she chided him gently.

"I'm a realist." He speared a piece of sausage.

Nicole looked sadly at him as he carried on eating. She thought that having the idea that the world was full of people who enjoyed picking out errors was somehow depressing. But did John really think that, or was he being flippant? She often found it difficult to decide whether he really meant what he said.

"You don't mean that," she said. "You don't really think that audiences sit there trying to pick holes in the show do you?"

"I think it depends on the show," he answered, "If you go to see something light and escapist, particularly a musical, or perhaps even better variety, or cabaret, even panto, you go in with the expectation of being entertained. You go to enjoy yourself. And unless the production is truly awful, which isn't really very often the case in the professional theatre world, you will enjoy yourself. And that's partly because you went in with that expectation, with that intention." He took another mouthful, warming to a theme he never missed an opportunity to rehearse to any captive listener. "But," he continued through munching, "if you attend straight drama, plays, except comedies, of course, and arts type shows, and particularly anything considered a worthy classic, heaven help us, you are condemned to a miserable evening. Our schools audiences are doubly cursed, because they are forced to attend a classic that won't entertain them and wasn't their choice in a staging that removes all the trappings of amusement and enjoyment... no glamour, no glitter, usually no bright lights."

He looked to see if she was following him. Nicole nodded slowly, perhaps unconvinced. Through another mouthful he carried on.

"You can't be surprised with a straight play audience if their attention wanders to pick up on scenic errors or props anachronisms, there's little else to amuse them. It gets worse once some director wants to try to impose a message on the audience. Lots of the fringe and small companies touring the arts centres are political. I can point you at companies whose sole raison-de-être is to spread some sort of propaganda. It's usually left wing, sometimes it's got some other axe to grind, Adam's keen on the left-wing you may have noticed, sometimes it's feminist or has a local mission bent. In a few cases, actually very few, their staging and presentation is very slick and clever, but it will never prevent any half sensible audience from realising they have just been lectured to. If I want to be lectured to I turn the tele onto BBC2 late at night and watch the Open University."

"Why are you working for Theatre Wagon if you feel so strongly that way?" she ventured.

"Well, despite ramming some set text down young victims' throats Theatre Wagon doesn't really stage lectures although Adam might wish to. But I wouldn't choose to be in this section of the industry. I had a few weeks of resting and this came along... you know how it is." He looked up from his plate at her, and she nodded, "When another entertainment show comes knocking I'll be off like a shot."

Nicole suddenly felt a chill of apprehension. Just as she was maybe starting to have a friend in the company he was casually suggesting leaving. She said "Oh," in a voice that conveyed enough disapointment for John to realise what he had said and understand her meaning.

"Don't worry," he told her, "it won't happen that soon, I expect."

The discovery that he might be leaving the company, if he got the chance, which would leave her back as the outcast of the group, made Nicole more subdued than usual as they finished the meal. Leaving the café the habitual separation to their respective digs seemed even more painful than ever to the girl. John was in an ebullient mood and failed to notice these symptoms.

"Let me know when we can go props shopping." she reminded him, "I'll have to tell Mrs Odet, she's my landlady."

"Do I have to ask her permission to take you out then?" he joked. "Sounds like a real tyrant."

"She probably means well," Nicole said generously. "But she is a bit bossy. And she can't cook either."

"Digs with a bossy landlady and bad food. You have been unlucky," he said, "See you tomorrow." And he was gone.

Chapter 10

The long awaited end of the schools tour accelerated towards them all with surprising speed. Lighter days, warmer days, and though the nights were still chilly, even cold, the certainty that spring at least was on the way. The overnight cold still meant that John was running the van's heater to clear the misted windscreen each morning, as they repeatedly waited for Penelope to arrive. Reluctant though he was to give the girl credit for anything, John did have to admit that her timekeeping had gradually become better. There were even occasional mornings when she climbed into the van with the others. He was more and more sure, despite this, that her tardiness was part of a concerted attempt on her part to avoid social interaction with the rest of the cast as much as possible. John could understand this in the case of their resident campaigning actor. After all, his scathing attacks on her had been relentless even when he had been told to give it a rest. He couldn't quite understand why she would wish so obviously to avoid the others.

He could admit some bias in thinking that Penelope should have no reason to avoid Nicole, who he had become more and more fond of as the show had gone on, and Hugh was usually willing to talk to anyone. It occurred to him that there was probably a critical mass for the size of a touring company, below which personal relationships would always founder and be under strain. You had to have enough people to make it possible to form cliques for people to join in with, he decided. Theatre Wagon's tiny gang was certainly too small to allow this. He wondered whether the slightly larger cast; Nick had decided to add another actor and another actress for the mid-scale version, would be enough to deal with this problem. He doubted it, he was sure that Theatre Wagon would never expand a cast beyond this point. There had been long, even acrimonious, discussions over the financial situation caused by a couple of extra salaries. Nick had overriden the accounts section's doubts, but only because he wanted to have more freedom of staging, not for social purposes. More cast, though not more crew John noticed, reduced the pressure to be inventive with the scripting, and Nick was always on the lookout for an easier time for himself as director. With the school version he, or at least the company, had had to be creative with doubling parts and giving the gist of the plot. Now with the script writer working on the show with more actors there would be less compromise, and so less effort to cover the story.

John had the advantage over the cast of having been kept informed about the venues they would be playing as each booking was made. He was pleased with some of them, old familiar stomping grounds in the case of some of the larger theatres, where they would be 'playing underneath' another show which was already running in the evenings. Some smaller venues he had heard of, some he knew by repute, arts centres and council owned theatres mostly. In some cases he knew little or nothing about the proposed venue, and little or no technical information had been sent by them. He rummaged through the files that the office assiduously kept of show reports and frequently found that the company had never visited some of these places before. In those cases he resorted to looking up their entry in the 'British Theatre Directory', well aware as he did so that the specifications were usually a year or two out of date, and had been written by managements that were keen to show their theatre in the best possible light. He had been let down too often before by discovering on arrival that the equipment stock was a thin imitation of what was listed in the publication. Usually this was due to the original stock list being reprinted year after year with no allowance for losses and failures. 'Ambitious' was a word that sprang to his mind for some stock descriptions. Despite this, the directory did at least give him an idea of the general style of unknown venues if that had been needed. The title 'arts centre' really said it all to John. It implied meritorious, possibly experimental, venues with some sort of idea of educating a public who would, he was sure, consist mostly of professional people who attended, not to be entertained, but to be seen.

He was more than grateful, despite this, to find that enough of the venues were 'proper' stages to ensure that the company would not be expecting to employ thrust or in-the-round staging. He was relieved that this was the case, removing, as it did, the niggling problems of lighting and sound in such spaces at the same time as saving him personally from his dislike of formats where the audience surround the performers.

The last few schools of the tour were, he was pleased to find, ones where the staging was inevitably end-stage, even in one case actually on a platform stage, and where some minimal equipment allowed for rudimentary lighting.

Making their way to one of the very last schools the long journey took them across country. On the way John pulled the van off the road into a petrol station. A black rubber hose stretched loosely across the entrance sounded a bell as the tyres squashed it which they could hear in the van.

John stopped by the pumps and got out, and was greeted by an elderly man in greasy overalls who said, "What'll it be?" as he reached for the pump nozzle.

"Oh fill it right up please." John told him. He was out of practice with attendant service these days. He would probably only have put a few gallons in if he had been serving himself, but felt that the small remote business should get all the sales it could.

The cast were climbing out of the side door, stretching, and looking about at the wild countryside around the wayside service station. Adam strode away to the edge of the forecourt and stood on a low mound surveying the land. Hugh and Nicole went the other way to admire a view of rolling hills. John saw that Penelope stayed close to the van, watching him, but even she couldn't help stretching and luxuriating a bit in the sunshine.

"This is nice," said Hugh to Nicole.

Nicole thought how much nicer it would have been if she and John had been together looking at the countryside, rather than being with Hugh. She didn't dislike Hugh, but a rural idyll with John was much more attractive to her. She looked back to where he was standing beside the attendant near the pumps.

"Yes," she agreed "it makes a nice change from all those schools."

Pumping complete, the attendant wiped his hands on a rag which he then rubbed on the filler cap and led the way to the tiny wooden hut kiosk. Squeezing himself behind the little counter, which was black with age and oil and wear, he asked, "Will it be cash or card?"

John waved the company card at him, and while the man laboriously wrote the amount onto the blank greaseproof paper and carbon slips, and carefully inserted them into the machine before sliding the roller back and forth over the garage's embossed plate, said what a nice setting this was, and asked if trade was good. John signed, and received the customer copy, as the man shrugged.

"We're in the middle of nowhere. Some days we hardly see anyone."

Sorry for him, John rounded up his cast and pointed out "Last chance to stock up on sweets and crisps today," which swelled the man's take by a little, before herding them into the van and setting off again to the distant sound of bells pinging as he drove over the other rubber pipe on the way out.

"What a nice old-fashioned place," said Hugh

Everyone agreed, and Adam's comment that the attendant shouldn't have had to 'serve' them as it was demeaning was cut short as he was shouted down by the whole company who for once were united in enjoying the rare trip in the country.

The very last performance was a let-down however, with the all too familiar school hall, stinking of the all too recent school dinner, its floor grubby with spilt food and with an inattentive audience marshalled by disinterested teachers. John felt it was a fitting end to the run as it encapsulated all that he hated about theatre in education.

"That was a duff way to end," said Hugh, as they loaded the van for the last time.

John, who was bent over in the vehicle wrestling items into place and trying to soften the worst excess of carelessness that the cast were demonstrating, now that they believed they would no longer be needing the furniture and rudimentary scenery, grunted.

"You're not surprised are you?" adding "Try not to break that, we'll probably need it on the revamped tour."

His caution was mostly ignored by his tiny cast, who, like schoolchildren on the last day of term, were eager to escape. They had arranged among themselves to have an after tour get together in the pub nearest to the offices, and had invited the new actors who were to join the revised version of the show, along with the office staff and Nick. John realised that he hadn't been asked, but had decided he had better show his face. He was pressured into attending mostly by Nicole. She initially had failed to notice that the others had omitted John from the informal guest list and was eager that he should be there, partly so that she would not be alone in the crowd. The omission wasn't a deliberate slight by the cast, it was just an example of the way John's presence was a constant that they took for granted, much as one might with a servant. Perhaps therein lay the root of some of his dislike of the schools tour he thought.

Late in the day the cast, or at least Hugh and Nicole, discussed whether John was coming.

""I have asked him," she said.

"Oh, good." Hugh seemed slightly relieved, "I just realised that probably no one had mentioned it to him. It would look very bad if we'd forgotten him entirely."

Nicole noticed that even Hugh was more concerned with 'how it would look' than with actually wanting John there, or even thinking it would have been a friendly thing to do.

"You wouldn't care if it upset him would you, just so long as it didn't 'look bad'." she snapped at him.

Hugh was surprised at her vehemence. He was conscious of the girl's crush on John, which of the cast wasn't, but he had not expected the little mouse to roar. Caught out he said, "I'm sorry. I didn't mean it like that. Of course we want him there."

She was only slightly mollified by this response but let it go.

John would probably not really have minded missing the end of run party. They had pushed a few of the pub's tables together and were gathered in the slight bay of a window overlooking a drab street. The tables didn't fit together, as they were the small round type with the ornate cast iron legwork frame, painted and overpainted in black gloss, with the animal head at each leg picked out in heavy gold till the original casting had all but vanished below the coats of paint. Each heavy table bore the signs of having been moved about before, with large chunks missing from the paintwork and the edges of the mahogany tops. By the time they had all crowded around their cluster of furniture life was uncomfortable and far too snug. The sticky tabletops had a selection of card beermats, many of which had been stripped of a few layers by previous customers idly delaminating them paper layer by paper layer, and in each case a large, slightly grimy ashtray, advertising beers. Wherever you sat there was a good chance that you were either contending with a gap in the tables, where two curved edges met, or rather failed to meet, meaning you had limited options as to where to put your glass, or your legs were constrained by the forest of curved ironwork below. Or in some places both these inconveniences. John was suffering from both discomforts.

He'd arrived a bit late, to find Nicole valiantly saving a place for him beside her. Nick was at the bar fetching drinks, having realised that he would be expected to buy a round, and hoping that he would get out of further cost if he 'got them in' first. His wife had attended, and was clearly not enjoying the experience of being wedged in among the cast. When Nick did return from the bar, grappling with several glasses, including one for John, he found that the space he had occupied before he left had somehow shrunk and he spent the rest of the time standing just too far away from his wife for either of them to be able to suggest leaving to each other. He would find himself told off about this almost the moment they eventually passed out of the door.

From where he was John could look round the gathering, but he was trapped in a way that made it impossible for him to speak to anyone apart from those immediately either side. Nicole, of course, and on the other side Alison, the secretary. Sitting beside the office worker in a social gathering like this he realised how little he knew about her, and more noticeably how little they had in common. She had, he would find, no interest in theatre at all and saw the job as exactly that, just a job.

"Whatever made you come and work for Theatre Wagon then?" he asked when he realised this.

"What?" The noise in the bar had become too much for real conversation.

"Why did you come to work at Theatre Wagon if you don't like theatre?"

"Oh. It had its attractions I suppose."

"Don't tell me you fancied Nick," he shouted in her ear jokingly, at exactly the moment one of those sudden and unpredictable lulls in the noise level make bits of conversation audible to all around. Several heads turned John's way. He was a bit embarrassed to see that one of them was Nick's wife.

Alison, oblivious to the momentary spotlight on their chat, said "Certainly not!" in a way that was unambiguous.

This time it was Nick's head that turned to them, and John had the brief impression that there was a flicker of disappointment on his features.

As always the chatter swelled back up and the interlude was lost in the mêlée.

"I wanted to be able to stop work in time to get the kids from school. Obviously a TIE team wouldn't need me after school hours, so I told Nick that was when I was prepared to work till."

John contemplated the endless occasions when he had had to extract details of the next day's performances from the files himself on return from an afternoon show. It galled him that even though this was not really what he understood as the 'entertainment industry' there should be people in it who saw their personal lives as more important than the show. It flew in the face of everything he had always believed in all the years of working in the business. He was wryly amused to discover that Nick had tamely agreed to terms laid down by a prospective employee. She was, after all, just a fairly fast and accurate typist. So far as John could tell she had no initiative, and, now he discovered, no sympathy for show biz. He was formulating a reply to this revelation when Nicole on the other side of him tugged at his sleeve.

"This is Laurence," she indicated the newcomer on the other side of her. "He's taking over from Adam when the new tour starts. He's been in tele and everything." She was clearly impressed.

John leaned across to shake hands with the new actor. He was conscious of brushing against Nicole to do so and put his other hand on the back of her chair to steady himself. To most of the assembly it looked as though he had his arm around her. Laurence's handshake was the firm confident business-like shake of someone very much in command of the situation. His eyes studied John steadily in the way of people who are making a judgement.

"John," he pronounced. "How good to meet you. Our general factotum I understand."

"Oh John does everything for us, don't you?" Nicole looked up at him leaning over her, his face just inches from hers. He had a sudden, almost irresistable urge to kiss her, but he sat up straighter, released from the handshake, and quipped,

"All the things I'm supposed to do for the show, and all the things that lazy actors can't be bothered to do for themselves."

He kept his arm round the back of Nicole's chair as he looked meaningfully over to where Penelope was, next to Nick's wife. She had chosen a seat as far from Adam as practical in a small gathering like this. It was her choice of seat that had caused Nick to end up standing after buying the first round. Penelope saw John looking her way and gave one of those seemingly snooty slight tosses of the head, but her eyes stayed on him.

Laurence was picking up the social interactions very quickly, or maybe someone had filled him in. He said,

"Perhaps we can change things a bit, you know, all pull together, that sort of thing. When I was in soap the cast was one big happy family."

John had a flash of recognition. The face had been familiar, now he realised that this new cast member had been a regular on the screen in a daytime soap, he'd not watched it but knew it had been playing to millions. He wondered about that fall in status. Not that Nicole had given that much thought, he could see that she was slightly in awe of Laurence.

He craned his head this way and that to see if he could identify any other newcomers. By his reckoning there should have been another actress and another actor joining the company. Just as he was about to ask Alison Nick banged on a table and started into what was obviously a prepared speech.

"Firstly I would like to thank the original cast for a tremendous schools tour. The response from the schools you played to has been excellent. We are sorry to see Adam leaving us to move on to pastures new," there was a general mutter from the company at this, in which John was almost sure he heard Penelope saying 'good riddance' under her breath, "and we wish him success in his new venture."

The stilted speech continued:-

"It is with great anticipation that we are getting ready for the mid-scale touring version of the show. The revised script is nearly ready, and when we start rehearsals in a couple of weeks time I am sure we will be able to give you a full list of the bookings. To do this expanded version we have increased the size of the cast as you know, so three new faces are joining us. Laurence," he paused and pointed dramatically, " is taking over Adam's part. If you think that he looks familiar, then you are right. We are very lucky to have a famous TV soap star in our midst."

A small ripple of applause greeted this statement. Laurence made an exaggerated bow from his seat. Adam shrugged, and Hugh looked rather downcast at his former position as a television actor being quietly sidelined.

"Two more members of cast will be added, but couldn't be with us this evening. You will meet them when rehearsals start. Meanwhile have a good evening." Nick finished abruptly, looked for somewhere to sit down, still failed to find a seat and looked hopelessly at his wife, who frowned at him.

There was a momentary quiet. The time for applause passed, no applause came, and the cast went back to their private conversations.

"Another drink?" asked John.

Laurence accepted, Nicole hesitated, of course, but was persuaded, and John felt obliged to ask Alison, who said 'no' and made immediate preparations to leave. He fought his way to the bar. Returning with the drinks he had more room, as Alison had left, but he returned to the previous position, even putting his arm around the back of Nicole's chair again on the excuse of leaning toward Laurence during the conversation.

The evening wound down quite quickly. Nick and his wife made excuses and left. Adam struck up a conversation with some of the locals on the other side of the bar, and eventually slipped away with only the barest of goodbyes to anyone. Laurence declared that he had to catch a train back to London, as he had not yet got himself digs in the area.

Unexpectedly Hugh was to be heard persuading Penelope to join him at the local Chinese restaurant, and they left together.

John looked at Nicole. "Another? Or do you want to join those two?"

"I don't want to join them I don't think. Anyway they didn't ask us."

John thought Hugh might not have roped them in because he thought they wanted to be alone.

He said, "But?"

"Is there somewhere we could go for a coffee?"

Nicole held her breath, and crossed her mental fingers, hoping.

"Do you want to come to my flat?"

"Oh yes!" she gushed, too eagerly.

John smiled at her in an almost fatherly way. "Come on then." he said, standing and helping her on with her coat.

She'd never been exactly sure where he lived. It turned out to be a mere couple of streets from Theatre Wagon's office, the first floor of an old Victorian terraced house that had been divided and let out. The narrow shared hallway was unprepossessing, with wood panelling to waist height, and heavily textured patterned wallpaper above, painted in a cream gloss. There was a small shelf where the walls angled for the staircase which was piled with what seemed to her to be a huge quantity of post. John flicked through it briefly as they passed. He selected one envelope from the pile and dumped the rest back on the shelf. She could see that most of the envelopes were circulars and that Reader's Digest seemed to predominate.

He led the way up to the landing and opened the door with a Yale key which was on a very large bunch he pulled from his pocket.

"What are all those for?" she started to ask, but he was standing aside to let her in to the flat, reaching round the doorframe to flick the light switch on as she passed him. She took one step inside the room and stopped staring, taking it all in. He came in behind her and put his hand on her shoulders.

"Oh it's lovely!"

He shut the door.

"Let me have your coat," he said, but she was looking round the big high room.

It was decorated in colours that were perhaps a few years out of date, with deep purple carpet, and turquoise walls. There were double sash windows opposite them which she found out looked over the rear garden. The other walls contained doors off to the kitchen, bathroom and bedroom, and each spare space between these housed an alcove with an arched top shelved and crammed with books and files. There was big soft furniture, and an old fashioned table and chairs, and against one spare piece of wall an old rolltop desk stood, open, crammed with papers with a typewriter balanced on them and a swivel captain's chair at it.

The light switch had turned on a big Victorian glass bowl light in the centre of the room, but John moved round the room now, turning on a standard lamp, the desk anglepoise and a switch that lit the alcoves by concealed lamps in the top hidden behind the arches. He turned off the main light and the room was warm and friendly and welcoming.

"Oh John!" and she suddenly thought that it might have been the first time she had said his name like that to him. "It's really nice."

"You didn't have to be so surprised," he joked, "What did you expect, a squat?"

"I don't know. It's just that I've been in digs so long, and living out of a suitcase, and I've never been able to afford anything.... well 'nice', and this is a home."

"Well you make yourself at home while I put the kettle on, unless you want something stronger?"

She hesitated.

"I've got wine."

"Yes, wine please."

"Red or white?"

"White please. Is that a model of a theatre?" She was looking at a model of the settings for a show on one of the shelves whose stage had become the resting place for the phone. She moved the phone to one side.

"It's the set model for a show I worked on a few years ago," he said, and disappeared into the kitchen. There were clinking noises, and he re-emerged dangling two glasses by their stems and holding a bottle and a corkscrew in the other hand.

"What show was it?" closer inspection had revealed a thin layer of dust on the detailed intricate model, but although she had seen such things before briefly, usually on the first day of rehearsal at a crowded read through, she had never seen a professional set model at close quarters.

"'Chuzzlewit'" he said casually. He started to screw the corkscrew into the top of the bottle.

"The musical? You worked on that?" she was agog with envy, for it had been one of the hit musicals running briefly in London during her student days, one of the shows she had yearned to see and had been unable to afford.

"Yes, I was the stage director." The cork popped out of the neck of the bottle and he poured two glasses. "Do sit down."

There was, she decided, no boastfulness about the statement, it was just a fact. She took the proffered glass and went and perched on the edge of one of the big soft armchairs. He flung himself onto the sofa.

"Come on here if you like," he said.

She stood up to cross to the sofa, but stopped as she was distracted by the contents of the shelves. The files had worn spines and were clearly scripts or prompt copies. Several well known show titles jumped out at her, and she began to appreciate the extent of his background in the business. The books were almost exclusively theatre related, mostly text books, or directories of artists, actors and actresses, or of theatres themselves. In a rather dusty corner of one shelf a small framed photo was half hidden by the books. She pulled it out and examined it, wine glass in one hand, picture in the other. It showed a young woman, in a skimpy, glittery cabaret style costume with a feathered head-dress.

"My ex-wife," he said.

"I'm sorry. I shouldn't have been nosy." She was trying to balance the picture back where it had come from.

"It doesn't matter, it was a long time ago," he said. "Water under the bridge. The wounds have healed... even the cuts and bruises."

"Cuts and bruises?" Nicole was surprised at the implication.

"We had a love – hate relationship. She loved to hate me. Sometimes she could be very violent."

The girl was silent. Not knowing what to say to this revelation.

"Oh don't worry, in return I hated to love her."

Nicole had the feeling that these plays on words were well rehearsed and were saved for exactly these sorts of moments of explanation. She said "And now you are divorced?" and came and sat beside him.

"We don't have to talk about her." John said.

Nicole swigged some of her wine. John topped the glass up and she said, "But you obviously still have feelings for her. You've got her picture there." She pointed with her free hand. "I guess she was a dancer?"

"Yes. Still is I suppose."

"You don't know?"

"All right, yes, I know. People tell me when she turns up in shows they are working on. It's not a big thing, we aren't going to get back together you know." He nearly added 'don't worry' but bit it off, thinking it might be forward, and frighten her with the implicit message.

Nicole thought about this. She wanted to ask if he would like to get back with his ex. She wanted to know about how they had split. Yes, she admitted to herself, she wanted to be sure that she wouldn't prevent that happening if she got closer to John. She was dismayed at the picture, partly because it had been kept more or less on display, and partly because it showed an evidently sexy and attractive woman. She couldn't help comparing herself to the dancer in the picture.

John couldn't help comparing her to his ex-wife too. Nicole's whole personality was almost the reverse of hers. She was modest and retiring, not raunchy and pushy. She was gentle and thoughtful, not brash and domineering. Her curves were sexy, but not in the pin-up brazenness of his ex-wife. She had, he realised, been for the past few weeks, an unfulfilled fantasy for gentle, caring loving, quite unlike the uncontrollable desire that his ex had inspired in the early, happy, days. Now he was very unsure what to do next. He still wanted to avoid hurting Nicole in any way, but there was a growing desire which he couldn't completely ignore. He held out an arm to indicate the seat beside him. When she was seated he let his arm rest softly on her shoulders. Nicole looked at him, her expression clearly implied that she wasn't sure whether to move away, or move closer. They covered the awkwardness by each draining their glasses. John refilled them.

Nicole knew she was getting a bit dizzy from the drinks in the pub, and now the wine. Her mind's suspicious part wondered if John was deliberately getting her drunk; the trusting part was feeling relaxed and happy and wanting to be closer and closer to him. She rested her head on his shoulder and they talked.

She'd admitted before to her penniless training and the struggles of a not very successful actress life. He'd been less forthcoming about his past, limiting the information to a series of reluctant admissions of having worked on what she thought of as huge and glamourous productions. Now, as the evening grew much later, and the wine in the bottle vanished, she told of her childhood, and he opened up about the highly successful backstage life he had been leading until recently. She remained impressed at casual mentions of star names and big theatres and he was even relaxed enough in her company to describe some of the violent arguments and fights he and his ex had had before their split.

Gradually the talk grew intermittent, and John realised that the girl was dozing off on his arm. Vaguely he wondered if her landlady would be concerned at her absence, and then he too slept.

It was the cold of the early morning hours that woke him. Nicole was still asleep and he worked his arm out from behind her and spent a few moments restoring the circulation. Then he carefully picked her up and carried her to the bedroom, laid her on the bed, removed her shoes and tucked her under the covers. He got himself a blanket and returned to the sofa to sleep.

Chapter 11

Hugh and Penelope left the pub together and walked the few streets to the Chinese restaurant in silence. Penelope was still thinking about John and Nicole as she walked. They got a table about half way back in the long thin building. The waiter gave them menus and flicked casually at the thick, slightly stained tablecoth. A few discarded grains of dry rice came off the cloth and went onto the floor. Penelope was a bit disgusted by this, but Hugh, seeing her reaction, said as the waiter went off: "Always go to places that are too busy to change the cloths, it's a guarantee of popularity."

Penelope wasn't sure if he was joking, but let it pass and they made their choices. Returning, the waiter took their orders, and almost miraculously the table was suddenly filled with gleaming glasses, fresh, linen napkins folded in fancy shapes and shiny cutlery, as well as, (she worried), wrapped packets of chopsticks.

"Did you know it was smarter than it appeared?" she asked him.

"Haven't you ever been here before?" Hugh said in genuine amazement. "There's only here and the Indian down the road that are worth going to in this town."

"I hardly ever eat out, my digs feed me and I'm not keen on eating alone. Anyway I never really know what to order in these foreign places."

"Ah, I thought you were copying me when we ordered." said Hugh, and it was true that she had said 'I'll have the same' a couple of times. "But I don't think you can call this, or the Indian further along 'foreign'. It's all very anglicised, specials for the English palate. The Indian was telling me last time I was in there that they mostly sell Chicken Tikka Masala."

"Well that's foreign isn't it?"

"Good Lord, no! It was invented in Birmingham by people running curry houses in this country. There's nothing remotely like that in proper Indian cuisine."

"Have you been to India?"

"No, but I used to share a flat with a bloke who was Indian. He was on the crew of one of my films. He had lots of Indian friends and they used to come round regularly and they'd take over the kitchen and cook up what they said was proper food. They let me have some, of course."

"Did you like it?"

"I loved it. Well apart from the time I bit into a chilli by mistake. I thought I'd never be able to deliver a line again. I couldn't speak for half an hour." He laughed. "Anyway, trust me Indian restaurants in this country bear no resemblance to the real thing."

"And Chinese restaurant menus?" she questioned.

"Pretty much the same problem I think. But I still like them."

As he said this the starters arrived. They had both ordered soup. Penelope toyed doubtfully with the strange shaped porcelain spoon that had been provided but was eventually surprised at how well it worked. She found the soup watery, with occasional bits of vegetables she could not identify floating about in it. She also decided she liked it. Hugh was slurping unashamedly, while her upbringing made her try to eat daintily.

There was a similar difference of approach with the main course when it came. Penelope looked dubiously at the chopsticks, but Hugh grabbed a fork and began an untidy shovelling action. It explained to her the stray rice that had been on the table, but she copied his method. Once they were well into eating the food the conversation resumed.

111

"Well, like it?" Hugh asked.

"Yes. Very much. I haven't had anything like this before."

"You must have had Chinese before surely." Hugh was an inveterate 'after show', or perhaps in the past 'after shooting' restaurant diner.

"Only a Vesta Chow Mein." she admitted.

Hugh spluttered through a mouthful of beansprouts.

"Vesta!" He was genuinely horrified, expressing his shock so loudly that one or two of the other customers turned to look. Penelope could see a few faces in the dim light of red and gold lampshades against red wallpaper looking their way. "That's not Chinese," he finished more quietly, "that's Cup-a-soup in a fancy packet."

Penelope, whose self-catering experience was quite limited and whose dining-out had previously only extended to fairly posh restaurants with her family, or reluctant visits to pubs or cafés with fellow actors, due to living in digs which provided bed, breakfast and evening meal ever since leaving acting school, bristled at the feeling she was being mocked.

Hugh saw that he had offended her. Conscious of how easy that was, from weeks trailing round schools in the back of a van with her, and not really wanting a scene, he said, "All right, all right, I'm sorry. It's easy to forget how different people have different experiences. What sort of things did you used to eat when you lived at home with your parents?"

"Our cook did a lot of traditional English meals. So breakfast tended to be bacon and egg, or possibly porridge in the winter. We always had a very light lunch, because father didn't like to leave the company for too long at lunch-time."

Hugh knew about her father's big company. Everyone did. "Didn't he trust his managers?" he said.

"He didn't want people saying he was taking long lunch breaks when they only got an hour. Anyway," she was defensive of her father for a moment, "he worked very hard."

"Oh I'm sure."

Momentarily she thought he was being disbelieving, but he was meeting her gaze quite seriously.

"And so we had afternoon tea and then dinner at night."

"On weekdays?"

"Every day. Except sometimes on a Saturday if mother and I went into the city shopping. Then we might have afternoon tea out."

"What did cook give you for dinner then?"

"She did whatever mother told her to." Penelope was still eating the meal. "Always a starter, and either a roast, or something like chops, traditional English fare, and desserts. Mrs Hobward was very good at desserts."

"Have you got a sweet tooth then?"

Penelope nodded munching.

"And what became of Mrs, what was it, Hobward?"

"She's still there. When her husband, he worked for father, died, they moved her in to the house. She's getting a bit old now, and mother says the cooking's getting erratic, but she's still feeding the family."

"If she was there when you were a child how old is she now?"

Penelope considered. "Seventy something I suppose."

There was a longish silence, during which she finished her meal. His mention of desserts had made her think of a sweet, but she'd already stretched her budget by coming for this meal at all. She could survive the next week or two on Mrs Bray's homely if cheap meat and two veg meals if she stinted on the midday meal out. She was tempted by the thought of something simple and reliable, a comfort food like ice-cream.

Hugh had changed the subject and was questioning her about what she really thought of the coming mid-scale tour. She wasn't sure that she wanted to confide many more private views and information. Still Hugh was saying that he'd only taken the on-going role till something else turned up, because he clearly thought that one day a film director would get in touch and whisk him away to Hollywood. She admired his confidence and wished she had the same.

She nodded at appropriate moments, and agreed that she too awaited the call of the big time, even if in her case she aspired to live, rather than film or TV, parts.

Quietly she ran through the disappointment of the missed door opening contacts in the letter a little while ago. But said, "All our turns will come."

The waiter removed the empty plates, revealing and leaving a ring of spillage where Hugh's plate had been. He asked if they wanted desserts.

There was one of those awkward moments when people look at each other hoping for a lead. Penelope had almost persuaded herself to go mad and risk her budget but said, "Only if you do." to Hugh. Hugh suddenly had a flash of insight and guessed at her true financial state. He, like the rest of the cast, had become so acclimatised to Adam's constant repetition of his assertion that she was a spoilt rich kid that he hadn't considered that she was actually struggling to make ends meet on the same wages as the rest of them. He was comparatively financially secure at the moment, as despite the previous period of low paid menial jobs his income had just been swelled a little by some repeat fees from his childhood work. It wasn't enough to make any sort of song and dance about, but it had taken the strain off the past few weeks to the extent that he almost forgotten the way the others must be counting the pennies.

"Come on then. We'll have an ice-cream each." The waiter acknowledged this and turned to go, "And two coffees." Hugh added.

He saw the worry on her face.

"My treat," he said.

For the first time since joining 'Theatre Wagon' Penelope had a realisation of people's kindness. In the gloom of that Chinese restaurant, with its heavy red décor and rice splattered table cloth, she saw that Hugh had noticed her uncertainty, had worked out why, and had been generous enough to subsidise her dwindling finances. She couldn't say why she knew this, but some intuition made her sure.

"The bank of Mum and Dad stopped after I left drama college." she explained.

"With Adam having a go at your background all the time I think some of us found it a bit difficult to remember that we are all in the same boat."

Somewhat guiltily she considered her behaviour throughout the schools tour. Maybe, she conceded privately, her insecurity had let her to treat the others a little badly. She was wondering how John felt about her, for she knew that it was probably he who had been the recipient of her worst off-handed snootiness, and whether he would be as forgiving as Hugh, as they ate their ice creams. She'd been thinking more and more about John as the weeks had passed.

She looked at Hugh. Would the bigger tour be more bearable if she made a friend, even a 'boyfriend' within the company? No. Not Hugh. He was pleasant, and this evening's meal showed his generosity and compassion, but she kept finding herself making comparisons with John. But wasn't John now paired up with Nicole? It had looked like it at the end of run drinks in the pub. Again a stabbing twinge of jealousy, then she burst out with,

"Is John going out with Nicole?"

Hugh, whose mind had been occupied by the firm discovery of Penelope's financial insecurity, and how at odds that was with the company members' ideas of her status, gave a slight start and thought for an instant before saying,

"I know they have the odd meal together, and I am pretty sure she fancies him, but she's far too shy to put herself forward, and he's too much of a gentleman to try anything with her, no matter how fond of her he is." He paused, "And he is."

"How do you know? Has he said anything?" it was important to Penelope to be sure.

"No, not said anything, but as I said, they meet occasionally, and you only really have to see the way he looks at her. And he's always carrying her bag for her, or helping her to sort her props." Hugh took a spoonful of ice-cream. "No, scrub that, he does that with everyone."

"So he might just be being polite?" Penelope's question was over eager.

Now Hugh decided he had found something else out about

Penelope. It was even more unforeseen than her straitened circumstances. With his usual perception he deduced that she fancied John. This, he thought, could put a whole new dynamic into the company's relationships. He wondered how long she had nursed the secret. He wondered if John had noticed. He wondered, a bit sadly, how this would affect the way John and Nicole had been getting along. He had been watching their relationship for some weeks now with a voyeuristic interest.

"I don't think John is consciously being polite, it's just the way he thinks things should be. He can't leave jobs undone. To him the show is all important, and anything, no matter how trivial, that affects the show just has to be dealt with."

"Even this show? I mean I thought he felt Theatre Wagon a bit beneath him."

"Penelope," Hugh said, "we all think Theatre Wagon is beneath us."

And Penelope was silent, sipping coffee, and knowing how true a statement that was.

Chapter 12

It was a comfortable sofa, but John still woke early. He turned a few times, wrapping the blanket around himself and eventually coming fully conscious when he had managed to trap himself within the makeshift bedclothes and had to reverse his turning in order to escape. He sat on the edge of the sofa with the blanket around his shoulders and tried to guess the time by the angle of the light leaking in through the gap above the curtain track. Giving it up he looked at the clock instead. Half past seven. A bit early for theatre people not constrained by a school performance, but he decided to get up anyway.

He walked quietly into the bedroom. Nicole was curled like an infant asleep. He half expected to find she was sucking her thumb from the position she had adopted. He crept to the wardrobe and got clothes, then left, shutting the door silently behind him. There was one thing, he thought, years of backstage theatre work taught you how to move silently.

Washed and changed he rummaged in the bathroom cupboard and found a new toothbrush in its packet, which he placed on the shelf over the sink, next to his toothpaste. Returning to the kitchen he made mugs of coffee and carried them through to the bedroom. Gently he woke Nicole.

She sat up with start and said, "Oh no! Is it morning?"

"Nearly eight."

She dragged the duvet up to cover herself, then realised she was still dressed. "We didn't..." it was momentarily unclear what she worried that they had or hadn't done, till she said, "Mrs Odet will be furious!"

He handed her the coffee mug.

"What's it got to do with her?" he asked, though he guessed that the landlady probably kept a strict controlling eye on her lodgers' comings and goings. Just maybe the woman might have worried at one of her tenants failing to come home at a usual time.

Nicole sipped the coffee and said "Well I had told her we were having an end of tour drink, but I expect she would have assumed that I'd be back when the pubs closed. She'll make such a scene."

"I'll take you back." John said. It was more of a question than a statement.

"Would you? Thank you. That might be better."

Now, slightly relieved, Nicole looked around the room as she drank the coffee. It was plain emulsion painted, but in shades of orange, or red, she couldn't quite decide, with heavy curtains at the window, which John now opened to let the morning light in. It was, she thought, a bit theatrical. Then she grinned to herself, thinking 'it would be', and hugged her knees up to her chest under the covers. John turned back from the curtains and caught her grin.

"Penny for them," he said.

"I was just thinking how theatrical your flat is."

"Well it would be," he replied. She smiled, finding his words had echoed her thought. "Anyway the props department has found you a new toothbrush and set it in the bathroom, and front of house catering is about to start cooking breakfast."

And with that he was gone. Shortly she heard the clatter of a frying pan, and hurried to wash.

When she had freshened up from the night sleeping in her clothes she joined him in the kitchen. There was a shelf table on one wall and he had laid cutlery for them.

"Ah, good timing." he whisked plates of bacon and egg onto the table and sat down patting the seat next to him.

It was rather reminiscent of their café meals she felt as she ate. It bothered her briefly that perhaps fried breakfasts were John's staple diet. Even the table had an elderly formica top like the café.

"When do you start hunting for props and furniture?" she enquired.

"Almost immediately. In fact I might have a drive out to a couple of second hand shops today. Want to come?"

"I've got to go and make my peace with Mrs Odet, and change my clothes." She looked down at the creases that had resulted from sleeping in them. "But I'd like to, if you don't mind waiting."

"We'll pick up the van and I'll run you over to your digs and wait for you," he said.

It turned out to be anything but that simple. After dawdling over breakfast they made the short walk to the theatre company's yard and collected the van. John drove to the lock-up garage that the company rented for storage and they off-loaded the remnants of the schools tour props and furniture. Nicole thought that it was just as though they, and they alone, were touring all over again. She thought how pleasant it would have been if it had been just John and her on the road with the show, free from the slights, bickering and unpleasantness that had dogged the tour. These operations took some time and it was very late morning before they closed the garage and got back into the van.

John drove to her digs. There the trouble started. She was

accosted as she turned her key in the door by an outraged Mrs Odet, who had clearly been awaiting her return and had presumably been surveying the street from behind the net curtains so as to be able to confront her lodger in the hall. John, who had paused to wipe some bird muck from the windscreen, heard the outburst start from where he was in the street, and although the words were indistinct there was no doubt of the tone. He threw the rag back into the van, locked the door and made for the house, in no doubt that the onslaught was directed at Nicole and would be upsetting her.

".... and to stop out all night! I assume you were in some man's bed. Ah! Here he is if I am not mistaken." She rounded on John. "Proud of yourself are you giving me all the worry while you were seducing and corrupting this poor innocent girl. You thoughtless lecher!"

John couldn't decide whether to laugh, protest his innocence, or berate the woman for her presumption that she should control Nicole's activities.

"Look at what you've done to her." the landlady continued in full flow, "..dirty, untidy and abused." She pointed at Nicole, whose clothes, creased from having been slept in, had acquired a coating of dust and cobwebs from the company's scenery store which she had not had time to brush off. Off-loading the van had untidied her hair and there was a small dirty mark down one cheek. He had to admit she was not her usual smartly turned out if impoverished self. Actually he found her exceptionally appealing he decided.

Mrs Odet went on, "Well I can't risk my house getting a reputation for late night cavorting. I certainly can't have the stress of not knowing what has happened to ladies in my charge."

'In your charge?' That's pushing it a bit, thought John.

Nicole finally managed to butt in to the woman's tirade, "I'm really sorry Mrs Odet...."

"You should be. You don't know the worry you've caused me. I expected better of you.... To stop out doing who knows what all night!"

Nicole burst into tears.

"No, it's no good turning on the waterworks. I'm not going to be swayed. I must ask you to leave, and at once."

Both John and Nicole were astounded.

"I've packed all your things for you, here's your case." Mrs Odet announced, dragging Nicole's case from behind the door where it had been standing, and sliding it towards the doorstep.

They were both at a loss for words. Their confusion was redoubled by the arrival of a middle aged man, who was clearly a commercial traveller of some kind, holding a suitcase in one hand and a briefcase in the other.

"Ah, my new tenant!" said Mrs Odet, with an air of finality.

John started to protest. It was the sort of high-handed behaviour that he would usually have been unrestrained in arguing with, but Nicole, still with tears making the dirt on her cheek into grey rivulets, grabbed his arm, pleading, "No, please John, I couldn't stay here now." so that he contented himself with a glare at the woman as he grabbed Nicole's suitcase and put an arm around her waist to lead her back to the van.

He opened the passenger door and let her in, slid the side door open and put her case in the back, walked round to the driver's side and looked back toward the house. The door had shut behind the landlady and her new tenant. He got in. Nicole was sobbing uncontrollably. He took a handkerchief from his pocket and reached over, gently wiping the girl's wet face. She tried to control her tears and her sobs changed to short gasping intakes of breath like a child.

"Please...can we....go..."

He started the engine.

"That woman's a control freak."

"Please.... please.... just go..."

He shoved the van into gear and drove away from the girl's digs, unsure where to go.

"I just want to get away from her." Nicole's gasping was subsiding.

"Do you want to go prop hunting to take you mind off things, or..."

"I'm sorry, I just couldn't. Not today."

He swung the van though the streets till he pulled up in front of his own flat, fetched Nicole's bag from the back and got her out of the passenger seat and led her to his door. Opening it he guided her inside and shut the door behind them feeling relief that none of the residents of the other flats had been around.

Once he had installed her on the sofa he made coffee and came and sat beside her, putting an arm round her shoulders and urging her to have the drink. He was not used to giving this sort of care and attention to women. His ex-wife had never been the sort to need sympathy, or indeed to give it.

They sat there for most of the day. Early in the evening John went out and fetched fish and chips, and they ate them, side by side. The conversation was slow and rambling with numerous long gaps. As the previous night Nicole asked John about his previous career, but he also managed to persuade her to talk about herself more. She told him more about her struggle to get into acting training, her financial constraints through that time, and, as all actors do, about failed auditions once she left the theatre school.

No matter how John tried, however, the talk returned time and again to Mrs Odet and her peremptory eviction of Nicole.

"I just can't understand how she managed to get a new lodger so quickly. She must have decided to chuck you out during the night, rung someone like tourist information and taken a new booking first thing in the morning."

"I suppose she thought the worst of me because I didn't go back for the night."

"Did you find her name and address on the theatrical digs list?" he asked at one point.

"Yes, I think so. Alison in the office gave me some addresses."

"Humm. That would be the one," he said thoughtfully, "I think I'll get her removed from that. All the city theatres issue the same list."

"Would she know who took her off the list?" she worried.

"No, of course not. And I wouldn't care anyway. I think my milk of human kindness has curdled as far as that woman is concerned."

Despite herself Nicole smiled at the turn of phrase. Her upset had lessened in the security of John's presence throughout the day. There was none the less the unspoken doubt as to where she would be able to live. Eventually in mid evening she steeled herself to ask, "Can I stop here tonight?"

"Of course you can. Stop as long as you like." he said, surprised that she had not assumed that this would be the case, for he had gone to some lengths to reassure the girl, and hadn't dreamt for a moment that she might think he would be throwing her out onto the street like Mrs Odet had. He was finding her company more and more enjoyable despite the downbeat content of their conversation. If he was honest with himself he was finding how strongly attracted he had become, and welcomed the prospect of at least sharing the flat with her for a while.

"I don't want to be in the way." Nicole's usual natural reticence was showing again. "I'll sleep on the sofa. I can't turn you out of your bed again."

"You will not. You have the bed. I've had plenty of practice sleeping on sofas." He went on to tell her pointless tales of sleeping on theatre fly-floors and in control rooms during long and arduous show fit-ups, while in the back of his mind he was accepting the fact, the disappointment he realised, that she had so blatantly telegraphed separate bedding arrangements.

Under normal circumstances John was used to going to bed very late. A career composed, for many years, of working till at least eleven o'clock each evening, after which there would have always been the journey home, a meal and possibly a TV programme on the video recorder to play back and watch, had trained his body to a routine that operated much later than that of the average nine-to-five office worker. He'd been forced out of this style of existence in the past weeks by the TIE team's school timetable based operation, but old habits die hard, and already he could feel his body-clock urging him to stay up. He frequently had to explain this rotation of active hours to people he met outside the profession. In the early days of his career he had been apt to grumble at what he saw as the ridiculously early close down of the television broadcasts, which left the poor choice of a succession of bland simplistic Open University lessons for night owls like himself to watch. Now videotape recorders were common he generally made great use of the machine, recording, later watching, almost every light entertainment and variety show that was screened.

For Nicole it had been a long, and traumatic, day, and she was evidently tired even before she started to yawn. By mutual consent they cleared the debris of the fish and chips and he made sure she, and her luggage, were installed in the bedroom.

He gave her a reluctantly chaste kiss on the cheek before pulling the bedroom door shut behind himself as he returned to the living room.

For some time he bustled about, arranging the blanket on the sofa and putting the cushions at one end as pillows. He discreetly ignored her hurried scamper from the bedroom to the bathroom and back and when she had shut herself in again he undressed and got into his makeshift bed. Had he been conscious of it he would have been surprised how swiftly he fell asleep.

When he did wake again it was because someone was gently stroking his hair back out of his eyes. Lying on his side he opened them and in the shaft of light spilling from the open bedroom door he saw Nicole's pale thighs in front of him. Seeing him awake she squatted beside the sofa. She was wearing one of his shirts he noticed. It was mostly unbuttoned, and only just long enough to cover her. His surprise at the girl being like this, so unlike her usual reserved nature, was doubled when she took him by the hand, pulling insistently for him to follow her as she made for the bedroom saying, with almost desperate persuasive plaintiveness "Please".

Chapter 13

Penelope sat at the dining table in her digs. The two salesmen had been unusually quiet over the evening meal tonight. Mrs Bray had produced pork chops, which was a step up on the usual fare, Penelope decided, because the chops did not involve any active preparation on Mrs Bray's part, so unless she managed to burn them, which she had not, they were not likely to be spoilt. Penelope was growing increasingly critical of Mrs Bray's culinary skills, having found that her pie crusts and other pastries were of very variable quality and not at all the 'home cooking' that she remembered from her childhood and was starting to yearn for in her uncertainty.

She herself had remained silent throughout the meal, thinking about John. It was now reaching the moment when the landlady would come and remove the plates to make way for the sweet course. Penelope might have wondered what slightly unsuitable dessert Mrs Bray had decided on had she not been doing her very private and rather sad contemplation. She had been deep in this brown study for a day or more now, ever since the Chinese meal with Hugh in fact. Glumly she was considering whether her behaviour throughout the schools tour had soured John's opinion of her to the extent that she had lost any hope of winning him over. Because she had decided that her attraction for him was stronger than she had admitted to herself and was spending the idle time, waiting for the new show rehearsals to start, indulging in more and more fantasising.

"Ee lass, you do look reet sad."

She looked up with a start as one of the salesmen addressed her. Mrs Bray chose that very moment to come in and start collecting the plates so she was saved from having to reply.

"Treacle sponge for afters," the woman announced with the air of someone giving out winning raffle ticket numbers in the certain knowledge that everyone in the room had won.

Penelope had a flash of memory of Mrs Hobward's gloriously sweet, soft, luxurious treacle puddings soaking in hot flowing syrup and wondered what Mrs Bray's version would be like.

The salesmen made suitable appreciative noises, then one said, "Isn't our Penelope looking right glum Mrs Bray?"

"What's the matter Penelope?" the woman asked with concern, and Penelope found herself saying that she was fine, which her questioner clearly didn't believe, because once the meal was over, and Penelope's prediction to herself that Mrs Bray couldn't live up to Mrs Hobward's standard had been proven correct, the woman made a great deal of fuss, clearing the room of the salesmen so that she and Penelope could "have a proper girly chat."

Penelope didn't want to have a 'girly chat' with Mrs Bray, or anyone else, but was trapped into the situation with her as she shut the door behind the retreating backs of her other guests telling them, "Now you boys go to the pub, and don't come back till we've had time for a nice long tête-a-tête."

The actress found herself manoevered into one of the over-deep armchairs with a wobbly side table bearing tea in a china cup and saucer as Mrs Bray pulled one of the dining chairs up in front of her so that she felt as though she was about to be interrogated. There was no escape. Even if she had tried she would probably have had a struggle to lift herself out of the depths of the armchair.

"Now," the woman put her hand on Penelope's knee, "Tell me why you're upset."

"Oh it's nothing Mrs Bray. Don't worry."

"Of course I worry. I like to take care of all my guests. Tell me all about it."

"There's nothing to tell. Well nothing anyone can do. I think I've been a bit silly."

"You're not in trouble are you?" The woman's idea of 'in trouble' was transparently obvious.

"No. No. Nothing like that, it's just...." and suddenly Penelope wanted to tell someone, and the landlady was there, and being sympathetic, and all the bottled up uncertainties of weeks of tour and the stupid, yes stupid, jealousy of silly little Nicole were bursting to come out. She'd never see Mrs Bray again once the show moved out onto the bigger tour, so why not confide in her?

"You see I was a bit selfish with the other members of the cast during the tour, and I don't think they like me very much. They all think, well not Hugh, that I've got lots of money, and I haven't really, and so I didn't mix with them, well apart from having to travel in the van with them and.... oh it's just silly."

The woman, who only half understood the concepts of touring and of TIE shows nodded gently and encouragingly and said "Go on."

"Well I was horrid to John and now I think..."

"That's who you are really worried about isn't it?"

"I don't know. I think I really like him, but he's with Nicole now and he isn't going to be attracted to me after the way I behaved."

"Do you know that he's with this Nicole?"

"No. But he was next to her at the end of tour party."

"So in a party of half a dozen people he happened to sit next to her. And let me tell you something about men. They are fascinated by the unobtainable. If he's seen you as standoffish and distant for the whole of this last tour he's certain to be interested in you. It wounds their pride you see. They can't imagine anyone not fancying them, so when they don't get approached they will start to try to attract your attention. If he's making friends with this Nicole it's a fair bet he's just trying to make you jealous. What's she like anyway?"

Penelope considered. "She's a bit younger than the rest of us, and I suppose she's pretty. She's no good at acting though and really quite embarrassingly nervous and shy." she thought for a moment, "I think he might want to take care of her, you know, look after the little waif. And she's got even less money than the rest of us. They say he's been buying her meals sometimes after we get back from shows."

"I don't think you've really got much to worry about. Sympathy and pity aren't the basis for a permanent successful relationship." Mrs Bray was an avid consumer of magazine agony columns and was delighted to be able to draw on her wide knowledge of the sort of things said in the advice replies. "What's this John like?"

"Oh he's really nice, and he'll do anything for anyone," Penelope gushed. "He has to, of course, because he's the company manager. We can't really find out too much about his background. We know he has been company manager or stage manager on really big shows, and he used to be married, but they've split up."

"Divorced?"

"I don't know. He never talks about it. He never says anything about why he is working in a small company like this one when he had been in the big shows. Oh! You don't think he did something wrong do you?" Penelope gasped in sudden concern.

"Has anyone said so?"

"No. Never."

"Then you're worrying unnecessarily, as you are with thinking you've lost him."

"I haven't lost him, I 've never had him, and I have been so silly to be off hand with him. I really fancy him Mrs Bray"

There was much more like this as the older woman tried to reassure the actress and the evening grew darker till at last Mrs Bray rose, turned the dining room light on and shut the curtains.

"Fancy comes and goes Penelope. When I was your age I fancied a boy in our street, but he moved away and I married Mr Bray and we've been together for forty years next August."

Penelope nodded. "But did you stop fancying this other boy?"

The older woman thought for a bit. "When I first married I didn't think about anyone else. Perhaps I did after a number of years. But by then he wouldn't have been the same boy I'd fancied, even if I chased him down and he was free and I had been willing to split up... he wouldn't have been the same. Anyway, I doubt he was even aware of me except as a neighbour. He certainly never did or said anything to make me think he was. And I think that was some of the attraction. He was, sort of, out of reach. Just like your John. But your man knows who you are, and sees you every day, well not at the moment, but usually, so he knows, and he'll be thinking about you. I bet he's fantasising about you in his room right now."

"You really think so? Fantasising? That's a bit..." Penelope wasn't sure how to put what she was thinking to this older woman.

"There was an article in one of my magazines just the other day," Mrs Bray offered as though it must be true if it was in a woman's magazine, "they said that the average man thinks about sex every thirty seconds and because of that they are completely controlled by their, err, lust."

"Libido?" Penelope offered.

"That was a word they used. Anyway it's a certainty that John is thinking about going to bed with you at this moment."

There was a noise at the front door.

"That's the men come back. Off you go to your room quickly, And remember what I said. He'll come round to you soon enough, you're too attractive for him not to."

With that endorsement ringing in her ears Penelope fled upstairs. Mrs Bray came out into the hall to see the men looking up, watching the girl's shapely bottom vanishing round the corner onto the first landing.

"And you can all stop ogling the lass!"

Mrs Bray's husband slunk quickly into the kitchen, while the salesmen, emboldened a bit by drink perhaps, muttered things like 'Eee tha's just spoiling our fun' before wheedling a night time coffee out of their landlady.

Chapter 14

John was standing looking out of the window, the phone receiver in one hand and pressed to his ear, the phone itself in the other hand, dangling casually with his fingers tucked beneath the rest.

"... and make sure those rooms get taken off any future versions of the digs list too will you please...   Many thanks....   Yes good to talk to you again too, see you sometime."

He was hanging up when Nicole came up to him, coyly wrapped in a towel. She pressed against him and reached up to put her arms around his neck and stand on tiptoe to kiss him. Released, the towel slipped down. They kissed for a while and then John broke away.

"Come on. Breakfast, then we've got work to do."

Nicole made a disappointed noise, stooped nakedly to pick up the towel which she then held cheekily half revealingly in front of herself saying, "Not even just quickly?".

"No. Not even just quickly." She turned in a mock sulk and he gave her a light smack on her exposed bare bottom as she made off into the bedroom to dress wondering to himself how long she would keep this tempting game up, and whether he really should have gone along with her 'come-on'. He shrugged. She was a grown woman after all. But then she was still the nervous, waif like young actress he'd been attracted to caring for.

Their round tour of second hand shops successfully loaded the van with a selection of bits of furniture that John said would suit the show's requirements. Nicole was not always certain how some of the pieces that John haggled over and bought fitted with either the period or style that she expected him to be on the look out for, but John was, as ever, sure and confident.

Some of the time Nicole shadowed him around the dusty shops closely, at other moments she found herself distracted by items on sale. John lost sight of her completely for a long period during which she prowled a whole gangway given over to old children's toys, in which she lost herself looking at playthings she had yearned for, but never had, as a child. Incongruously the end of the aisle was dominated by a large Victorian bookcase with a scattering of broken spined books on top of which sat a large stuffed parrot on a heavy branch inside a square glass case. Nicole was stood staring, fascinated by the bird, whose fixed glass eyes seemed to look knowingly at her, as if it was critical of her recent behaviour.

She was on the point of shaking off the spell, and the feelings of guilt that it somehow raised in her, and going off to seek out John, when the shop proprietor came up.

"Nice bit of stuff isn't he?"

"He makes me feel as though he's watching me," she replied.

"It's the trick of the way the taxidermist set the eyes."

"And judging me," she added.

"It's very old. They knew their craft in those days. Was it the sort of thing you were looking for? I have a few more in the store room."

"No. Thank you. I'm with.." she looked slightly wildly back and forth and was lucky to catch sight of the back of John's head over some stacked up chairs, "John." She pointed. "We're looking for props for a show."

"Ah. The haggling negotiator," said the owner, "I hadn't realised you were hunting in a pack. If he negotiates many more deals I'll be bankrupted," he joked. Nicole noticed that for the last statement he exaggerated what she now recognised had been

134

there all along, a slight Jewish accent. As if to enforce the point the man spread his hands outwards with the palms up in a gesture as old as trading. John appeared.

"You haven't let this old fraud sell you anything have you?" he asked with evident jocularity.

"'Old fraud' he says. When have I defrauded you, you skinflint?"

"Not for lack of trying." John laughed.

"If you can't take a joke.... Now is that everything you need my old friend?"

"It is, for now. And I'll let you know about that packing case once I've talked to the director. This is Isaac," he told Nicole, "Nicole, Isaac, Isaac, Nicole. Isaac owns this place and I've bought props and furniture from him for years."

"Nicole," the owner held out his hand to her, "delighted to meet such a lovely lady. I hope you'll make my good friend John very happy."

Nicole blushed visibly at this, and John said quickly, "Anyway, I think that's everything..."

The owner called a gangling youth over, and there was a flurry of activity as John's selected pieces of furniture were taken to the door ready to be loaded into the van. Nicole made to assist, but had her efforts overtaken by the combined energy of John and the youngster. She loitered in a corner near the door as various items were dragged to the door, and eventually loaded into the van. Finding herself beside a stack of framed pictures and posters that leant against an old sideboard she idly examined them. They were an eclectic mixture of posters and reproduction advertising. She flipped each one forward to allow it to rest against her knees as she stood there. The first, at the top of the pile, was a gaudy print of a woman in a red Spanish dress, next an alert colourful toucan surveyed her beside the word Guinness. Behind that a girl tennis player, with her back to the camera, lifted the hem of her skirt and scratched her bum. She flicked over a batch to see what would be further down the pile, and came to a slightly tatty piece of hardboard to which had been pasted an original poster now covered by a sheet of perspex clipped to the edges. It advertised "Chuzzlewit". Nicole saw the shop owner approach out of the corner of her eye. She was impressed at the way he could apparently sense the exact moment to step towards a potential customer.

"Found something of interest my dear?" asked Isaac.

"I thought I might get this old poster for John, but I haven't much money. How much is it?"

A sad expression flashed across the man's face and he grabbed her wrist.

"If I thought it was the right thing to do you could have it free for John, but it would be a terrible mistake."

Nicole was confused. "Why?"

"Look, obviously he hasn't told you everything about himself. Maybe he doesn't want to. Trust me when I say that a reminder of that show is probably the last thing a pretty new young girlfriend should be giving him."

"Now you must tell me. You can't just drop a vague hint like that."

"All right, All right. But don't say I told you. "Chuzzlewit" was the show on which John met and married that dancer wife of his. She was a real devil to him. They're divorced now, of course but he's not over her. Be kind and gentle to him, treat him well, he deserves it and needs it, but don't give him that show poster."

Nicole let the pile of pictures drop back. She was frightened by the intensity of Isaac's admonishment.

"I'm sorry. I didn't know," she stammered.

Isaac became gentler. "Of course you didn't. But there's a skeleton in that closet that you ought to get him to confide in you about. It would be good for him to let it out. Do him, and all of us who are his friends, a favour and try to make him talk about it." He let go of her wrist just as John, who had finished loading, came looking for her.

Amid the 'goodbyes' Nicole said quietly to Isaac "I promise to take care of him." and the man nodded seriously saying, "You must. He can't lose another."

Chapter 15

Nicole and John spent the rest of the daylight hours off-loading the results of the shopping trip at the company's stores and parking the van back in the yard. They talked about going to the cafe for what would be a late supper, but Nicole persuaded him that they should stop at one of the tiny family run supermarkets that dotted the route back to John's flat. She bought a basket full of different food items, which were loaded into a plastic carrier bag printed with the shop's name, 'Steve's Mini Mart'.

She and John disputed with each other at the check-out over who should pay for the shopping, setting eventually on both contributing some cash towards it and Nicole finding the change pressed into her hand.

Back at his flat Nicole set about cooking, producing a meal of sausage and mash, with the addition of tinned peas.

While the potatoes were boiling she came back into the living room to find John once again dangling the phone from one hand and holding the receiver to his ear with the other.

"Thank you Jimmy," he was saying. "Just leave them in the box office in my name and I'll pick them up before the half. I owe you a drink sometime." and he hung up.

"Who was that?" she asked.

"The house manager at 'The Imperial'," he replied. "Proper feel-good entertainment tomorrow night."

"We're going to the theatre?" she asked, delighted, and trying to remember what was on at 'The Imperial'. She was not used to attending performances as a member of the audience.

"Something light and frothy. Just what you need."

They ate, and afterwards, when the washing up was done, they sat on the sofa with glasses of brandy, and talked.

Again Nicole found herself telling him about the struggles and setbacks she'd endured, taking the tale right back to her school days. She was determined in this to lead around to making John talk about his ex-wife and the failed marriage as she had promised Isaac that she would.

When she began to ask she found John very reluctant to tell her anything, but as the evening grew later and the brandy warmed them more she slowly discovered more and more about his past.

He'd been a known and successful stage manager when "Chuzzlewit" had come calling. He'd joined the production in that position and seen it through its pre West End trials and tribulations. Despite frequent re-writes and even the substitution of completely new numbers the show had been a roaring success from the very first out-of-town previews. In the early days John had been far too busy to pay more than passing attention to individual members of the cast, and they too were concentrated on the extra rehearsals and re-blocking that a new show entailed.

Still he knew all the company by name, and even if his duties brought him into much closer contact with the half dozen stars, some of whom were household names that Nicole recognised as he mentioned them, than with the ensemble. He was aware of the dancer. Her name was Melanie. He was physically attracted, he honestly admitted to Nicole.

Within a very few days of the show settling into an established routine they had started what John described to Nicole as 'a passionate and ill-advised affair', which led to a hasty wedding.

"We got a special licence, married on a Monday morning in Nottingham in the second week playing there, and were doing the show as usual in the evening, Mel dancing, me running the stage management team."

Nicole pouted. "You were happy then?" She was probing as gently as she could, but her jealousy was making some of her questioning a little sharp. She cuddled tighter to him on the sofa.

"I don't really know about happy. We were sex mad. It was like, oh I suppose, you know when you have an itch, how once you start scratching you can't stop, and then when you eventually do it needs scratching again almost immediately." He squeezed her tightly. "It's all over you know. We had the most enormous bust up."

"How long did it last?"

"Not long. When we first got married we spent a lot of time ripping each others clothes off. In fact there was a bit of 'Chuzzlewit' where Mel had exactly eight minutes between dance routines, and we found we could do it then, so we did, a couple of times, in the stage manager's office. Not very easy when one person is wearing a Victorian stage costume. 'Chuzzlewit' was one of those shows that didn't display the dancers in the least."

Nicole covered her ears and shrieked, "I don't want to know!" After a pause she said, "Actually, yes, I suppose I do want to know. If it was so good why did you spit up?"

"New paint fades, fresh cream goes off.... I reckon. When 'Chuzzlewit' went into London we bought a basement flat, well actually I suppose I did, because I paid the mortgage, Mel was supposed to pay the shopping and some of the bills, but she usually didn't. Anyway the show only ran a few months and then we were working on different things."

"And that's when you split?"

"Not immediately, but you should understand that Mel was, is I expect, sex mad. The word nymphomaniac was invented for her. And she had rather rough desires." Nicole was looking up at him wide eyed, saying nothing. "So once we had the flat she and I would come home from work and, of course that was the middle of the night really, and she'd deliberately pick a quarrel so that she could start a physical fight to lead into sex."

"Did she hurt you?"

"Physically? Not really, though I got hit by a few things that she threw. Mentally, I guess so. Break-ups always hurt, and I suppose that goes with the territory."

"You mean all couples hurt each other?"

"I mean that all break-ups hurt both parties."

She wanted to know more, but she wanted to change the subject.

"Why did 'Chuzzlewit' close? I heard it was really good. I wanted to see it but, then I couldn't afford to of course."

"You could probably have got comps towards the end. It was a good show in its way. There were some great numbers, you know them, you've heard them...will still hear them played on the radio. They made some bad mistakes with the script though."

"Mistakes?"

"All the Dickens books are too long. You know he wrote them as serials, and the longer he could spin them out the more episodes were published and the more money he made. They are universally dreary and 'worthy'. There's nothing worse than worthy. It results in children being set exams in them. The intelligentsia forget that Dickens and Shakespeare and all those 'classics' were just hack writers churning out product like Catherine Cookson, or Dick Francis or.. who's that MP? Will schoolchildren be forced to study them in a few hundred year's time? Anyway 'Chuzzlewit' at least had a 'love makes it all turn out all right in the end' plot...."

"But not for you."

"....No. Not for me. Anyway Dickens, in fact none of the classics are any good as entertainment."

"What about 'Oliver' and 'Pickwick'?" Nicole asked.

"Exceptions that prove the rule. 'Oliver' covers only a tiny bit of a vast sprawling book, and 'Pickwick', well it's a romp culled from some rare slightly amusing short stories. Did you know the original book of 'Chuzzlewit' is over five hundred pages long? They made some cuts naturally, but stupidly they kept in the whole American bit because they thought it would appeal to the American tourists and maybe even sell to Broadway. They failed to notice that that section is all satirical anti American political propaganda. As usual political theatre eventually fails to entertain."

"And when it folded you were out of work."

"I went straight on to another show, and Mel got a job in a cabaret club very soon. She liked that. She preferred costumes that showed off her body, like that," he pointed at the photograph, "to Victorian period stuff. The split was pretty soon after that."

"Would you have stayed together if you'd been working on the same show?" Nicole wanted to know.

"It probably accelerated the inevitable. She was finding new friends, I was working with a different group of people. You've probably noticed that any theatrical company hangs together as an informal family. There are people you like, people you hate, but you all stick together because the show is like a sort of glue, linking you."

"I'm not too sure about Theatre Wagon," she said, "we haven't stuck together like glue." She thought of the bitchiness and arguments of the past few weeks that had upset her so much. John stroked her hair and said,

"Theatre Wagon isn't big enough for it to work properly. There has to be enough people for you to be able to walk off and talk to someone else without causing offence. A big cast show, like 'Chuzzlewit' if you want, allows for that. If people pair up, like Mel and I did, it doesn't make a hole in the family."

"But if we've paired up it will make a hole in the Theatre Wagon 'family' because there's too few people? You've made me feel guilty now, Will the others resent us?"

John wondered about what she was asking. She certainly now seemed to consider their relationship more serious than he had. He had realised from the moment the girl and he had slept together that she might want more security than he could probably give. Clearly their casual friendship has gone further than he had intended and though he was happy to admit a physical attraction as well as his protective concern for the naive girl's welfare he wasn't sure that he saw their relationship as permanent.

He brushed aside her worries about the rest of the cast. "They'll get over it, especially now the new company is starting soon."

"And have you got over your wife?" again Nicole probed, remembering Isaac's suggestion again.

"Enough of me. Tell me about the trail of broken hearts you have left behind," he said.

Nicole shuffled with embarrassment. Her shy disposition meant that she had never discussed anything about her private life with anyone. Not that there was anything to discuss, she thought. Where fellow students, and then colleagues had sometimes chatted openly, even boastfully, about their amorous adventures she had cringed silently in corners away from the conversation, and no-one had ever tried to drag her into their ribald talk. Perhaps, she was honest enough to suspect, they knew that she had nothing to add to the girly confessional.

"I haven't... well once, with a boy from the stage school, but it wasn't like with you. He just did it, and afterwards I sort of thought 'is that all that happens?' and he went home and we never spoke about it again."

"And you never had another boyfriend?"

"No. Never. Well not till now if you're willing to be called my boyfriend."

John didn't reply, but took the glass out of her hand, put it on the floor, put his arms around her and they began kissing.

Chapter 16

Penelope stood in her bedroom in front of the dressing table mirror feeling that a wall full of MGM lions were watching her as she stripped to her underwear and examined herself critically.

'Attractive' was the word Mrs Bray had used, and her fellow residents made no secret of a certain, unwelcome, randy fascination for her body. Penelope wanted John to exhibit some of that interest, not perhaps in a coarse, vulgar way like the salesmen, but at least enough to allow her to seduce him and capture him. She turned and looked over her shoulder at her bottom reflected in the bevel edged octagonal shaped mirror She reached out and tilted it to an angle that allowed her to admire herself. It was possible, she thought, to get into a frame of mind where you overlooked the plus points. She was sure that her curvy lines were sexy and attractive, she turned back to face the mirror, just as Mrs Bray said. She'd long been conscious of the effect her physical appearance had on the opposite sex, whether salesmen in her digs or schoolboys in audiences. So she resolved that she must start the new show with a concerted campaign to win John. She would mix 'hard to get' with suitable 'come-on' behaviour. She decided that she would win him. From a selfish viewpoint she felt she had to win him, as she was quite aware that it would be he, of all the company, whose theatrical future would be fairly secure once this tour finished, if half the rumours about his background were true, as well as a need to satisfy her increasingly frustrated lust for him. The longer you wait for the unobtainable, the more desirable it becomes, she thought.

She dressed, and went to the Theatre Wagon office, partly to see if anyone else, why not admit it, to see if John, was about, and partly to fill the vacant time.

She was disappointed. Alison told her that John was out in the van, prop hunting when she enquired. Penelope's new 'leading man', Laurence, was there though, wedged on a chair to the side of Alison's desk, reading the new script.

"Oh are copies here somewhere then?" Penelope asked.

Alison shook her head, "Not available yet because Nick hasn't read it and he might want to make changes."

Penelope wondered why the new cast member, Laurence, would have been granted a preview if this was the case. She also found she was irritated by the suggestion that Nick would make any changes, and that her look at the new script should be delayed while he did. Like all the company she was well aware that Nick's input to the new show would be negligible.

Laurence turned another page of the typewritten script, read to the end of a speech, and looked up at Penelope.

"We're the leads in this thing then are we Penny?" he said.

"Penelope," she corrected automatically. "Yes I suppose so." The soap star's face was very familiar, she'd not been looking at him during the end-of-tour drinks session, being fixated by John and Nicole. Which soap was it? She couldn't place it. Alison saw the question on the actress' face.

"Soap star," she said to Penelope in an intentionally loud stage whisper.

"I know," she whispered back. She was not a soap opera watcher, she knew why the face had seemed familiar but had no idea from which soap. Mrs Bray would know she decided.

"I think we can probably do something with this." Laurence waved the script about and loose unbound pages fluttered precariously in his grip. "You just follow me, Penny, and you'll be all right," he told Penelope, patronisingly.

"Penelope," she corrected him again.

146

She wished she hadn't come to the office. She had a worrying instinct that this new actor would be pushy and self important. The irony of her being the recipient of that was lost on her, buried under the aggravation of his using 'Penny' instead of 'Penelope' despite her correcting him twice.

Alison heard Penelope's sigh, looked up from her paperwork, and tried to decipher the complex emotions from the actress' face. She made completely erroneous deductions. Ignoring Penelope's first question on arrival having been about John she decided that the girl's reactions were either due to her fancying the new actor, or to her being star-struck by him. Alison's lack of interest in the world of theatre didn't mean that she was immune from the general public's fascination with 'stars' and she was impressed by Laurence's presence in a way that she had failed to be when Hugh had joined the company.

Laurence himself failed to pick up any reactions from the women in the office. It was not that he was wholly absorbed in the script, which he was finding a bit tedious. He was used to soap scripts that comprised a series of short scenes between a kaleidoscopic selection of characters culminating in the 'cliff-hanger' type ending that was usual for each episode. He was finding that this play, based as it was on a long-winded classic, was too slow moving to capture him. He had resolved that he would press through some cuts to speed the pace. If the powers that be in this little company didn't agree he would unilaterally cut bits once they were out on the road and away from any direct control. The thought that John might use his 'in loco parentis' status to put him back onto the scripted straight and narrow didn't cross his mind. But then he'd never run across a stage manager of John's dedication and expertise before in his mainly television career. He rather failed to realise how numbing routine repeated performances of the same script could be, nor how glaringly conspicuously a slight change would stick out once that routine was established.

Alison made up her mind to tell Nick of what she thought was

Penelope's attitude to the new man. To have an excuse for going into Nick's office to do this she rose, and boiled the office kettle, saying:

"Do you both want tea or coffee?"

"Tea please," said Laurence decisively. "With."

Alison looked enquiringly at Penelope, but before she could answer Laurence said "And Penny will have some too. I'm guessing white without."

"Penelope," she corrected him, and in doing so lost the chance to turn down the offer of a drink and make an escape from the office. She found herself indecisive and with nothing to do while waiting for the tea. She didn't try to make conversation with Laurence.

There was the rattle of mugs and a spoon, the noise of the kettle boiling, and eventually muttered thanks as Alison handed round the drinks, and took one through to Nick's office. She shut the door behind her once she got in.

"Laurence is outside reading the script," she said to Nick. "Penelope's just come in, and I'm sure she only came to see if he was here. I think we've got a real fan for him right here in the company."

"Well that might make the luvvey scenes easier than they were before with Adam," Nick said. "Why's he reading the script? It's not finalised yet."

"He asked to see it, and after all the existing cast have done it all before, so it was only fair to let him have a peek to get up to speed, so to speak, before rehearsals start."

Nick gave a resigned 'humph' knowing that he couldn't change the situation now and frowned at Alison's back as she went back out. Sometimes he wished that he had more control over his staff, his actors, the shows. Alison was an efficient enough secretary, but she had her own views and methods, and was decisive on matters that she probably had no business interfering in. He had never even managed to get her to work the hours he wanted her to do, as she arrived after the tour van had left each morning, and went home either before, or as it returned, because of attending to her children.

In the outer office Penelope gulped down the hot drink as fast as she was able, wishing to make a quick exit. John was not there and she was finding Laurence's attitude unattractive. At least Adam had gone. The newcomer might be full of himself, but he wasn't openly antagonistic to her.

Would John bring the props back here? she wondered. What time had he set off? When might he be back? She thought about hanging around in case he turned up. If Alison had been alone she might have done. Her decision to leave was delayed by the arrival of a small car outside, from which emerged a man and a woman. They came in squeezing into the already crowded space. There was a series of 'hellos' exchanged, and Alison started to make introductions,

"These are the other two new actors. Roberta..."

"Bobbie, please." She was a lively, confident and shapely, long-haired woman, dressed in jeans and a rather fussy blouse, which made her look younger than she was. Penelope fleetingly thought 'mutton dressed as lamb'.

"..and Robert."

"Bob to you all." Another confident character, also in jeans with rather effeminately long hair. He too, Penelope decided, was older than he superficially seemed.

"These are a couple of the other actors, Penelope, and Laurence.

Actually they are your two leads," finished Alison.

Laurence broke through Penelope's 'Hello' to say "Penny and I welcome you to the company.."

"Penelope!" she interjected sternly.

"We hope you'll be happy with us." saying which, in a proprietorial manner he shook hands with that double handed grip that people use when they are trying too hard to appear genuine.

"We only dropped in on our way to book in to our digs. We wondered if you'd got a map here. We're not too sure where our digs are."

Alison reached into a drawer of her desk and produced a city map, asking "Where are you staying?".

"Glendale Avenue," said Bob.

"Oh Mrs Lambert's place. That's near the Thomas Lincoln. It's said to be very nice, but it's a long way out."

"That won't matter, I've got the car, and it's just for the rehearsal weeks."

Alison unfolded the map, found the index wedged in among the adverts, looked up the street and said "G2" turning the big sheet of paper back over and running her finger across it to the right square. "There you are." She picked up a pencil and drew a circle around the road, refolded the map, with some difficulty, and handed it to Bob. He immediately passed it to Bobbie.

"Thank you. Bobbie will have to navigate if I'm driving. We'll see you all at rehearsals then." And with a chorus of 'goodbyes' the brief, crowded moment was over.

Penelope said her goodbye as well and followed the pair out, just in time to see them climb into a tatty Fiesta and drive away, turning left out of the yard gates.

Chapter 17

John and Nicole made their way to 'The Imperial' that evening where John left her, briefly, to go to the box office. She could see him chatting cheerily with the House Manager before he returned to her holding a pair of tickets overprinted 'Comp' in bold black ink. The audience crowd was starting to build in the foyer and he took her hand to lead her unhesitatingly to the circle level and across to the side their seats were on before entering the auditorium and showing the tickets to an usherette.

Once again Nicole noticed the brief but friendly few seconds of inconsequential chat. It was as if everyone knew him, though she suspected it was more likely that his confident manner made him stand out from the bulk of the public who were now starting to filter in to the great theatre's auditorium. People who knew where they were going and didn't need directions were a boon to hard pressed house staff.

Once seated Nicole looked around the theatre. She'd been in big theatres occasionally, but the opulence of 'The Imperial' was in a league of its own. Like most newcomers to its auditorium Nicole's first reaction was "Wow."

John smiled indulgently. He was a lifelong fan of the style of theatre building that is known as 'red plush and gilt' and had always believed that this particular venue was among the best of its type. As they waited for the performance to start he pointed out to her the more dramatic parts of the décor, the geometrically arranged plaster vines, twisting among the naked plaster cherubs and the glittering chandelier hanging huge in the centre of the ceiling. The red velvet house tabs were glowing warmly in the lights and there was an air of expectancy, the feeling that entertainment was about to happen. Musicians in the pit made preliminary noises with their instruments, and from where they were, above, they could just see a portion of the pit with its occupants moving about and settling in for the performance.

152

From John's point of view he could imagine the quiet activity backstage and the steady, measured rhythm of the dressing room calls in their established formulaic wording.

Nicole was eager in anticipation of the start of the show.

Eventually the houselights dimmed and the overture played. The performance of the touring version of 'Annie' was under way. Neither John nor Nicole had ever seen the show before, though its success meant that it was known to them and that some of the numbers had entered their consciousness by radio airplay.

In the interval John fetched ice creams for them. She noticed how even though, like the rest of the customers, he was obliged to queue he still managed a laughing smiling exchange with the girl with the tray of tubs around her neck.

"The kids are good, aren't they?" she said when he returned with their ices.

"Mm." John's mind was full of analysing various aspects of the show from a technical point of view, and his mouth was full of wooden ice-cream spoon.

"They're really working hard."

Freed of the spoon for a moment he nodded and said, "Yes. Good cast discipline there."

"Oh you are incorrigible. Don't you ever just sit and watch a show for entertainment?"

"I only ever watch entertainment shows."

The houselights started to fade again and the buzz of conversation in the auditorium died away as music started up again from the pit. She noticed John glance at his watch. 'He's

153

even timed the interval' she thought to herself. With the ices dispatched she was happy to sit, holding his hand in the dark, watching the show making its way to its happy ending.

When it was over, and she had clapped till her hands stung, along with the rest of the audience, they walked back to his flat arm in arm. There he made coffees, with a dash of whisky in them, and they talked about bits of the show that had attracted their attention. John talked of the technical aspects, Nicole of the bits she had like most, musically, or from the point of view of the performers.

A night-time routine had established itself now and Nicole went off to wash and clean her teeth first. By the time John returned from his wash she was sitting up in the bed with the covers pulled up to her chin and a wide eyed childish look on her face. Sometimes now John wondered if the childish helpless innocence she exuded was a bit coy.

He began to climb into bed certain as he did so that he would find she was naked under the sheets. He was right. As he put his arms around her she whispered, "I'm your Annie, you look after me, so you're my Daddy Warbucks."

"If those are our characters you probably shouldn't be in my bed, and certainly not with no clothes on, it would be weird and very illegal, " he said, as he turned the light off.

Chapter 18

John had put a pair of trestle tables next to each other in the centre of the rehearsal room with chairs round all four sides of the resulting big surface. The trestles were not identical, and there was a quarter of an inch height difference which formed a ridge up the centre. The cardboard model of the set straddled this line. Most of the chairs around the tables suffered from some loss of free leg-room due to the struts and frames of the table legs. The seat at the end gave the occupant a decision to make as to which side of the multiple legs they should sit.

John set himself up with a small square table against one of the walls with the show file on it. The cast began to arrive, clattering the stacking chairs in the echoey hall. Whether for dramatic effect, or by accident, Nick was the last to arrive, interrupting the chatter and introductory 'hellos' that had begun. Apart from Nicole, who had come straight over to John and trailed her hand across his shoulders as she made her way to a seat at the table, and Penelope, who he saw had positioned herself so she faced directly towards him and was looking hard at him, no-one paid John any attention.

Laurence had strode in with an air of importance, and taken the seat at the head of the table. John thought this was rather rude, but contented himself with the knowledge that the actor would find he had got cross members of the trestle ends right in the way of his feet. Laurence was unconcerned by this expected inconvenience, placing his feet on the cross members and tilting his chair back onto two legs at a jaunty angle. John, who was starting to find the man's approach a bit bumptious from the brief acquaintance he had had so far, nurtured a quiet hope that he would tilt back too far and over-balance.

Nick was also surprised and thrown by this seating arrangement, particularly as the centre seat on either side and the end seat at the opposite end were also unavailable to him. He found himself on the end of one side of the tables in a place that might normally have been reserved for a secretary.

Nick's opening remarks were predictable. He told them all how excited the company was to be expanding the scale of the show for this tour, and gave a nod to those members of the original cast, pointing out that their roles might have altered a bit from the previous version. He surprised John by inviting the cast to comment as they went through the reading. John had not met that approach before. Usually all comments on a new work were saved up till the end. This cut out lots of delays due to people picking up on things that probably got explained later as well as meaning that many of the petty gripes that actors are able to invent might have been forgotten by the end.

He went on to welcome the newcomers, Laurence, then Roberta, "she likes to be called Bobbie" and Robert, "he likes to be called Bob." He introduced Nicole, Hugh and eventually 'our leading lady' Penelope. There was a bit of a delay to the start of the read through while he listed the allocation of the parts. With such a small company covering a sprawling novel doubling was inevitable. Nick pointed out the set model and explained how the occasional changes would be done by the cast moving a truck themselves, either at the start, or the finish of a scene. Eventually they started.

John sat, aside from the main gathering, making very occasional notes in his copy of the script.

The reading was slow, with many interruptions. Every one of the cast stopped at some point to query the script. Laurence, reclining commandingly in his place at the head of the table, was particularly frequent in his comments, which ranged from 'I don't think my character would say that' to the more blatantly self-promoting suggestion that he should be onstage and other cast members or characters should enter and come to him, rather than, as was frequently scripted, they should both enter and meet.

The set itself caused some friction, with both Laurence and the other newcomers feeling that they shouldn't be moving scenic pieces when they had just, or were about to, deliver lines in character. Nick was at pains to explain that if done correctly this technique helped the pace and smooth running of the show. They remained unconvinced, and during the rehearsal period that would follow there would be a number of scene changes that were re-allocated to the venue crew. John glumly noted these as the weeks went by, knowing that the rehearsal and cueing of this sort of thing added to the get-in time and always introduced an element of risk into the first performance at least at any venue. Aside from that he would now have to get the office to modify the contract riders, some of which had already gone out, to ensure that the venues had a couple of stagehands available for performances. In some of the arts centre type venues this would not necessarily be the normal case, and if they were working on casual volunteers to make up staff he would probably find himself teaching them the cues very close to the start of a performance if those volunteers had 'proper' jobs during the daytime.

He was more interested in the way the relationships between the members of the cast had developed, and changed from those in the first company. Hugh seemed more subdued than in the past, accepting that his position as the 'famous name' had been trounced by Laurence's arrival. Penelope had previously always given an impression of aloof superiority and despite the antagonism between Adam and herself had never seemed to be in any way subservient. Now Laurence's various opinions were holding sway and being given more weight that hers as this read-through progressed. John thought that she seemed to have lost the fighting spirit that had backed her demands in the past, and was distracted, frequently looking at him rather than the script and quietly allowing the debates to pass over her.

Nicole was unsurprisingly quiet. John couldn't quite get a grip on Bobbie and Bob. They were clearly great friends, and had arrived together in Bob's car but he puzzled as to the exact nature of their relationship. In many ways their characters were as similar as their names, and whenever a consensus opinion was being sought, a thing Nick frequently did in his unassertive style of direction, they would say the same thing in what was almost like choral speaking. It became, to John's mind, almost like an old, established, comedy double act as the long session wore on.

Nick called a break at lunchtime, and the company scrambled to their feet, scraping chairs back and stretching from the cramp of sitting through the morning. Someone suggested the pub, and Nicole came over to John.

"Coming with us to the pub?" she started to ask, but was interrupted by Nick saying,

"John, can you come and have a word."

"I'll catch you up." John told Nicole, "You go with the others."

In the end he never caught up with the rest, as Nick, once they were in his office, launched into a long string of stage administrative details for several of the venues they were booked to tour to, and a discussion about the set and lighting.

John missed the lunchbreak. Nick had punctuated the discussion they had with taking bites out of sandwiches and drinking coffee from a thermos that stood on his desk. He didn't offer John any.

When they returned to the rehearsal room the cast were straggling back in. Everyone resumed their previous places. Nicole caught John's eye and mouthed 'have you eaten?' to which he shook his head. She wagged a gently concerned and admonishing finger at him, and he shrugged.

The reading continued. Whether because of the lubrication of the pub lunch, or frustration at the slow progress, Laurence became more and more vocal in his interruptions, making directorial 'suggestions' on everything from delivery to blocking, which wasn't really on the agenda yet. The only occasions on which he dropped his chair forward onto four feet were those when he reached across the table to move parts of the set model to new positions he felt should be used. Somehow his suggestions became set in stone and would remain with the show throughout the run. John privately admitted to himself that the actor's ideas were usually correct, even though it was not his place to say many of the things he did. From his side table John was also aware that Penelope was irritated by many of these interjections. There were a couple of moments when Laurence held forth authoritatively on some aspect of the production and John and Penelope's eyes met and there was a second of unexpected understanding in their mutual annoyance. Was there something else? John was not sure, Penelope's expression was different, not the superiority that he had found so off-putting all the previous weeks. He became sure that she'd met her match in Laurence and realised she was no longer top dog, 'or bitch' he thought to himself.

"When she comes to 'Thornfield', and it's in ruins," Laurence said as they neared the end of the play, "the lighting should be gloomy and low, so we can have a spot highlighting me coming on being blind in that scene."

He leant his chair even further back confidently. Nick made umming and erring noises muttering something about John dealing with the lighting design,

"And that means when Penny reacts to seeing me..."

"Penelope."

"...the audience will be getting the same shock and react as well."

"Let's see how it works when we do it with moves." Nick

offered as a compromise.

There was, John decided, some merit to this, the last of Laurence's suggestions, even if it was clearly a means of bolstering the importance of his character yet again. He scribbled a note in the margin of his copy of the script.

Bob read the final speech, wrapping the plot up and suggesting to the audience that the curtain call was the leads' wedding, and Nick said, "Thank you everyone. A long day, but very constructive. We'll start blocking tomorrow morning. John can you mark the rehearsal room floor ready for tomorrow?"
John pulled a handful of rolls of coloured tape from his pocket and waved them at Nick with the air of someone who had already prepared for the request. 'As, of course he has', thought Nicole fondly.

The cast went their separate ways. Nicole stayed behind with John. Penelope, last of the departing cast, looked back over her shoulder at the two of them as the door swung shut leaving them alone. John began re-arranging the tables and chairs.

"Can't you do that in the morning?" she asked.

"I'll get it done now. Less of a panic tomorrow. And easier than getting half way through it and finding the early birds are trampling all over you while you try to mark the floor."

He laid out a production table at one end of the room, with chairs behind it for Nick and himself, and the model to one side, and began sticking long strips of tape to the floor to mark the positions of scenery and furniture, measuring each distance carefully with an old architect's cloth measure. Nicole helped, holding the end of the tape measure in place where he indicated.

When they had finished the floor was criss-crossed with different coloured markings that matched the shape of the scale model that stood on the table. He took a roll of white tape and stuck a dot-dash centre line from the back to the front of the stage area. Theatre Wagon was lucky in having premises, old warehousing, which afforded the space to lay out at least an average stage size for rehearsal.

John stepped back and looked at what they had done.

"It will all get scuffed up of course," he remarked, "but it's a guide." He grabbed Nicole's hand and added, "Come on. Time to go and eat."

They turned the lights off and locked the doors.

"What do you want to eat?" he asked.

"What do you want?" Nicole countered.

"Let's have something more than a pub meal," he said, "do you like Indian?" He saw her hesitate, "All right, what about Chinese?"

She nodded. "But I can't afford...."

"Come on. Start of a new show, I'll pay," he promised. So John and Nicole found themselves seated, had they known it, at the same table that Penelope and Hugh had occupied at the end of the last tour.

"What did you think of the newcomers?" John enquired as they ate.

"Bob and Bobbie seem very nice," she said. "They're really quiet and not at all pushy. But very cheerful"

"Did you find anything out about them?" John already knew about their careers, minor tours and some repertory work, from seeing the audition paperwork. "Are they a couple?"

"I don't know," Nicole admitted, they're obviously very friendly and I think they've worked together a lot. They're in the same digs, but I don't know if they're sharing a room." She blushed, and thought to herself 'why should I be embarrassed about it?' disguising her thoughts by concentrating on chasing rice around her plate with a fork.

"Well they certainly aren't in digs with Mrs Odet if they want to share," John joked.

"Oh, don't remind me. I was trying to forget all about her."

"Sorry."

"I was so ashamed. I've heard people say they wanted the ground to open up.... but I think I really did."

"So did I, but the ground under Mrs Odet would have been my choice."

Nicole laughed. "That's unkind."

She ate some more. She was enjoying herself. Her under-financed background gave her more in common with Penelope than she would have guessed and although she had eaten the occasional meal in a variety of cuisines on special occasions it was unusual enough for her to feel that each experience of it was special.

"I wonder how, if they're together, they manage to get cast in the same shows."

John said 'Humm' as he thought about this. It was a question that rang a bell from his personal debate with himself about Nicole, and his concern that any relationship would be under immediate strain once this show ended and new jobs needed to be found. He decided that Bob and Bobbie were probably at so similar a level in their careers that the problem was less for them than it was going to be for himself and Nicole. The difficulty was on the distant horizon for them, but he realised that she had not thought far enough ahead to see it.

"Anyway I think they're nice, and we're all going to get along very well."

'Yes', he thought, that's her main concern. No friction, no fights no-one upsetting the applecart.' He said "What about Laurence? You haven't said what you think of him."

Over the top of her dish he could see her cheeks redden. She had lowered her head towards the plate to scoop up some food, and now she raised her eyes towards him, wide, and almost guilty. She fancies him, thought John.

"He's very nice. Of course he's famous so he might not take much notice of the rest of us." She meant take notice of me.

"Think he's a bit bossy?"

"He's the expert, so obviously he's going to say what he thinks. I don't think Penelope likes him much." she said after a moment's consideration. There was a further pause. "I don't think Hugh likes him either, because he's jealous, because it means he's not the star name any more."

"Perhaps neither of them really want the public to know about their past stardom. I mean the obvious question that comes up then is 'why are you in a little show like this then?' and they might not want to answer that."

"You don't think something went wrong for him on the soap do you?" Nicole was clearly concerned. Then with an unkind candour she added "You wouldn't be expected to be working at this level in the industry either really."

"Touché." said John, spearing a king prawn. "We're probably all out of our proper positions on the ladder.”

“I didn't mean... I know why in your case. It wasn't supposed to be any sort of....”

“Don't worry so much. I promise we'll kiss and make up later.”

Nicole squirmed slightly on her seat and smiled.

“I'd like that,” she said.

Chapter 19

Rehearsals started the next day. Nick was immediately aware that it was Laurence, not he, who was directing. The new leading man naturally assumed the mantle of control, taking it upon himself to position the cast in relation to John's meticulously marked settings, and passing comment on most of the company members' deliveries of the script. Nick was not averse to this arrangement because it relieved him of most of the directorial decisions. The cast raised no real objections, in part due to Laurence's previous reputation, and the acceptance that his skills were probably greater than Nick's. In any case the new man's character did not appear in the opening scenes, so he was outside the action, looking in, and his comments did not strike them as terribly out of place.

Hugh felt a certain annoyance, but couldn't make his mind up whether this was due to the man's domineering, or to his own natural frustration at a loss of status that the newcomer's arrival had caused. In any case he remembered in rehearsals for the original schools tour he, himself, had offered numerous suggestions which Nick had accepted without question. In many ways the company ethos was that of a collective, with each member contributing from time to time.

Penelope had different views. She smarted under the realisation that she had probably lost her position as the leading actor due to this new 'star'. She also had some considerable resentment whenever directorial style 'suggestions' were addressed to her. She didn't argue, much, but she stored up a number of moves and deliveries that were being changed from the original show in her mind, and spent the next couple of weeks subtly changing these things back to the old comfortable way she had been used to performing the part. It all upset her more than she chose to admit to herself and she occasionally looked over to John with an expression that was supposed to imply 'help, please save me from this' with an underlying sub-text of 'be my knight in shining armour and rescue me.'

Annoyingly, for Penelope, John almost always failed to notice these glances as he was usually scribbling blocking notes furiously into the prompt copy of the script.

As the days passed Laurence's character was gradually appearing on stage in scenes they were working on, yet he still continued his self-elected directorial position. John thought that he reminded him of descriptions of the old style actor managers, or of characterisations of such men in films like 'The Dresser'.

There was considerable excitement one morning, when, as they were in the midst of an act one scene, they all became aware of a car transporter reversing into the yard outside. The vehicle's bulk blocked the light from the windows and everyone was drawn to look to see what was happening even though the scene ploughed on in a half-hearted way. The actors involved at the time, it happened to be Penelope, Nicole and Hugh, carried on saying lines, but their heads were turned unavoidably to the darkened windows and their lines came in a lifeless automatic way.

Coming to a halt in the yard the truck proceeded, amid much clanging and clanking, to lower its tailgate ramp to the ground and decanted a small car.

It was not new, but it was showroom shiny, pink and glinting in the sun. The winch whirred and it was lowered down the ramp to the ground. Once there the driver of the truck and his mate unhitched the little Fiat, for that is what it turned out to be, re-wound their winch cable, raised the truck bed back to horizontal and were seen to come into the reception office. There was a short delay. Penelope delivered a line with more force than it warranted in an attempt to draw attention back to the rehearsal and her performance, and the door to the room opened and Alison appeared.

"Sorry to interrupt, Nick, but I think Penelope needs to come out here for a moment."

The scene shuddered to a halt.

"All right we'll have a break everyone," said Nick, "Go and deal with whatever it is Penelope."

She put her copy of the script down on a chair and, saying 'sorry', went out. She felt a small chill of fear. What had happened she wondered. Had there been some accident?

When she got to the little office it was filled by the two men from the truck, clad in somewhat greasy boiler suits. The older man, who was obviously the boss, bulged in his overalls. He held out a hand, oil stained from the winch cable, which grasped a wad of paperwork.

"Penelope Carson?" he asked.

"That's me."

"Just sign here please."

He laid the wad of papers on top of some newly delivered show posters on Alison's desk, leaving a greasy smudge on the top one.

"What's this for?" Penelope was confused.

"Your father sent this," the man explained a little curtly. He handed her an oversized greetings card which he produced from the pile of documents with a flourish, like a magician pulling a handkerchief from his sleeve.

Penelope read, 'You'll be needing this to get from town to town on your tour. It's taxed, MOT'd and I've insured it in your name, and the garage should have filled the tank for you. Drive carefully. Love from Mum and Dad.'

Penelope was dumb with surprise, signing the document in a

kind of daze and having the car keys pressed into her hand by the delivery man. She hardly managed a coherent 'thank you', though all her upbringing told her that she should be polite to these workmen.

The men left and the truck turned round and drove out of the yard into the traffic.

"Well aren't you lucky," said Alison. When there was only a sort of stunned silence she added, "You'd better go and look at it."

Penelope looked at the car, she opened the driver's door and was sitting in it studying the interior, which, like the outside was waxed and polished to a slippery finish, when most of the company appeared and surrounded the vehicle. She saw that they were holding coffee mugs and thought how she would have liked one too. There was a babble of chatter and variations on the questions, was it a present? Who was it from? She explained that it was from her father, and a total surprise, climbing out of the car and shutting and locking the door carefully. It was another surprise to find John beside her handing her a coffee.

"You looked as though you might miss out in the excitement."

Penelope thanked him, more grateful for the attention than for the drink. She was also grateful, she admitted, that Adam was no longer with them, for she could just imagine some of the things he would have said.

The cast, having walked around the car and admired it, drifted back to the rehearsal room to resume work. The interruption had broken the concentration however, and after Laurence had made a few sharp biting criticisms, which Nick had tried to smooth over without great success, the director called an early lunch.

"Isn't Penelope lucky?" said Nicole to John as they sat in the café with tea and sandwiches.

"I suppose so."

"Well not everyone has parents who can just give them a car. It isn't even a special occasion like Christmas or her birthday... Oh! It isn't her birthday is it?"

"I haven't heard so. I was just wondering what it must be like to be in a family where people can hand out big gifts like that. I mean Penelope can't possibly reciprocate on a Theatre Wagon wage, so Christmas, for example, must be a bit of an embarrassment. I just wonder if her father is a bit controlling. Does he let her do what she wants, or is he always looking over her shoulder?"

"I wish I had the sort of family that looked over my shoulder and controlled me by giving me a car"

"Don't get all jealous, it doesn't suit you."

Nicole pouted at him.

"She's got so much more than the rest of us."

"Ah. But you've got me." John joked.

Nicole reached across the table and held his hand.

Later that evening in Mrs Bray's dining room the salesmen had discovered Penelope's new acquisition, and where it had come from. Conflicting reactions were apparent in the room. Mrs Bray herself was delighted on behalf of her tenant, though she was reminded that this car signalled the approaching end of Penelope's stay there. Once she left on tour Mrs Bray was certain she would not return. This saddened the woman. She had grown genuinely fond of the girl, and interested in her welfare. She was nearly as frustrated by the failure of

Penelope's campaign to woo John as Penelope herself, even though she personally had never met him. There was also the need to find a replacement lodger, and she knew only too well how often that resulted in a resident that you didn't really like. The salesmen were no real trouble, but their booking didn't include Friday and Saturday night, as they both vanished to their homes for the weekend. It was not easy for digs such as hers to fill a couple of odd nights, so the rooms almost always stayed empty. Penelope had been a continuous resident since the first rehearsals for the school tour and had come to be Mrs Bray's solid steady income.

"Lass," said one of the men "it's very pink!"

"Is tha talking about her car?" asked the other, and they both roared with laughter.

"She could get a chauffeur, and be Lady Penelope sitting in the back."

"I'll be her chauffeur, you can tell me what to do any day."

There was more laughter.

Penelope resisted the temptation to tell him what he could do, and the leg pulling was halted by Mrs Bray's arrival with food. She thought that this was an aspect of her digs that she was not going to miss in the slightest but she dreaded the whole business of arriving in strange towns and cities and having to find, and book in to accommodation.

Mrs Bray was still a bit in awe of anyone whose family could hand over a car as a present and had pulled out a few stops for this meal, which resulted in them all escaping the chewier items in the larder. The meat was not as grey as usual, possibly even identifiable, and the veg less boiled to a pulp. If the salesmen noticed they said nothing, and the actress thanked the landlady as usual, while making another daily comparison with the food in her parental home. Mrs Bray hung around the dining room as they ate and made small-talk about where the first dates of the tour would be, and how much driving Penelope would have to do to get from one town to another. The salesmen were acknowledged experts in the travelling field, and the meal descended into detailed discussion as to the best routes from various towns to others, with no reference to where Penelope had actually got to go to and from. By the sweet, and subsequent coffee, she had been plied with advice about 'best routes' that consisted almost entirely of strings of road numbers that she couldn't have remembered even if she had wanted to.

Occasionally she couldn't help but look out of the window at the patch of pink that was the top of her car just showing over the low wall and hedge that formed the front of Mrs Bray's house.

Meanwhile in John's flat, with tea finished, he and Nicole were in the kitchen washing up.

The conversation was usually about the show, but tonight Penelope's car was still very much in the front of Nicole's mind. After they'd talked about it a little she asked again about the transport arrangements for the tour. She had been pressing John off and on to be allowed to travel in the truck with him. His argument that this would leave her arriving early and hanging around the venue while he did the get-in, put the set up, got the lighting hung, focussed and plotted, ran through technical and scenic cues with the local crew and generally dealt with the hundred and one jobs that were part of his remit was falling on deaf ears.

It struck John that Penelope's new car would help someone if she were willing to take a passenger. Bob and Bobbie would presumably travel together, Laurence had a car so Hugh would probably cadge a lift from him. Perhaps Nicole could travel with Penelope, though John knew that Nicole might not welcome that arrangement.

Nicole dreamed idly of travelling with John in the van carrying the set and other items. She pondered long leisurely days cruising pretty country lanes and stopping occasionally at roadside pubs for ploughman's lunches. The fleeting moment at the wayside filling station towards the end of the schools tour had given her an image to base her fantasy on, even if that rural idyll had been one she had had to share with Hugh. Sometimes she found that the driver in her fantasy world had quietly morphed into Laurence, and she pulled herself back from that version of her imagined tour. In neither case did the more realistic vision of pounding bleak motorways and A roads against tight deadlines or being stuck in frustrating tailbacks and jams as the clock ticked against them spring to her mind. Nor, despite her experience of the schools tour, did the journeys culminate in desperate street by street searches for the destination, involving erratic guidance by well meaning but ill-informed passers-by who were accosted from the wound down passenger window, and who frequently only 'thought' the venue they sought was 'that way'.

Nicole's insecurity made her wonder if there was some hidden reason for John's attempt to discourage her from travelling with him. Secretly she worried that he had lovers in all the venues they were to visit, for she knew that his previous career had taken him the length and breadth of show-biz country. Secretly she worried that he didn't like her enough to spend time cooped up in the cab with her on long journeys. Secretly she feared that if she was not with him he would meet someone else at one of the venues before she and the rest of the cast arrived.

Logically she knew these fears to be exaggerated, but her nature made her prone to worry.

Washing up completed she settled onto the sofa to watch as he began to draw set plans and lighting plans for each of the venues. He had a large drawing board, and a seemingly inexhaustible supply of blank plans for venues large and small that would be visited. Clipping the plan to the board he deftly overlaid the set layout, marking where they would need masking and backings that might be supplied by the venue, then, using a set of blue specialist stencils, and consulting the printed details of the venue's equipment, either from sheets he had been sent or from a directory, he drew symbols where the lighting equipment should be hung.

She watched for a long time, deep into the evening, as he repeated this exercise for half a dozen of the theatres. Eventually he finished a plan, stretched, leant the board against the side of the sofa and said,

"I think that's enough for tonight."

"How do you know where to put the lights?"

"This is pretty repetitive actually. You'll find that it will seem the same in each theatre, but it's only a case of getting a suitable angle really." He pointed upward and outwards with straight arms toward the corners of the room, "Forty-five degrees up and forty-five degrees out each side will do. Then we just put a few specials in, for things like the fire, and tell them what gel colours we want."

"Is that what those numbers are?"

"Yes. Fairly standard system. Different colour manufacturers use different numbers, but it's mostly just the first digit that changes, the last numbers are as near as makes no difference the same whoever the theatre buys from. Those numbers got sorted out.. oh round about the 1950s. Some of us old lags still use the original numbers as a shorthand and don't bother to add the newer prefix number. Of course I've written it on these," he indicated the plans that were gently rolling themselves up scattered around on the floor, "but it's not really vital."

"And will they have rigged all this before we get there?"

"Very unlikely. We're not a big priority show, even for an arts centre, so the get-in crew will probably have to do any rigging. I've mostly indicated positions where their basic standard rig would be expected to be hanging. We can be flexible about most of it, just a few specials need to be sorted, and I'll be less fussy on the odd one night dates than on week runs."

"I wish I could help," she said. "How do you know how to do all these things?"

"It's all bluff," he joked, "all my knowledge comes from the back of matchboxes."

"What?"

"'England's Glory'. Always some useless fact or saying on the back of the box."

She swung a cushion at him in disgust and when he retaliated they ended up laughing and fighting on the settee.

Chapter 20

Bobbie had the most important part, or parts, for there was much doubling, of any of the newcomers apart from Laurence. Nick soon found that she was adept at both learning the script, and at absorbing direction. He was conscious that this direction was mainly coming from Laurence, but recognised that the new actor had abilities and vision that not only bettered his own, but also were not jaded by having directed a previous version of this show and having, in any case, run out of ideas as he had.

Bobbie had worked in small companies before, and was not fazed by the doubling of parts, though she preferred larger and more conventional companies. She and Bob were willing to compromise on the level of the show in order to get work together. Theirs was not a formal relationship, but whenever they could be in the same company, or sometimes just in theatres in the same town, they would share digs, and many of their acquaintances saw them as a couple.

She was getting some wry amusement from the interactions in Theatre Wagon that she was observing as the rehearsals wore on toward the opening night. She made a mental list of the protagonists with their foibles which she then listed to Bob.

Penelope, she had decided, was a strong actress, confident enough in her own abilities to be aggravated by any invasive direction. Bobbie's female intuition led her to deduce that Penelope was increasingly infatuated with 'that stage manager bloke'.

Laurence was riding high on his television fame and was pushy enough to have taken over as a sort of 'ex-officio' director, and making quite a good job of it. He seemed to have taken a fancy to that little girl, Nicole, but it hadn't come to anything. "Yet," she added thoughtfully.

Nick, she thought, perceptively, was too vague to direct, and had very few ideas.

Hugh had also been in television, though it was too long ago for Bobbie to have seen him in anything. She knew this from his regular use of 'when I was in television' as a preamble to some long-winded comment or suggestion. Bobbie said that she thought that he resented Laurence's greater fame. On the whole, she felt, Hugh was friends with everyone and would be the best person to turn to if there was any trouble.

Nicole was clearly in a relationship with the stage manager, but had a hero worshiping attitude towards Laurence. Bobbie told Bob that she was "a good enough little actress, but she's totally insecure. That's why she's with the stage manager bloke, because it's his job to fix everything".

...and the stage manager bloke, what's his name, John. "I think he's slumming it for some reason. He's too good at his job for this little show, knows too much about the business. I don't know if he's followed Nicole here because he's smitten by her, but if so he'd better watch out, because if Laurence snaps his fingers she'll be going to him like a shot."

Bobbie thought about John for a moment and added, "Mind you, if John snapped his fingers Penelope would be with him like another shot. I can see why. Perhaps we'll suddenly see them all change partners."

"As long as it's polite and civilised," said Bob.

Elsewhere Bob and Bobbie were the subject of John and Nicole's conversation that evening.

"I'm sure they're a couple." Nicole said, out of the blue.

"Who? The florin?"

"The what?"

"Florin... Two bob. Old money," he explained. "They're both called Bob, so that's two bobs, two shillings, a florin. Collective noun for Bob and Bobbie therefore is a florin."

Jokes are never as good when they need to be explained, but somehow this one escaped from their private conversation and became the company's invariable way of referring to the pair. John couldn't remember using the nickname to any of the cast, but was equally fairly sure that Nicole wouldn't have done so. Perhaps he had used it in conversation with Nick in the offices one day. It remained one of those mysteries as to how the expression leaked. However it was Bob and Bobbie made no complaint, and it cemented their acceptance in the group.

Rehearsals continued. But John was more absent now, visiting and chasing scene builders and collecting from props and lighting hire companies. In due course the hired truck appeared in the yard, dwarfing the company's van when parked alongside. It was a small lorry, at the limits of what could be driven on a normal licence with a box body behind a separate cab, roller shuttered rear door with a tailgate lift and a rather sooty look to it due to its slightly smokey diesel engine. It was elderly, and had done many hard miles with the hire company, which was delighted to have a long term booking for it with Theatre Wagon for this tour.

John made some adjustments to the truck to suit himself, wielding a spanner on wing mirrors which had rarely been adjusted before and fidgeting the driver's seat to a position that was comfortable for him. He stacked the supply of tachograph discs in the glove locker and wedged the gallon can of engine oil and some rags behind the passenger seat, well aware that this old truck used copious amounts of oil.

Nicole stood beside the truck while he did these things, watching, and clutching a pile of loose maps and a big road atlas. Eventually he took these from her and slid them into the pocket set into the driver's door.

"Time for tea," he announced from the driver's seat, looking down at her.

"We haven't got much in. We might have to go shopping."

"Let's go to the cafe," he suggested. "Lorry drivers like a fry up."

Once they were seated, and waiting for their food, he asked her, "How are the rehearsals going now?"

"We've done most of it, and it's much better than the old version, but they just never seem to get to the last couple of scenes. They say 'we'll run Act two' and never get to the end."

"It's perfectly normal in my experience. Though I think it's unfortunate in this case given what happens in the latter scenes. I'll be making a fuss if we aren't given a clear tech run of the fire scene, without a lot of blocking and stuff taking up technical time."

"But they must give you time for lighting and things on the fire, mustn't they?"

"They should, but I've had a few occasions when the tech side has given way to the acting as the show gets nearer. Let's just hope we don't have that on this one."

Their meals arrived. Mary loitered by the table as they sprinkled salt and picked up their knives and forks. John and Nicole looked up at her, aware that she wanted to say something more than the usual 'enjoy your meal' style comment.

"I hear you're going away for a while," she said, making it sound a bit like a prison sentence.

"Yes," John mumbled, through his first mouthful, "off on tour for thirteen weeks from next week."

"You will both be coming back at the end won't you?"

"Have to come back to my flat," said John.

Mary looked at Nicole, who blushed and said, "I hope so."

The woman saw her uncertainty, and left it at that, simply adding as she turned away, "I do hope so. We'd miss you. Both."

Chapter 21

Over the next few days the company transferred to a local arts centre, where the last rehearsals and the previews would be held. Nick had negotiated a deal for them to have the use of the space for technical and dress rehearsals, in return for which the venue was to take the lion's share of the box office for the Thursday, Friday and Saturday performances there.

John didn't see the venue as an ideal place for previews. It had been converted from its original use as a warehouse to provide a 'flexible space'. As he put it: "In other words it doesn't do anything anyone wants well, it just does a lot of things very badly."

There was of course no stage; the flat floor gave a performance area, whose shape could be changed a bit by repositioning a number of cumbersome and obviously mechanical seating units. There were a number of lengths of scaffolding in the roof that provided both lighting positions and hanging places for a worn selection of black drapes, and a few rooms behind the wall at the back of this stage space that were grandly called dressing rooms, having a few loose stacking tables and some chairs in them and an assortment of slightly grimy mirrors screwed to the walls. Two of these rooms also boasted a sink, and John allocated these to the actors, taking one without facilities for himself as the company office.

An anonymous handful of amateur volunteer helpers assisted him in off-loading the truck and assembling and positioning the set, hanging black drapes in positions he indicated and adding the shows own extra lighting gear to the art centre's own rig.

By the end of the day, with these tasks completed, and the lighting coloured and focussed, loudspeakers plugged in and some rough sound levels set from the show-tape, now threaded on the venue's own tape recorder, John found that the volunteers had dwindled in number. Left on his own he sat at the inadequate lighting desk and laboriously wrote down channel numbers and levels for each of the lighting states that the show required, leaving the pages clipped to a board propped on the desk, before telling the front of house staff that he was leaving and that they would all be back in the morning.

Having parked the truck in the company's yard he walked home to his flat. Nicole was in the kitchen stirring something in a saucepan with a worried expression.

He kissed her. She said, "I didn't know what time you'd be back, so I couldn't start the spuds, so it will be half an hour or so yet." as she turned on a ring under one of the pans.

"What are we having?"

"The tin says it's stewed steak."

"OK. How did the rehearsal go today?"

"We finally got to the end. Laurence has had these really great ideas for the fire and for the finale," she enthused.

John recognised the eager praise for the new leading man was somewhat influenced by an element of hero worship and let her tell him all about it as he drank instant coffee and waited for the potatoes to boil. It was a long time before she asked him what the venue was like.

"Typical arts centre," he told her, bluntly, "but the set fits, which is a bonus, and the posters look quite good along the frontage."

Actually he had been quite surprised to find that the arts centre had a quite traditional canopy over its front of house doorway, as the warehouse conversion was using what had been an entrance to the original owners' offices as a foyer. The building's unimaginative title 'Western Approach Arts Centre' took its name from the road it stood on and was emblazoned along the edge of this canopy. Below, flanking the main doors were several cinema style poster frames, flat metal boxes, with clear perspex covers. These frames were twice the size of the Theatre Wagon posters, so these had been mounted two to a frame, side by side. This had resulted in a striking symmetrical pattern of four posters each side of the entrance screaming repetitively and in very bold type 'Eyre'. John wondered, striking or not, how informative this contraction of the book title to a single word would be to potential arty audiences, though it was, he conceded, modern fashion.

He told Nicole odd details of his day before they ate the tinned stew, then settled wearily onto the settee.

The advertising on the front of house gave the cast, and the official director, a significant frisson when they arrived the following day. Suddenly the show was a reality. The grim, even tedious, routine of preparing the show for performance now gave way to an awareness of immediacy in their minds. Parked in the arts centre's tiny car park they offloaded hand props and costumes through the back door to the dressing rooms, but they had all passed the frontage, with their billing displayed on it and a babble of chatter surrounded them as they explored the stage, the dressing rooms and, cautiously opening the doors at the rear of the auditorium, the foyer.

Inquisitive hands picked up, and in some cases purloined, copies of the programme from an open cardboard box standing by the foyer doors. As a schools tour there had been no programme, but now Theatre Wagon had produced a couple of sheets of A4, folded and stapled as a booklet programme which included mug shots and brief potted career histories alongside the cast and crew list. There was some explanatory text about the show and about Theatre Wagon and a couple of adverts from local firms who had been generous with goods or services. This same booklet would, in bigger venues on the tour, be placed inside a generic glossy cover to produce a more pretentious saleable book of the show.

Some of the cast were surreptitious about acquiring a copy of the programme, some were blatant, picking a copy up and walking back to the dressing rooms holding it dangling by their side, visible and open to challenge, but hoping no-one would say anything. No-one did.

Nick called them all together for one of his pep talks. He stressed that for today it would be a case of much stopping and starting as they sorted technical things for the first time. John was having a quiet talk with the two casual stagehands and the board operator that the arts centre had supplied. He was conscious that they were volunteers, and hoped fervently that they had enough experience to tolerate the dragging tedium of the next day or two. He was right to have concerns.

All in all it was a bad day. Scene changes that looked so simple on the model turned out to be more complex with actors around the set. Laurence made a habit of pronouncing "You can't move that yet!" if a change started before he had completely left the stage, which slowed the pace of the show until John, in frustration, appealed to Nick to allow the changes to happen around exiting actors. For once Nick made an executive decision that John was right about this and things became smoother as a result, although John could tell that Laurence did not welcome having been over-ruled.

Sadly all this caused hold ups that the volunteers were less able to cope with and their concentration was considerably disrupted by the situation. This in itself caused delays due to them not being ready and waiting on occasions.

Laurence made a habit too of questioning lighting states. John had had to fend off comments by Adam during those rare times on the schools tour when they had been able to light the show, but was surprised at an actor of Laurence's standing complaining that he thought he was not lit. It took John a while to realise that Laurence's experience with television soap meant that he had grown to expect a plethora of lanterns to be pointing at him wherever he stood. Over lunch he drew Laurence aside and had a quiet word.

"Stage lighting is a bit different to television, you know. The audience's eyes can accommodate much greater variations than a TV camera tube, so we get to paint much more interesting pictures with light on the live stage. I expect it probably feels a bit strange to you, but trust me it looks right out here."

"But I'm the lead, I have to be lit." Laurence complained a bit petulantly.

"Of course you do, and I can assure you you are."

"Well it doesn't feel like it."

"Theatre uses much softer lighting than a TV studio. I'm sure you'll grow accustomed to it."

The attempt at mollification was not wholly successful, and Laurence could be seen, throughout the afternoon, dodging about slightly on the stage looking up at the lanterns, trying to position himself in the exact centre of some beam or other. John knew that this was going to be an ongoing battle and prepared himself for complaints at every venue, especially those that were at the less well equipped end of the scale.

Laurence did, however, fail to make any complaint at the lighting for the fire sequence, for which John had introduced a number of bits of effect lighting that the show would be touring with it.

The shortage of rehearsal of the final scenes became conspicuous as they reached that stage, with Laurence making directorial blocking changes for Penelope as they reached the scene in which they are reunited. John was wryly amused as she accepted his instructions without argument, and wondered whether she would slyly creep the stage positions back to her preferences as the tour ran. He decided that she was cowed by Laurence, that her attitudes in the past had left her without any real supporters in any argument, and that she now realised this. He failed still to recognise that her repeated appealing looks toward him were anything more than pleas for support on matters concerning the show.

On the other side of the behavioural coin John did notice that Laurence adopted a very different approach to Bob, Bobbie and Nicole, using phrases like "do you think it would be better if..." where he wished to impose his will. John saw that Nicole was taken in by this slant on instructions.

Nick decided not to give notes at the end of the technical run through, John felt that it was less of a run and more a stagger, saying that he would go through comments tomorrow morning. John let that promise pass, for as a technical rehearsal it was no business of Nick's to give notes at all, except possibly to him, John.

The volunteers and the cast slunk from the arts centre building, tired from the tedium of the day, with the promise, or perhaps threat, of another lengthy day tomorrow which would include the dress rehearsal.

Nick and John stood in the car park beside the truck and talked though the next day. There were no surprises, except that Nick wanted to complete the dress before the evening, so that the cast could have an evening off, and that he didn't want to run anything the next day, prior to the press preview first night. In John's experience most directors want to keep rehearsing their cast, and crew, every available moment until the audience is literally waiting outside the auditorium doors. John was both surprised, and pleased, having always maintained that such last minute rehearsing is a waste of time, as no-one learns anything new that late in the proceedings, and also that running bits of a show at the last moment is an admission of bad time-tabling by the director throughout the rehearsal weeks.

He broke this news to Nicole once they were back at the flat late that evening.

"Will we get the day off then on the first night?"

"You might. I shall have a go at tweaking a few of the lighting states probably."

Her disappointment was evident.

"Don't worry, I promise to take you out for lunch."

Like a child, promised an ice-cream, her face lit up and she hugged him.

Chapter 22

It was an uneventful dress rehearsal. From the moment John gave a half-hour call over the makeshift dressing room tannoy system, till the end of the curtain calls, which in the absence of proper front of house tabs were conducted by a series of blackout, lights up, bow and repeat actions, no-one had much to complain about.

Nick was clearly perfectly happy with what had been created in his name by the cast. Laurence was obviously biting his lip about a few details, but seemingly awaiting the opportunity to do one of his 'wouldn't it be better if..' type alterations to the show. Penelope had, almost unexpectedly, for she had been quite inconspicuous throughout the whole rehearsal time, suddenly pulled out her star-quality for the occasion, and seemed likely to steal the show, despite the presence of Laurence. The supporting actors were all acceptably competent and even the local volunteer stage hands had done what they were asked to do reasonably discreetly when they should. In fact these scene changes were probably John's biggest bone of contention with the show. He was a fan of scenes changing by the simplest trick of some piece or pieces of scenery moving into different positions. He was not a fan of this happening because a couple of black clad stage hands had walked into the middle of the stage and grabbed some piece with the obvious intention of shifting or adjusting it. He had tried again quite recently to get Nick to put his foot down and make the cast move things. The scenery had been built to allow a single handed drag to move it smoothly on its castors, and John believed that it was perfectly possible for the exiting cast, or the entering cast to do this at the end or beginning of a scene. He was sure that this would result in a quicker, smoother show. Nick clung to the method of using stagehands because Laurence had argued against the cast being involved.

On the day of the first night John and Nicole sat in a country pub restaurant a few miles outside the city and had lunch. It was a good lunch, better and more expensive that their usual fare, and the table they were at in a bay window allowed them to see customers arriving and leaving by the front doorsteps, and to observe the rest of the diners too.

Nicole, particularly, was enjoying people watching, and the low conversation tended to run something like, "She is, she's wrapping it up in her serviette and putting it in her bag. No! Don't look round! Perhaps they've got a dog at home."

"Perhaps she's a health inspector and she's taking it away as a sample."

"No, she doesn't look like a health inspector. I think she's too old, and he's far too old."

"Maybe they're under cover. Perhaps it's clever make-up."

"They're leaving."

"Well if they get onto the front steps and then make a run for it we'll know won't we."

"All we'll know in that case would be that they haven't paid."

...and so on.

And eventually, when the people in the dining room, and one or two of the staff, had provided their parts in the speculative conversation Nicole and John returned to what was really their only common ground, Theatre Wagon, and 'Eyre'.

John expressed his opinion about the scene changes, and sounded out Nicole as to how she felt about his views. She thought for a few moments, trying to decide how much trouble these extra tasks would be to her, and the others, for she was under little illusion, the bulk of this sort of thing would doubtless fall to her and the other small part players.

It was not that she, or she imagined the others, were trying to avoid extra 'work'. There was a clear feeling among the cast, she knew, that to move scenic pieces would take them out of character in a production where establishing your current persona at any moment was potentially difficult due to the parts doubling that was required.

She didn't want to contradict John. She believed his experience to be so much superior to the general level within the company that she was willing to accept his viewpoint. But surely it was now too late in the proceedings to make such a dramatic change, especially when the company feeling was so against it.

"I don't know," she admitted, "I think the others wouldn't like it." but she didn't offer any explanation for the cast's reluctance.

John merely gave a slight shrug.

"We'll see when the press reviews come out whether any of them mention it," he promised.

And Nicole was even more convinced that he must be right about this, even if he was in a minority of one, for apart from Nick, who was giving virtually no opinions on anything, John was the only person who had sat out front watching the whole show through. She made up her mind to test out the others when the opportunity arose. She found she was hesitant about this, not due to her habitual reticence, but strangely, because she had heard Laurence's strong opinions against the idea. She wouldn't want to do or say anything that ran counter to Laurence's opinions she realised. And there was a seed of a puzzle that would occupy her waking hours for some time to come. She admired John. She saw him as both the font of some considerable wisdom and the source of comfort, for he certainly had taken, and did still take care of her. In the case of Laurence she was a little awed by his fame and admitted an attraction of the same kind that she had for John. It was unlikely that Laurence would be inclined to 'look after' her as John did, but his robust, over confident, attitude, born of his fame, she supposed, was both scary and exciting, producing an unexpected emotional response in her.

She poked her food about with her fork and said, "I expect you'll be right."

There was the slightest hint of criticism of him for being right in the tone of her comment, but John completely failed to pick up on it.

The discussion turned, as it did so often now, to transport. Still she attempted to hitch a ride with him in the truck. Still he discouraged this, pressing her to ask one of the car owning members of the cast if she could share.

""They'll be happy to give you a lift if you share some of the petrol cost," he told her.

"You wouldn't make me share the petrol cost if I came in the truck," she said, a bit grumpily.

"No, though I probably should. What would Nick say if he found out his tour truck was running a taxi service," he joked, "but you know why I don't think it's a good idea. You'd end up having long days hanging around and getting tired."

"They expect you to have long days and get tired, and they don't worry about you."

"How true. But that's just the nature of the beast, as well you know."

"I could help you."

"You shouldn't have to. You ask around and see who's got a spare seat."
There the matter rested again, John firm in his resolve not to

inflict the boredom of loitering round a get-in, fit-up and technical on the girl, for her own good, and Nicole resolved to make yet another attempt at changing his mind when the next opportunity arose. She wanted to go with John to be with him, even though there was a growing idea that journeys with Laurence might be nice, and to keep John company, because she had some slight concern about him falling asleep at the wheel. There was also the niggling doubt that maybe he had girlfriends along the route, 'a girl in every prompt corner' was a phrase she had invented in her mind, and that if she was not there old flames might re-ignite. Her insecurity fed this thought. She also wanted to have someone with her to guide her through the worrying maze of finding, and booking into, whatever digs were available.

Theatre Wagon, under John's guidance, was already taking care of that for the cast. Rooms were being booked on their behalf, though they would have to pay for them, in towns and cities on the tour for the dates they needed. Using the local digs lists, and a certain amount of local advice they were able to extract from venues, they were selecting digs at the cheap, but acceptable, end of the spectrum. As it happened this opening week would see Alison asking each of the cast in turn whether she should confirm the reservation she had made for them in each of the first few weeks. Nicole, caught surprised by this question, not having experienced being remotely organised in this way, fended Alison off by saying, "Can I let you know tomorrow?"

In her mind the girl had assumed that she and John would share accommodation, as they were at the moment, and she had to ask him.

"I tend to stop in more expensive digs than they are offering you when I'm out on tour," he said. "Of course you can share a double with me, but it might cost you more than singles in the company arranged digs would. They'll have probably got a bit of a discount for taking several rooms at once too."
"But if we shared the room cost?"

John had to concede it might not work out too badly for either of them financially, and admitted to himself that there were attractions in sharing a bed with Nicole while on tour. He booked his digs as double rooms, with the usual extras that he always paid more for, like telephone access and en-suite bathroom.

The opening night was, to John, unremarkable. The cast were backstage in their dressing rooms. The stage was set, and a preset lighting state dressed the fragmentary scenery. The houselights were up, working lights off, and gentle period style play-in music was running.

John gave the actors a half hour call via the dressing room calls system, and told the arts centre's mostly volunteer front of house staff 'Your house', a perfectly standard term, that he then had to explain to them. Doors were opened and the premier night audience began to come in.

John rarely went front of house when an audience was present, but on this night he succumbed to a mild curiosity, and abandoning the prompt corner for a few minutes he slipped through the pass door into the foyer.

He'd left the black emulsion painted world of the studio theatre, but he hadn't entered a warm welcoming bright world of bars and foyers as one might have hoped. The part of the concrete walled entrance nearest to the studio was unchanged from when it had been the reception of an industrial building, except that it looked as though the people who had painted the studio black had found they had some paint left over, and had extended the finish out through the doors and into the public areas, only stopping where they met obvious corners and brickwork. Thus the theatre going public entered a brick and concrete area which abruptly turned to black emulsion.

Downlights over the bar and box office counters tried in vain to give a welcoming or even sparkling appearance to this space, but succeeded in giving the impression of a council bus station.

Despite this discouraging outlook the foyer was already filling with an audience that included both the local 'great and good', John saw that a mayor had turned up, complete with chain of office, and a number of grey looking men who were clearly press reporters or reviewers. They mingled with obviously 'arty' types who, John suspected, were members of a supporters club for the venue, who would be making use of a first night discount which their membership entitled them to. None of these customers had chosen this particular show because they were fans of the book, or been dragged in by enthusiasm or even curiosity, and he recognised that the cast were going to have to work hard from the outset to woo them.

The truism that half of any audience doesn't actually want to be there, because in couples one person chooses and the other strings along with that choice, seemed to him to be optimistic on this night, for he estimated that very few of the audience he could see so far actually wanted to see this show. Mostly they were there out of duty. He could see Nick in the background, also looking as though he was there because he was obliged to be.

The house staff had the doors open now, and the first members of the public were abandoning the entrance to make their way to the auditorium seats. He watched them shuffle past for a few minutes before returning to the backstage areas.

The minutes ticked away and the backstage calls were given routinely, till at last the house manager gave clearance and the first night began.

Chapter 23

During the first week the arts centre housed their performances, and business was brisk, following universally good reviews from both the local city papers and from a national who had been an unexpected attendee on the first night. John felt it was reasonable to assume that the national had been tipped off about Laurence's presence in the cast, and had his suspicions that Laurence himself might have been responsible for that. However it had come about the effect was briefly advantageous to the box office, and gave the 'Theatre Wagon' office some treasured critical quotes to print up and paste across all the posters that were used on the rest of the tour.

At the end of the week the show was loaded into the truck. The cast left the Western Approach Arts Centre while this de-rigging and loading was still going on, all except Nicole, who stayed with John, although he made her sit in the auditorium to be safe from any possible accident. So while the rest of the cast returned to their digs for their last weekend in them, Nicole watched John quickly, efficiently and smoothly organising the dismantling and stowing of the show. She had seen him before with the small load that their company van had carried, but this was different. Previously she'd admired his patience, the way he took trouble over all the company's needs and requirements, now she saw, at least in part, the extent and complexity of the job when it was scaled up. She realised that even now this was only a simple little show to someone of John's experience, but had a dawning realisation of what he could really achieve.

She was a little frustrated by him keeping her out of harm's way as the scenery was dismantled and the company's own lighting was lowered from the scaffolding bars in the roof even if she did see the logic. Still she was here, and with him, even if he seemed to be completely ignoring her as the get out went on. And there was the weekend, or what remained of it, to look forward to, for the next date was only about forty miles away, and the truck, and John, would not leave till early Monday morning. She daydreamed for a moment. Was 'daydream' the right word she thought; maybe nightdream, though that probably meant when you were asleep, and she wasn't. She gave a start. Or was she? John had vanished, and the now empty stage was deserted. She got to her feet and went to the outer door, but the truck stood, unattended, with its roller shutter door half closed. Back into the building, and then she saw John, coming from the dressing rooms.

"Just doing an idiot check of the dressing rooms... to make sure we've got all our idiots," he joked, unaware of the momentary scare he had given her. "Come on, you keep saying you want to ride in the truck." and he led her outside again, shutting the back door of the vehicle with a rattle, and padlocking it.

He followed her round to the passenger door, reaching up over her shoulder to unlock and open it. She was a bit unnerved by the height. Reaching up she managed to grasp a grab handle beside the seat and began to climb the steel steps. John waited protectively behind her and then, seeing she was finding the short ladder to the cab a struggle gently pushed her up with a hand on her bottom. Nicole gave a startled 'Oooh' and pulled herself into the passenger seat. She looked down at him.

"Any excuse will do for you won't it," she said, smiling.

Back in the company yard he had to reach up to catch her and lift her down, and she held on to him tightly as she landed.

"Come on, home, supper and bed," he told her, locking the truck, and they set off for his flat.

The cast spent their Sunday quietly and, aside from John and Nicole and Bob and Bobbie, in varying degrees of isolation. In most cases some of the afternoon was occupied by packing, a task that took longer for those who'd been in their current digs for some time due to the previous tour.

Hugh left his digs on the Monday morning after breakfast. The inmates of his bed and breakfast lodgings had either gone off to work, or taken up their positions on the bulging furniture in the TV lounge where they would probably remain for the rest of the day. Breakfast television was occupying them at that moment with a bland mix of news and cooking tips. After he'd settled his account, and had failed to receive much in the way of a farewell during that transaction, he dithered in the hallway, trying to decide whether to say goodbye to the remaining residents. Looking through the open door he could see that their attention was entirely on the television. Shrugging slightly he picked up his two suitcases and, negotiating the inner and outer doors of the porch with some difficulty, started to make his way toward the company office. Occasionally he stopped and swopped the cases from one hand to the other by way of a change. No-one saw him leave.

Laurence, with whom Hugh was to travel, was waiting by his car in the company yard. The slightly pretentious Lancia looked out of place in the utility surroundings of the Theatre Wagon yard. Hugh deduced, from his own experience, that this car was a hang over from Laurence's more affluent period in TV soap. As they loaded the suitcases he made a silent bet with himself that unless Laurence found his way back into the higher earning world of television the car would soon be downgraded to the more familiar small family bracket that most of the actors he knew drove.

Laurence was quite subdued as they got ready for the journey to the first real date on the tour. His departure from his digs had been very similar to Hugh's, with no real acknowledgement of his leaving from anyone there. He left behind no memory in the minds of the owner or residents except a signed 'Walker Print' publicity photograph jammed into the frame of one of the pictures behind the tiny desk in the hall where people checked in and out. This was not how he felt he should have departed as his whole attitude cried out for some sort of flamboyant exit.

It was Penelope who had made the most flamboyant exit as things turned out. She was all packed as she slowly ate her breakfast that Monday morning, needing only to return to her room to clean her teeth and put her wash-bag into a suitcase. Over breakfast the two salesmen kept up a long and sorrowful account of how much they would miss her to a background dissertation by Mrs Bray which consisted of multiple repetitions of 'have some more' and 'you don't know when you will next get a proper meal' as if she were leaving for some long cross-desert trek over unexplored territory rather than an hour's journey from a city to a neighbouring county town.

She submitted to these comments with a good grace partly because she knew she would not have to tolerate the salesmen's innuendo again, and partly because she still had some hopes that once the little band of players was out on the road she would be able to engineer the circumstances in ways that might win John away from Nicole and over to her. There was a slight fly in that ointment, because transport arrangements had ended up so that she was having to share her car with Nicole.

Once breakfast was finished she went back to her room to close her case. She was aware that the salesmen were not dashing away to their work as quickly as usual, but thought nothing of it. Fastening the catches she took a last look around her room. She would not miss it, she decided. She would not miss the old fashioned dressing table and bedside chair, or the wallpaper of ribbons and roses and the illusion of lions. She picked up her cases just as Mr Bray appeared in the doorway.

"I'll take those down for you," he said.

Penelope wondered if that was the first time since she had moved in there that he had spoken to her without her speaking first. It was certainly more than the brief 'hello' which had been the extent of their interaction when he was not hidden away in the kitchen.

He hefted the bags and vanished down the stairs. She followed slowly, finding the front door and the gate at the end of the short path open. The two salesmen were standing, a bit self-consciously, outside, one either side of the path, and Mr and Mrs Bray flanked the single wooden gate onto the pavement. It looked like a small, but rather intense, guard of honour. She finished descending the stairs and went along the hall and out of the door. The first salesman grabbed her wrist and stopped her, turning her toward him and saying,

"Lass we will miss ee," upon which he gave her a unwelcome, and, even at this hour, beery, kiss, before turning her round to the other man who repeated the kiss, and said,

"Ah hopes thee'll come back soon."

She could think of no response to these farewells, which were probably genuinely well meant. Briefly she wondered if John would smell of beer in the unlikely event that she got to kiss him.

Further down the path Mr Bray shook her hand, and Mrs Bray hugged her, whispering in her ear as she did so,

"Go out there and win that stage manager of yours, love."

"Thank you." said Penelope, and she loaded the bags which were at the roadside into the pink Fiat 127, then opened the driver's door and climbed in. She was surprised to find that she drove away with a bit of a lump in her throat. She parked up in a side street for a while and waited till the clock wound slowly round to the time that had been agreed for leaving from the office.

At Bob and Bobbie's digs the departure was rather mundane. They alone of all the company checked out, climbed into their car and drove straight to the next town without calling at the company office.
John and Nicole had more clearing up to do than the others, and spent some time very early in the morning emptying perishables

out of the fridge, tidying the flat, and generally shutting down a home that would be abandoned, aside from occasional flying visits, for the duration of the tour. They had breakfast in the café the moment it opened, and John had the truck on the road, with Nicole's suitcases and his on board, by half past seven. Nicole wandered to the newsagent, bought a paper, and was sitting on the step at the company office before Alison arrived to unlock the door, reading it.

"Hello," said Alison, "Are you early, or have you missed your lift?"

"Well I'd have liked to go in the truck with John, but I'm waiting for a lift with Penelope."

Alison looked around the yard. She knew from the digs bookings arrangements that John and Nicole were together.

"I see John's left already, have you been sitting here long?"

"Not too long," Nicole lied.

The secretary studied the little actress and deduced that this was not true, saying, as she unlocked the door and went in, "come on in and have a cup of tea, the rest of the cast won't be leaving for a while yet."

And so it was that as Laurence met up with Hugh, and shortly afterwards Penelope appeared in her new car, Nicole had already been in the office drinking tea and chatting with Alison for several hours.

Penelope pulled her little pink car alongside Laurence's more pretentious vehicle in the yard, getting out and walking across to join the other two.

"Here she is. Lady Penelope in the pink Rolls Royce." said Hugh.

Penelope looked severely at him.

"It's getting to be an old joke," she chided.

"It's getting to be an old car," said Laurence, rather seriously.

In truth in the short time Penelope had had the car she had come to realise that the high gloss showroom finish was mainly superficial. Closer examination revealed that the pink bodywork was a respray over what had been a white car. This showed in a number of slightly hidden places like doorposts and inside the boot and engine bay, where the respray had been less than thorough. She'd also realised that the car had covered huge mileage, and tended to struggle a bit on steep hills. Despite this, and the colour, which she would not have chosen for herself, indeed had she been shopping for a car on a forecourt she would almost certainly have walked straight past this one because of the colour, Penelope was still in the early stages of pride of ownership, and still felt gratitude to her father for the gift. She ignored Laurence's quip.

Nicole joined them from the office. Penelope was glad to see that she did not seem to have any suitcases with her, rightly deducing that John had taken them in the truck, for the little car's boot was already full with her own luggage, and stowing more on the back seat would be awkward, involving tipping the front seats forward to gain access in this two door car. Penelope still hadn't quite worked out how to tip the seats properly, having only succeeded so far in folding the back forward, not tipping the entire seat. But the assumption that John had taken Nicole's cases brought a renewed surge of jealousy as it reminded her of John and Nicole's relationship. She felt that the girl was deliberately flaunting the fact that they must have slept together last night, and nights before that, by arriving in the yard with just a handbag. Her nose felt that it was being rubbed in the dirt by this reminder that John and Nicole were staying together in different, rumour had it 'posher', digs from the rest of the cast. The sexual jealousy that she felt made it difficult for her to be more than civil to her passenger. Mrs Bray's parting whisper came back to her mind, and with a reborn surge of self-confidence she found she could feel sorry for the little actress who, she felt sure, when she was in optimistic mood, was about to be ousted by her, Penelope Carson, in John's affections.

The four cast members stood around, and Laurence made an attempt to describe the route to their destination to Penelope. She mostly ignored this, partly because she was not good at following a string of road numbers, and partly because she had already had a look at a map, and had folded it with the necessary pages outward ready, and it was in her glove locker.

There was a strange reluctance among them all to embark on the journey. The great adventure of new and, to these actors and actresses, unknown, venues, was ahead, but driving out of the company yard was somehow final, somehow taking the step. They all knew that they would not be returning here till at least the end of the tour, possibly ever, if they were not invited into the cast of another Theatre Wagon show. This was where they had all met, this was where, with the exception of Laurence, they had all survived the drab round of TIE days,

It was Alison who broke the hesitation, by coming out of the office and saying,

"I just wanted to say good luck to you all before you go off. You know the office number, so if there's anything you need just give us a ring. Nick will be coming to some of the performances, of course. He would have been here this morning, but he's with the writers discussing another show."

They got a slight feeling of having been snubbed by Nick but they thanked her, and began climbing into the cars. Laurence turned to Penelope and said,
"I'll go first. You can follow me if you like," and then with a sneer, "If you can keep up."

Penelope pulled a face at him as he slammed his driver's door, started the engine and swept out of the yard.

Nicole said, "Goodbye Alison," and got in, fiddling with the seatbelt to find the clip to push the chrome blade into.

Penelope settled into her seat and they set off. They were four vehicles behind Laurence by the time they were out of the yard gate and she resolved not to try to keep up with him through the city traffic.

"There's a map in the glove locker. Can you follow it for us?" she said to Nicole.

Nicole was pleased. She had always quite enjoyed the occasions when being in the front seat of the van had allowed her to map-read, and, though she privately acknowledged that John had never really seemed to need the directions, she'd welcomed the excuse for a few words between them in the old early days of the schools tour. Now she saw that the map might serve as a bit of a bridge between Penelope and herself.

She was not sure why Penelope had seemed to be increasingly off-hand with her over the past few weeks. It was not as though they had ever been close friends. Indeed their conversation had been pretty limited, reduced really to the essential exchanges between two people who fate had made to share dressing rooms but who otherwise had nothing in common. Nicole had seen the other actress studying John from time to time, but Penelope's selfish awkwardness with everyone was so engrained in Nicole's mind that the assumption she made was that a complaint of some sort was on the way.

Penelope had been grudging when approached about car sharing for the tour, making clear conditions about sharing the cost of fuel and keeping the inside of the car tidy. The fuel cost sharing was in fact a boon to Penelope, who had been a bit worried about the expenses involved in the tour, for touring allowance or no touring allowance her finances were still tight.

They talked little. Nicole asked whether Penelope knew any of the venues in the first few weeks of the tour, and found that like for herself this was almost entirely new territory.

"I expect John will know them all," said Penelope.

"I don't think so. He only seems to have worked in big venues till he came to Theatre Wagon," Nicole replied. "I'm really glad he did though," she added. Then: "come to Theatre Wagon I mean."

Penelope felt the jealousy rising again. Maybe she wasn't so sorry for Nicole that she would feel any guilt taking John away from her. All's fair in love and war. 'Love?' She wondered if that was what she really felt, or was it desire? Her emotional experiences were much less than people supposed. Through stage school she had not formed any deep friendships with the men on her course, let alone had a boyfriend, fending admirers off with her habitual protective off-handedness. Now out in the big wide world she'd avoided any of the casual liaisons that might have been available in the succession of theatre companies she had been part of.

For her passenger this first journey also dispelled the wistful illusions Nicole had had about the travelling. There most certainly were not pretty winding country roads to travel along admiring the scenery. They left the city on dual carriageways lined with factory unit after factory unit, set back from the dirty grass verges filled with distressed looking parked cars, many with home-made cardboard 'for sale' signs wedged into the windscreens. The factory units were usually off the road behind steel fences and gates, with company names emblazoned on the building walls that mostly gave no clue as to the type of business. Once in a while an owner had indulged in a punny or alliterative title, 'Doug's Diggers' and the like, but few were amusing enough to comment on. After a while the industrialised buildings gave way to row upon row of domestic houses, terraced, semi-detached, even a few detached, and mostly dating from the 1930s, with tiny front gardens filled with dustbins and rusting children's bikes. Then for a mile or so there were dull flat fields before the houses started again. Nicole came to realise that the countryside she had envisaged in her daydreams had been eradicated between the urban conurbations.

It was early afternoon when they were aware that they were running into their destination town. The road, two way now, sprouted an endless succession of traffic lights, guarding every crossroads and pelican crossing, which slowed the traffic to a stop, start, progress. Penelope, who was not used to long journeys on urban roads, found that she was tiring from constant clutch control in these conditions and wished that she had chosen different shoes and that they were at their destination.

Nicole, as a passenger, could look around and study the houses and shops. Occasionally she commented on something she saw, but Penelope was clearly concentrating on driving and made little response. They passed through an area where the sides of the road were one endless procession of small shops with awnings sticking out. Butchers, grocers, estate agents, but noticeably numerous foreign shops selling Chinese, Indian and Jewish foods. Scattered among these the ethnic restaurants, and on the pavements were men and women in a variety of headscarves or turbans. There were no houses evident, and Nicole decided that everyone in the area must live in flats above the shops.

"Right at the next main junction," she said, for she had been following the map assiduously.

Penelope indicated and began trying to work her way across the continuous stream of traffic, succeeding only when a driver, more generous than the rest, held back and flashed her to come into the outside lane. They sat at the red lights. When they turned they found themselves on a tree lined road. Suddenly it was as though they had entered a different town. Smart detached houses with gravel drives lurked behind the grass verges and their trees and within a few moments they were pulling up in front of the little theatre they were to play.

The building was probably an old assembly room or church from the tail end of the Victorian era, but recent development and building work had given it a gleaming concrete and glass frontage with tall windows that showed an airy foyer inside. Their posters were displayed either side of the main doors, which stood open welcomingly. There was clearly some sort of parking on the right of the building, but it was blocked at the moment by the truck. Penelope parked against the curb close to the theatre. She was pleased with her successful parking manoeuver, she had become more accustomed to the car now after the drive through urban traffic but reversing into a space was still a worry to her. Further up the road she could see Laurence's car also parked.

The two actresses got out of the car and went in. Penelope's instinct was to find the stage door, but exploring the side of the building they could only find a locked and anonymous door in what seemed the likely area, so they went in through the foyer.

Hugh was stood just inside studying a display of production photographs and blown up edited press cuttings which had been stuck on some Marler Haley boards in the foyer with the title "Eyre" which had been cut out of a poster.

"Hello you two," he greeted them, "Find it all right?"

"Yes thanks. What's it like, is it nice? Where are the digs?"

Hugh laughed at the small torrent of queries.

"Yes it's nice. Actually it's rather posh for a small theatre, and the audiences are all good. It seems that this place is the local for all the culture vultures who live in the smart houses round this area. The digs are only just along this road, but Laurence and I haven't checked in yet, we thought we'd wait for you. I haven't seen the florin. I thought they might have been here before us."

Nicole was only half listening.

"Is this the way in?" she was asking, but she was already going through the obvious audience entrance door. Hugh grinned at her vanishing back and turned towards Penelope with some quip, about the love birds having been separated, on the tip of his tongue, before he saw the anguish in her eyes and kept quiet. He'd become increasingly aware of the potential love triangle in the company ever since the end-of-schools'-tour-meal he had bought for Penelope. Sometimes it amused him, sometimes it worried him, frequently the imminent heartbreaks he predicted to himself saddened him, for he liked both Penelope and Nicole, and had some concern for John as he pieced together more of his background.

Nicole found herself at the back of the auditorium, in darkness. A single spotlight pointed at the stage, its beam wiggling about as one of the crew adjusted its position. John was on the stage with his back to this light, arms outstretched, clearly indicating where the thing should be pointing. Nicole hurried down the side gangway and onto the stage to John, running up to him and going round to hug him and turn her face up to be kissed. He was taken by surprise, but he kissed her and said, "Hello."

She thought he seemed distracted, but she couldn't read his expression because she was looking straight into the lantern they were focussing.

"Just another ten minutes, this is just an alteration, it's all plotted and set otherwise. Sit in the auditorium, I'll take you to our digs in a minute."

She looked about, and despite the bright blur in her vision where she had been briefly blinded by the spotlight could see that their set was standing on the stage. She let him go and went to an audience seat, folded the tip-up down and sat waiting. It was a bit more than ten minutes, but eventually working lights came on and the ladder was cleared away. It was a nice little theatre, finished in warm colours, with a single raked bank of seating facing a floor level stage. Anonymous black drapes framed the company's set.

John thanked the crew, saying 'see you later' and came over to her.

"Want to see the dressing rooms?" he asked.

She nodded, and he led her across the stage to a door that brought them into a bleak white corridor with rows of numbered doors off it. She saw that he had allocated the dressing rooms with neatly written cards with the cast's names on. Hers said 'Miss Simmons & Miss Wade'.

"You and Bobbie are sharing, so are Hugh and Bob, Penelope and Laurence have got their own rooms this week. I'm just down there." He pointed to the next door but one, whose card said 'Company Office'. "Luxury this week! Don't get too used to it. Got anything to drop off before we go to our digs?"

She shook her head. They went back onto the stage and Penelope, Laurence and Hugh came in from the foyer to the rear of the auditorium at the same time.

"We've been having tea and cakes in the café," said Hugh, "what have you two been up to?" and he winked.

"Dressing rooms are through there," John gestured, ignoring the innuendo, "and we're going to find our accommodation. You might want to check your props but I think they're all in place. Costumes are hanging in the appropriate dressing rooms.

Absolutely no changes from last week, we go up at half past seven, everyone here before the half please.. though if you want to do a warm up that's up to you, no-one on the stage after the half because it's an open stage. Tell the florin when you see them, I reckon they've gone straight to your digs. Probably best to take your cars there as the parking here's a bit tight, but it's only walking distance. See you later."

With that he took Nicole's arm and led her to the foyer. He helped her up into the truck cab like before and drove a couple of streets to turn into the drive of a big double fronted house, taking the gravel roadway round to the back where he parked up on a wide parking area.

"Is this where we're staying?" Nicole looked up at the back of the building, which was almost as imposing as the front.

"Nothing but the best." And he lifted her down, and they went around to the front and up the steps between a pair of stone pillars that flanked the doorway. They were greeted by a friendly girl in a black skirt and white blouse that teetered on the edge of being a uniform, clearly chosen to give that impression.

"Hello Mr and Mrs Mason. Will you be eating here this evening?"

"Yes please," John answered, "but we'll have to be very early because of the show."

"Will five-thirty be all right?"

"Excellent. We'll see you then."
and John led Nicole to the ornate timber staircase and up to their room.

"She thought we were married!" said Nicole.

"She didn't think anything of the sort," John told her, "she's just keeping up a polite facade."

He unlocked the door to the room. Nicole peered in.

"Are you going to carry me over the threshold then?" she asked coquettishly.

"If you insist," he said, picking her up off her feet and carrying her, her arms around his neck, into the room.

Nicole felt that she had been booked into somewhere very luxurious, and perhaps, in comparison to the bed and breakfast digs she'd occupied, and that the rest of the cast were now in, this hotel was. It was easy to overlook the worn furnishings in a first impression of space and facilities. No shared bathroom along the landing, for there was an en-suite shower and toilet. There was a TV, and a phone, and tea making equipment and one of those ubiquitous Corby trouser presses. The young actress was slightly awed and explored the room making surprised 'oohs' at each minor discovery. John marched to the bathroom and washed and changed from the day's get-in, donning fairly smart black clothes from his suitcase which was balanced on one of the trestle style stands for cases. She saw one of her cases was on the other side of the bed.

"Be quick," he told her, "it will be a bit of a rush to eat and get back to the theatre tonight, as it's a first night."

She obediently hurried through her preparations, and they went back down to the dining room in time to be the first customers.

They ordered a simple omelette and chips meal. John said, "We'll dine properly the rest of the week, but I need to be there earlier tonight to check things."

She knew he wouldn't be at ease till he was back in the venue, and ate swiftly.

Afterwards they walked the few hundred yards to the theatre. Foyer lights blazed and made the frontage look more attractive than it really was in the evening darkness. They got in through the stage door, which was now unlocked, although unmanned. Inside she went to her dressing room and he prowled the stage and the control room, double checking all was ready.

A bit before the half he conscientiously visited each dressing room in turn, making sure that his little company had all they needed. Hugh and Bob were relaxed and professional, Nicole and Bobbie had laid their room out like a true home from home. Laurence was doing noisy vocal exercises, but stopped to assure John that he had all he needed. He came to Penelope's door last and knocked.

"Come in," she said.

For a moment he wondered if he had misheard, but knew he hadn't. After that he figured that perhaps she had been expecting someone else. But the only obvious conclusion really was that she had staged the scene. She was standing with her back to the door, in front of a full length mirror, the angles ensuring that anyone entering saw both her front, in the mirror, and back. She was in her underwear, with a short thin dressing gown hanging open and loose on her shoulders and with her arms raised to lift her blonde hair up from the back of her neck. There was a clear intention to titillate as much as possible, which was given away more by the look in her reflected eyes than by her state of undress, which, truth be told, was not that hugely unusual backstage.

John said, "Oh sorry, just checking everything is OK for you."

Penelope turned to face him, dropping her hair so it draped loosely over her bare shoulders, the gown flaring wider as she moved. There was an impression that she had thrust her hips toward him, and she regarded him steadily. He also wondered how long she had been waiting in this undressed state for him to come to check on her, she would probably have assumed that he would. He could hardly avoid noticing that she was more curvy than Nicole, or that her underwear was frilly and expensive.

"...and is there anything you need?" he added after the moment had dragged just a fraction too long.

She gave him an unexpectedly cheeky smile and answered "Perhaps not right now."

She was still flaunting herself as he turned away saying, "Break a leg," and shut the door behind himself.

On the way back to the prompt corner, where he gave a standard 'Ladies and gentlemen this is your half hour call,' over the dressing room paging system, and as he went onward to the foyer to look at the incoming audience, he thought about what Penelope was up to. He'd never been in any doubt that he found her physically attractive, even through the worst misery of her sullen and selfish behaviour he'd nursed a small secret fantasy idea that she might actually be someone he would like if she would just behave. He'd failed to ever notice any 'come-on' from her before. Then as he neared the pass door he began to convince himself that he'd misread the situation, that it was not a come-on at all, just one of those occasional backstage encounters with an actress in déshabillé. He pushed on the pass door, pondering whether it was his own secret fancying of her that had led him to interpret the event the way he originally had.

His meditations were immediately and loudly disrupted by running into Nick, who was in the swarm of public filling the foyer, who hi-jacked John into joining him in the 'meet and greet' with important members of the audience.
Important, John thought, either because they were from the press and might write a review, or because they were civic dignitaries. There were a few local councillors and their wives, who might possibly have a slight influence on the venue's booking policy too. Keeping a firm eye on his watch John

entered into the round of handshakes and false smiles that Nick required of him. Eventually, excusing himself, he returned backstage to give the calls that would start the performance.

The local audience, composed as it mostly was of the more affluent classes, who were accustomed to calling the shots in their daily lives, was tardy about taking its seats, and front of house didn't give clearance to him till nearly five minutes late. John had called beginners as usual, so Penelope and Bobbie had been hanging about in the wings for some time before he was able to take the houselights down. He could see them in the gloom across the other side of the stage from him, chatting quietly during this delay, and noticed that there were several glances from Penelope toward him, but he was still unsure whether these were open to any interpretation other than a slight impatience at the house keeping them waiting.

It was an uneventful performance. At the end Nick came backstage and had a few words with the cast, but John received no 'notes' from him, and he departed leaving them to it for the rest of that week at least. Press reviews that came out in the next couple of days in the local dailies praised the cast, mentioning Laurence's soap fame. John was interested to see that at least two of the reviewers also mentioned the undesirable business of stage hands entering to change scene.

John exercised some caution with his nightly dressing room visits for the rest of the week, at least as far as Penelope's room was concerned, and for the moment there were no more unexpected exposures, whether it had been a deliberate ploy on her part or not.

Now that they were more settled into the run of the show the company began to form regular patterns of behaviour during the performances. Maybe it was a growing confidence that led the actors to feel that they had time to observe more of the show than just the bits immediately before their various entrances. Maybe their costume changes had become faster through habit, and now they had more time on their hands. Whatever the causes the result was that at various times during any performance John would be aware of shadowy figures in the wings who were watching the play, but were nowhere near their next call. The week continued, and he began to suspect that there were more reasons for these visits to the stage than he had originally supposed.

Making mental notes, he saw that Laurence, whose onstage time was much less than might normally be the case for a leading man, was frequently to be seen intently observing Nicole performing in her various and varied roles. He also noticed that she, in return, was to be found watching Laurence. It was the fact that John himself realised that he was paying more attention to Penelope's performance than he had been, and realising this, feeling a slight guilt that the concentration on her was not due to her leading role but to an ever growing interest in her, that led him to wonder if the different wing watchers all had some hidden agenda too.

He saw also, though her time off-stage was very short, that Penelope was prone to watch the prompt corner, rather than the stage, when she was in the wings, and was unsure whether this was connected to her apparent come-on behaviour to him on the first night or due to keeping a professional eye on the stage manager.

Bob and Bobbie alone seemed not to have developed this habit of people watching, for Hugh was, it seemed to John, almost universally present. John could not decide if Hugh was watching anyone in particular, or everyone. As the week wound towards the final Saturday performance John became increasingly amused by the people watching activities of his charges, which were, by the weekend, obvious enough for him to make a margin note in the show reports that the cast were doing this.

After the last performance John and the local crew worked on the get-out, dismantling the set, de-rigging the lighting specials that the company had brought with them, and loading the truck, which John had driven round from the hotel before the performance. The cast slipped away to their digs, except for Nicole, who took upon herself the task of packing costumes in the dressing rooms and making a neat pile of props, furniture and a wardrobe skip close to the loading door.

"Thank you, but you should have gone back to the hotel," John told her.

"I wanted to help you," she said.

Although he trusted that she would have been scrupulously thorough about clearing the dressing rooms he did an 'idiot check' to make sure, finding only a 'good luck' card from 'Cynthia' stuck behind the mirror glass in Penelope's room. He debated whether to throw this in the bin, but in the end brought it out and tucked it into the show paperwork briefcase. From front of house he retrieved show photos and publicity that could be reused before saying good bye to the resident staff and hoisting Nicole up into the cab of the truck for the short drive back to their hotel.

John and Nicole had arranged to stay over the weekend in the same accommodation. Of the rest of the cast Bob and Bobbie had decided to move to the digs arranged by the company in the new town, while Hugh, Penelope and Laurence would make the journey early on Monday afternoon.

The cast, whether leaving on Sunday or Monday, all had to get up at what they, as actors and actresses, considered an early hour if they wished to get any breakfast. John and Nicole, with the luxury afforded by their more superior hotel, ordered breakfast on room service for Sunday morning.
They sat side by side in bed with the trays balanced on their knees, luxuriating in the laziness of a forthcoming idle day.

"Why do we do this?" John asked.

"Because we love theatre," she suggested.

"No, I mean why do we put toast in a rack so that it goes cold?"

Nicole, munching her buttered toast and scattering crumbs in the bed with abandon, looked around the room.

"I'll be sorry to leave here," she announced.

"Another week, another town," said John, adding "Another theatre, another week of monotony."

"You don't really mean that I'm sure."

"No, I don't suppose I do. But now it's up and running there's not much variation between one venue and another, well at least except for mechanical changes like backstage layout and where we can rig things."

"What's next week's place like?"

"Never been to it, but from the tech spec it looks quite well equipped. Funny venue though, I gather it's a converted disused church, so there's pillars all down the auditorium and rumour has it that the acoustics are terrible."

"Why did Nick put us in there then?"

"Nick, bless him, has put us in anywhere that he could sell us to. I think we'll just have to sit next week out. Then we do a week in a couple of real theatres. The week after looks much more interesting than this too, it's another conversion, old mill building I gather, and the sort of caretaker-cum-manager and his wife run a hotel in part of the building, so we're all booked in there together. At least it won't be a long walk to the venue each day!"

Nicole brushed idly at some crumbs. Then, rather shyly she rubbed her foot up and down his leg under the covers. The trays lurched dangerously.

"John?"

"Um?"

"Next week, will it be all right if Laurence and I do some rehearsing during the daytimes?"

"If you think there's bits that need going over. I can deputise for Nick. What bits did you have in mind?"

"Actually it isn't any specific bit. Laurence said he'd give me some acting tips, so I thought we could maybe have a couple of afternoons to do that. If you don't mind?"

"Of course you can. Why should I mind?"

"Well it would be just him and I and...."

Nicole stopped, for her mind was envisaging a caring one to one tuition with Laurence that went off into a number of vague fantasies which she didn't want to talk to John about.

"Silly," he said, and picking up both the trays in turn he put them down on the floor beside the bed, turning when he had done so to kiss her.

"There's a lot of crumbs in this bed," he said.

"Oh, I'm sorry, I think that's my fault."

Chapter 24

John had been right about the church venue. The stone slab floor made for noisy footsteps. The generous lighting was all fixed to the capitals of the pillars flanking the seating, resulting in strange angles. The stage area was backed by a row of plywood flats which hid the rudimentary dressing room spaces, no doors, just a pair of three sided oversized cubicles with a wardrobe rail each and an assortment of chairs that had been deemed no longer suitable for the public. John found that, although the venue had managed to come up with a pair of stagehands, there was no lighting or sound technician. The 'control room' consisted of an old, and noisy, scaffolding access tower at the rear of the seating. With a sigh, John set about assembling the set, focussing the lighting, rigging the company's additional effects and distributing the costumes and props to the so called dressing rooms.

Rummaging through the old church cupboards he managed to find and put into use a simple cue light system which would enable him to alert the stagehands when scene changes were needed. He experimented with the art centre's sound system, which seemed to be largely the abandoned equipment from its days as a church, with some column speakers on some of the pillars and an old fashioned mixer-amplifier with rotary knobs. He connected the company's rehearsal tape deck to this and was surprised and pleased when the lash up worked so that at least there would still be sound cues in the show. He would just have to live with the lack of quality.

He was nearly finished and had sent the local crew to fetch some flats to make wing masking from a store they said was just round the corner, when the cast began to arrive, Bob and Bobbie first, then Laurence and Hugh and eventually Penelope and Nicole.

"Hooray." Laurence greeted them sarcastically, "For a moment there I was worried that Penny's pink Rolls Royce hadn't made it."

"Penelope," she said flatly, tired after the long journey.

"Whatever." Laurence was dismissive. "Wait till you see the luxurious dressing rooms, you girls."

John joined them.

"Sadly Laurence is right, it's a bit make do and mend. The up side is that you haven't far to go for quick changes, the downside is you're going to have to be very quiet backstage and we aren't going to be able to have much light on."

Penelope, who had taken a swift look at the facilities, said "Where are the loos?"

"There's one, and I mean just the one, through that door." He pointed to a low arched doorway guarded by a heavy studded door in the wall behind the flats alongside the crude dressing rooms.

Hugh walked to it and opened it. There was an audible creak. Beyond the smallest possible lobby a modern door hid a toilet cubicle. Somehow the lobby also housed a tiny sink with a single cold tap.

"All mod cons," Hugh remarked. "We aren't going to be able to use this during the performance, too much noise."

"Really, how noisy do you intend to be?" asked Bobbie with an innocent air.

"Anyway," said John, "This is what we've got to work with this week. I guess we just treat it like we did all those schools."

"I guess we treat it with the contempt it deserves," said Laurence.

"I've got the locals bringing in some flats as wing masking, but you might want to try out a few lines. I'm sure you've noticed the acoustics are... well let's say challenging."

Laurence turned and gave a sharp single clap of his hands. The sound echoed around the old church predictably.

"Maybe it will be better when there's an audience in," he said, unconvincingly.

"It would need to be a heck of a lot. Are we expecting many?" Hugh asked.

John shook his head. "It's not looking a good week. Anyway are you all checked in to your digs?"

There were several murmurings, from which he gathered that most of them had come straight to the venue.

"Off you go then. There's no size changes to the setting, as it happens, so usual half hour call.. or earlier if you want to do warm up. There's no stage door, so you're coming in through the main entrance, same as the audience. Don't be late."

Nicole said, "I'll just get my other case from Penelope's car." and went out with the others. She returned with a small case, her main luggage having come with John in the truck. "Is there anything I can do?"

"I'd grab a chair and a space for yourself in the so called dressing room and mark your territory with something if I were you, this week is going to be just like going back to schools."

"Oh dear. Still, are our digs all right?"

"Ours are," he hesitated, "just about OK. I haven't heard anything from the early arrivers about the rest of the company, they're all together again, so we'll hear something from someone if there are any complaints."

As they spoke the church's old West door opened with a crash and the local stage crew came through carrying a pair of black flats. The timber frames were darkened with age and the black painted canvas flapped loosely. Under John's direction they positioned these either side of the stage area to produce some sort of wing masking.

"Well it's never going to mask properly, but at least we've tried," he said to Nicole. "Let's go and have our tea." And with a 'thank you' to the crew, and a brief discussion and a 'see you in an hour or two' with the volunteer lady in the little box office kiosk just inside the West door, they got into the truck and John drove to the nearby hotel he had booked them in to. There wasn't much to encourage them on the outside. He had chosen it because its car parking could accommodate the seven and a half ton truck for the week and it was within easy walking distance of the arts centre. Otherwise it had a dowdy, even run-down appearance, an impression which was not limited to the outside, for the hall carpets were worn and threadbare and the décor elderly and drab. No-one seemed to be using the small TV lounge off the hall, and the dining room was dark and deserted. John rang the desk bell and the owner appeared, wiping his hands on a grimy flowered apron, evidently in the process of preparing the evening meal. John checked that they would be able to eat before they needed to go to the theatre, and they went upstairs to their room, watched by the owner, whose doubtful expression made it clear that he didn't believe the 'Mr and Mrs' fiction John had checked in under.

The room was rather small, revelled in a loud abstract patterned wallpaper that had been applied in the seventies, and an equally loud plumbing system that seemed to be serving the whole hotel as the random noises started up unexpectedly when you were nowhere near the bathroom.

John had appropriated the dressing table for paperwork, but he hastily moved this aside so Nicole had somewhere to balance her case. She looked round.

"I'm glad noise doesn't keep me awake," she said, as a brief clanking came from a pipe.

"Sorry. We don't seem to have got the Ritz exactly."

She nodded, unpacking and hanging clothes in the cheap, if trendy, chipboard wardrobe.

"I don't think we'll be lounging around in here anyway, if you want to rehearse with Laurence, and, I've just discovered, I need to go back to the Theatre Wagon offices one day to collect some things..."

"That's ever such a long way, will you manage it there and back in the day?"

"It will be fine, if I set off early in the morning I'll be back before the show."

Nicole was quiet. She wanted to offer to come with him to keep him company, but a burst of naughty thought involving Laurence made her anticipate being able to choose that day for their one-to-one rehearsal, knowing that they would not be interrupted.

Back at the venue after an adequate meal John went through his pre-show checks and Nicole went into the dressing room area. Other members of the cast arrived piecemeal. No-one seemed to have any specific complaints about the cast digs, but no-one seemed very keen on them either. He could hear the cast moving about and talking to each other through the plywood flats as he loitered in the auditorium. There was no real foyer, though some attempt had been made to screen the entrance from the seating with ply faced shuttering style panelling. The audience had the luxury of some blatantly modern plasterboard enclosed toilets, which it soon became evident were not soundproof, for once members of the audience started to arrive the sound of flushing and filling cisterns was noticeable in at least the rear half of the seating area.

"Just like being back at the hotel," John muttered to himself.

He made his way backstage to visit the cast. There were no doors to knock on and he made a discreet 'are you decent' enquiry as he approached the girl's cubicle. He got an affirmative answer, and when he went into their space he noticed that Penelope was at least dressed, though the back of her first costume was undone and it tended to slip off her shoulder.

"Everyone coping with the situation?" he enquired.

There were some nods. Penelope had a table space near the outer end of one side wall of the cubicle, Bobbie the opposite side. Nicole had chosen an inner corner, from where she was looking at John with those doe like eyes she sometimes made.

"Oh, Penelope, you left this card behind at the last venue." He held out the good luck card, and was starting to reach past her to put it on the folding table that served as a dressing table when she stopped holding the shoulders of her costume, which slipped down slightly revealingly, and took the card from him. She looked very directly into his eyes and said; "Thank you, but I don't think I really want it," looked at it briefly and threw it onto the table.

John thought the reaction a bit strange, but nodded to Nicole and went next door to the men's space. Laurence, Hugh and Bob, who'd overheard his query to the girls said, "Yes thank you." and he returned to front of house.

The space inside the door that served as a foyer was only very thinly populated. He asked the woman behind the crude box office how many they were expecting.

"It's quite good tonight," she told him, "there's over thirty booked."

John had a dawning realisation that the expectations of this arts centre were very limited, and decided not to tell the cast. He felt this would be adding insult to the injury already happening to them. He went backstage again and told the cast to start on time by Hugh's watch, which was lying on the dressing room table, and seemed to show pretty much the same time as his, then he made his way to his scaffolding tower control room to await the start. There was an element of gamble in this, for front of house might not have got all the audience seated, but in the lack of any means of communication between the building's house staff and himself, or between him and the dressing rooms, he decided to take unilateral action. He was glad he went into position early for it was soon very clear that the tower creaked and squeaked loudly when he climbed it. Even after arriving at the top and perching himself on one plank facing the lighting desk and sound equipment balanced on another, he found that small movements caused mechanical noises from the tower that were rather audible, and certainly would be during the show. He resigned himself to sitting very still through the performance.

At about the appointed start time he could see movement behind the loose material of the side masking flats he'd had put in place, and, checking his watch, he slowly faded down the floodlights that acted as houselights over the seating. He was glad to hide the audience in the gloom for it was a poor house, with huge gaps of empty stacking chairs between the people.

The poor house was probably not the cause of the poor performance that night. In the absence of the nervous excitement that a full house generates to a cast there is often a falling off of energy. But this was not it. First night in a new town sometimes causes a weary show due to the tiredness from driving. But this was not it. What John deduced was that the company, having been encouraged to believe that the show was booked into 'proper' theatres, was discouraged by this poor apology for a venue, by the inadequate facilities, and just maybe too by the poor turnout once they were aware of it.

Lines were fluffed. Cues were not picked up quickly. Performances were stiff and mechanical. The disease spread through the cast with Laurence and Penelope both going through the actions on a sort of auto-pilot. The lesser roles suffered as a result, with perhaps only Hugh making the extra effort needed to try to lift the show. John's half time lecture to the cast in the interval failed to solve the problem and even seemed to raise resentment levels, although there was no doubt that they all knew that what he was saying was perfectly true.

He was glad when the whole thing was over and he could shut down the power and take Nicole back to their hotel while the rest wandered off into the dark, sulky and disappointed with the night.

"That was awful," said Nicole, when they were back in their room.

John was making them coffee with the room's kettle and cups, and wishing that the cups were bigger, and that there were more little sachets of coffee, sugar and milk.

"Well, at least there weren't too many there to see it," he commiserated. "I'm afraid the rest of the week isn't going to be much better by the looks of things. I'll ring the office in the morning and tell them what's going on, but I can't see what they can do about it. I don't honestly think that us going out leaflet dropping in the local streets would make much difference to the audience, and that was probably the main problem."

When he rang from their room in the morning Nicole could tell his prediction had been right. She heard him telling Alison about the venue, and then repeating the tale to Nick once he was transferred. Although she could only hear what John was saying she guessed that Nick was passing the responsibility of keeping the standard up to John.

"It's very unfair," she told him when he had hung up. "Nick's passing the buck to you to try to make things better, while he just sits in his office and does nothing."

John shrugged. "It was ever thus. That's why he pays me so much."

Nicole looked surprised, then realised he was being sarcastic.

The second night was similar to the first. John had managed to quieten his tower a bit by squirting the joints with WD40 and putting a couple of tightly tied sash lines across to hold the bits more firmly. Much as he disliked having to walk through the auditorium to the control point he changed the start procedure so he told the cast to 'go' by visiting the dressing rooms, and then returning to the tower to take the houselights out as a cue for them.

The cast still lacked pace, drive or energy. He'd tried a pep talk at the half, but the miserable conditions still seemed insurmountable.

On Wednesday morning in the gloom of pre-dawn he drove the truck out of the hotel car park and set off to the company's base. Nicole watched the flat roof of the truck pass under the window of their room in the grey light. She felt a naughty thrill, for this was the day, because of John's scheduled absence, that she and Laurence were to rehearse at the arts centre. She'd been vague about their plans for the day with John through a feeling of guilt at what she was thinking of as a date.

For John the long drive ended at the company office where he loaded a few pieces of furniture that had been acquired to replace parts of the set that Nick hadn't felt worked very well

225

during the very first week, a large quantity of posters and leaflets for up coming venues, and additional stocks of programmes which the printers had been slow producing. He discussed the company morale with Nick, and the way it had been affected this week, but Nick had no advice to offer, having himself slipped back into his earlier disinterested vagueness.

John was back on the road returning to the current venue before lunchtime, following a brief visit to his flat, where he checked that all was well and sifted the pile of junk mail on the shelf in the hall, picking out a couple of bills. He started back to the venue, stopping at a roadside burger van for a quick meal and a break on the way.

The arts centre was one that was open every day, though the reason for this was very unclear. A volunteer unlocked the building at ten each morning, and then a rota of such people sat in the kiosk by the door dealing with the very occasional enquiry there or answering, perhaps one or two phone calls a day. Laurence had called for Nicole at her hotel, and together they had walked to the venue. She was flattered by his attention, excited by being taught by someone she saw as a famous name, and eager to be in his company anyway.

In truth they had very few scenes together, but, with a dog-eared copy of the script in hand he led her through several scenes she had with other members of the company. She quickly discovered that he could learn lines very quickly, an asset from his TV soap work, so the typewritten script was put aside by him very soon. He gave her a refresher course on breathing, which, she was excited to find, involved him standing behind her and pressing his hand on her diaphragm. She had no doubt that he was taking every opportunity to make physical contact. There was a thrill in this, and she wondered whether he was attracted to her enough to want her to become more than just a pupil, a thought that filled her with guilt when she remembered John.

Laurence was a great believer in 'pointing' lines. He played his leading role, as he had done his soap part, very much in the style of one of the old famous greats of the theatre. He wished to dominate the stage at all times so that whether he was speaking or not the audience's eyes were drawn to him. For Nicole, in her minor parts, he was recommending a simple vocal trick which wasn't usually a major part of drama school teaching in the modern day. Pointing simply involved, he explained to her, inserting an almost imperceptible pause before a word or phrase to give it emphasis. They tried the technique with several of her lines. Nicole realised that Laurence was correct, that she could draw some attention to her unimportant lines by this, and become more than just a background to the action. She considered whether this was something that Nick or the scriptwriters might actually welcome from the selection of serving girls and passers-by in the street that made up the mass of her appearances in the play, but was sufficiently in awe of Laurence's ideas to accept his suggestions above any others.

She and Laurence had moved on to using some of his scenes with Penelope as exercises by mid-afternoon. Nicole had been delighted by Laurence's suggestion that they do this as the love interest between the two leads gave her an opportunity or excuse to get close to him. She wondered hopefully whether this had been in his mind too.

At the cast digs Hugh had become restless. He had been out briefly in the morning and bought the paper, but had now read this virtually from cover to cover, and was staring morosely at the adverts for escort agencies and lonely hearts on the last few pages. He roused himself, found his coat, and went out. With no particular aim in view he wandered toward the arts centre. Actors who were temporarily in strange towns frequently explored little more than the streets between their digs and the venue, and this week had not been one that had encouraged him to hunt out any of the city's attractions. They were, in any case, lodged very much in the suburbs, and the city centre itself was a considerable bus ride from the digs. He opened the arts centre's door and went in, saying hello to the volunteer manning the desk. He asked the woman about the sales for that night, getting an assurance that sales were picking up, a phrase he guessed probably meant nearly half a house in this venue.

"Some of your cast are rehearsing through there," the woman told him.

Hugh bought a cup of tea from her and wandered idly into the gloom of the seating facing the performance space.

With concern, rather than shock, he saw Nicole, with her arms wrapped tightly around Laurence's neck, they were kissing. The pair were unaware of Hugh, and he discreetly withdrew and drank his tea in the foyer area. Had he stayed he might have heard the actor telling Nicole that for a stage kiss you had to work out whose head was to be downstage, and, naturally, explaining that this had to be the lead actor's. As it was Hugh made assumptions that worried him. He was more aware of the possible complications of fall-outs between partners in small companies than most. He had seen it happen in big film unit groups, with the most unpleasant results. Because he was an inveterate people watcher he considered the likely outcomes more than his fellow company members might have done. He knew John was away in the truck fetching some replacement props and furniture and assumed that the couple he had seen were making the most of his absence. He was undecided what to do.

Nicole listened to Laurence's teachings, but both of them knew that the kiss had been more than acting schooling or rehearsal. Both had been quietly engineering the situation. Now Nicole clung more tightly round Laurence's neck and the kiss became real. Hugh would have had no doubts had he stayed watching a little longer.

Parking the truck at the hotel John went to their room and was slightly surprised not to find Nicole there. He'd envisaged her sitting in solitary isolation, awaiting his return. In many ways he was quite pleased that the girl had gone out and about in his absence. He had no wish for her to be hanging around waiting for him, she already suffered enough of that on get-ins and get-outs he felt, and the vague concern at the back of his mind about the possible future of their relationship had been growing as the weeks had gone by.

At the cast digs Penelope slumped on the bed in a manner that her mother would have described as most un-lady-like. She was wearied by the show this week, wearied by the venue and its make do and mend style when she had hoped for at least some small provincial theatre, rather than a barely converted church.

She sighed and made ready to go to the arts centre for the show. As she walked along the road to the venue she was joined by John coming from parking at his hotel.

"Hi Penelope," he greeted her.

She felt a flutter of excitement. As they walked she'd be alone with him, not in some cosy social location, but at least away, for a few precious minutes, from the rest of the cast or from a pub full of people. Could she attract his attention? She threw off her gloom and said hello to him as cheerfully, and she hoped winningly, as she could. They walked side by side.

"Is there any news from the offices?" she asked him.

"Well I talked to Nick about this week's venue, obviously," John told her, "and I don't think there's anything he can do about it. We'll all just have to sit it out I'm afraid. Chin up." And he touched her gently under her chin. She grabbed his wrist as he took his hand away and clutched at his fingers. They stopped walking.

"I'm sure you'll do everything you can for us," she said, looking almost pleadingly into his eyes.

"Hey. Don't get upset. It's only for this week," and he hugged her. She put her arms round him and held on, trying to make the moment last and looking up at him. He bent and kissed her. He'd intended a swift peck of friendship, but Penelope's desire and his feelings of attraction for the young actress combined to make the moment a drawn out sexual embrace.

"I'm sorry," she said when they separated, "I didn't mean..."

"It's OK." And he put his hand on her bottom and gently guided her in the direction of the arts centre.

Chapter 25

They prepared in their various ways for the performance much as usual; John pre-show checking and climbing and descending the scaffolding tower while the cast donned their first costumes and their make-up in the ad-hoc dressing rooms behind the set.

Hugh was quiet in his cramped corner of the men's cubicle, still contemplating what he had seen. Bob and Bobbie both provided the bulk of the small-talk, discussing their day in the centre of the city where they had made the rounds of the shops, without, it seemed, actually buying anything. Laurence silently pondered his day with Nicole, hoping that the messages of attraction he thought he had received from her would continue. Nicole was quiet, as she mostly was, hoping that Laurence really was attracted to her, and wondering about how upset John would be. Penelope was in a whirl of excitement at the possibility that John might be won over to her, but unable to talk about her feelings to anyone.

John was in a brown study about the situation. He felt his attraction to Penelope growing, perhaps more as a result of the kiss in the street that afternoon than it might have done otherwise. He knew that she was more mature in attitude, more confident, more likely to deal with rejection than Nicole, and he worried about Nicole being hurt if he were to break off their relationship. But, he kept telling himself, the relationship was one founded on his having taken pity on the girl. Maybe her attraction to him was just that of a victim to a rescuer, for he had rescued her from the landlady. He formed an image of Nicole as a little stray puppy that he had taken in. And that image made him feel responsible. He felt he could not face the pathetic reproachful look her wide frightened eyes might give him. But if there was a chance for him and Penelope....

He went backstage to give the half hour call.

Penelope, humming happily to herself, sneaked a look at the

audience through a narrow gap in the stage masking and froze in horror. For there, in the third row, was Cynthia. Penelope had not expected, or invited her one time friend to attend, and certainly not to attend at this, one of the smallest and least prestigious venues they were playing. It was unexpected. It was surprising. Most of all it was embarrassing. To be seen, after all her over-enthusiastic aggrandisement of this tour in her letter to Cynthia, playing a run-down arts centre on city outskirts to a less than full house was humiliating. She drew back from the gap, fearful of being seen, and dreading the coming hours of performance under Cynthia's scrutiny. There was only one thing for it, brazen it out and give the performance of her life.. but the rest of the cast were so disinterested this week, she must try to gee them up.

Back in the girls dressing cubicle she realised how much of an uphill struggle that might be. Through the canvas wall to the boys room she could hear a low conversation that clearly indicated that the men were considering this, and the other performances yet to come in this place, a bind and a duty. "We could be down the pub if it wasn't for this," someone said. In her own room Bobbie was dressing mechanically, still talking about her day's activities. Nicole was deep in thought, which Penelope was sure was nothing much to do with the performance coming up. Penelope couldn't believe that Nicole had any foreknowledge of what she hoped would be an affair between herself and John. She had some slight sympathy for the girl, but her own desires overrode this. She hoped that the girl would buck up for the show.

"We'll have to try harder than we have been tonight," she said. "It's a bit better audience, they deserve something for turning up to this dump."

The others looked at her, but no fire of enthusiasm lit their faces.

"Oh come on everyone, please," she begged, just as John

appeared giving the calls. "Tell them they've got to do their best," she turned and said to him.

"I hope they always do," he said, and winked at the other two girls. Hugh stuck his head round the end of the piece of scenery that separated the dressing spaces.

"Of course we do. Just sometimes the situation here distracts us," he said, and looked hard at Nicole, who, puzzled for a moment, guessed he must have gained some inkling of the growing relationship with Laurence she was nurturing, and looked down at the litter of make-up, brushes and combs on the table, blushing.

'How could Hugh know anything about what she and Laurence had been doing?' she wondered. 'Oh God! Laurence has been bragging to him,' she thought.

"Why are you so keen to give this dead and alive hole a good show?" Bobbie was asking Penelope.

"I don't know, I just think that they've paid and they shouldn't be penalised because the venue is so awful," she lied.

"I reckon they know what the venue is like already." Bob said from the next cubicle.

"Anyway," John stopped them, "hush, lots of quiet now. The house is open, and whatever the audience is like they shouldn't hear you bitching about the place." He paused and looked appraisingly at Penelope, "She's right though. Try to rise above the venue." And with that he was gone again.

Penelope's lack of success in encouraging her fellow thespians caused her to fear the worst for the performance in front of Cynthia. She dreaded the condescending comments that would follow and the glee with which her former friend would be relaying the details of the evening's performance to fellow acquaintances and even, perhaps, to her family. A cold chill of fear like the worst sort of stage-fright came over her. She went next door to the men's dressing room.

"Laurence," she said softly. He looked up. "Come out here, I've got to talk to you."

Laurence was surprised, but rose and stepped out of the enclosing flattage. He thought it was just possible that Penelope wanted to encourage him to pursue Nicole harder to clear the way for Penelope to win John, for Laurence's mind was very much on Nicole after the afternoon with her.

Penelope dragged him a little away from the entrances to the dressing rooms and began to whisper urgently. Briefly she explained the presence of her former friend in the house. She begged him to strive, with her, to lift the performance out of the lassitude that it was currently in.

Laurence was wryly amused by the situation, and indulged in a little banter, centred around a 'what's in it for me' approach, before offering "I'll see what I can do with the performance if you promise to work harder at winning over John."

Penelope was so anxious that it didn't occur to her at that moment to question how he knew of her efforts with John, or why he would be interested, or to consider the peculiar request.

In any case the show was due to start.

An unpromising venue, in the midst of an uninspired week of residency by a small company with no sympathy for the theatre or its audience, stage managed by someone who had no interest in the show and was tired out by driving a long distance back and forth to collect from the office, with a cast whose internal relationships were a mixed up mess of secret feelings was hardly the springboard for a memorable performance. Yet, unexpectedly, from the moment the crude floodlight houselights faded down and the stage lights came up and the first line was spoken the show took on a frisson that it had never had before.

John, wedged uncomfortably on the scaffolding tower, was startled; deciding, quite wrongly, that Penelope's pleas to the company had been successful, and wondering what she had said to them backstage to cause this transformation.

Penelope played her lead part with an intensity she had never previously given the role.

Laurence, partly due to the promise he had made, but largely because he would never allow anyone else to have prominence over him in a performance in the way that Penelope's performance tonight threatened to, commanded the stage in all the scenes he had.

Nicole, putting all the hints and tips that Laurence had offered that day into action, was suddenly a confident and competent supporting actress, as she made an effort to impress Laurence.

Infected by this unaccustomed effort by the others Hugh, Bob and Bobbie upped their games in the remaining minor supporting roles.

So far at this venue the audiences had been as apathetic as the cast. Tonight the show grabbed their attention and even John, with his personal dismissive attitude to classics, could see the way the public were held.

On stage, if she tried, Penelope could see through the glare of the ill positioned stage lighting on the pillars to where Cynthia sat. She had started the show in her C row seat in what might have been thought to be a slump, with her arms folded, no anticipation in her posture. Of course, thought Penelope, Cynthia would never slump. She was just not welcoming to the performance. As the first scene or two ran, however, she could be seen to sit more upright, and even to lean attentively forward slightly. By the interval Penelope felt that she might have got away with the performance in her erstwhile friend's presence. Mentally she thanked her lucky stars that the other members of the cast had risen to the occasion. She thought it was her appeal to them that had worked the miracle, not realising the various self-interests that had come into play to sway them.

By the fire sequence the audience was enthralled enough that the basic flickering lighting effects and enactment of panic by the cast even raised an unprecedented round of applause.

Once the piece concluded and the cast took their bows John went backstage to say a genuine 'well done' to them.

Back in civilian clothes and with make-up wiped off the cast began to leave the venue, gathering in a couple of little groups of two or three in the drab foyer ready to go out into the night and return to the digs. John had turned off all the power and took Nicole by the arm as they all left. Outside a figure emerged from the shadow caused by the gaps in the street-lighting.

"Penelope!" the figure exclaimed as she came out of the foyer door, "You were wonderful. But what a deadly place to have to do your little show."

Penelope had known the encounter with Cynthia was unavoidable and tolerated the gushing from her, though it spoilt the happy high that a good show for once had given her. The others walked away, leaving her to make small talk with her snobbish friend. Penelope looked wistfully and with jealousy at John's departing back as he led Nicole away. A little way down the road he looked back over his shoulder and grinned at her before carrying on into the darkness.

"Proper theatres for the next week," John told the cast before the show on the following Saturday night as they prepared.

"Do you know either of them?" Hugh asked. John's long

background made him the first person to seek venue information from in Hugh's mind.

"The first one's a real Victorian red plush and gilt place. The second half of the week is a converted cinema, which apparently used to do variety back in the day. Both mill towns of course, and not all that far apart, well, thirty or forty miles over the moors. But don't forget," he turned to include the whole cast, "it's a very long way from here to the first one, so leave plenty of time for the journey."

There were some nods, and Laurence, reaching behind his neck to fasten the collar stud on his costume, said "Have we ever let you down?"

He looked meaningfully at Laurence and then said, "Just a friendly word of advice, that's all," adding formally, "Ladies and gentlemen this is your half hour call, half an hour please." And he left.

Penelope watched him go, still with yearning. She mentally scolded herself for feelings that were not unlike a schoolgirl crush.

The show had never again reached the dizzy heights of the night of Cynthia's attendance, and that outstanding performance had come too late in the week for favourable reports of it to have lifted the box office much. The last house was barely over half full, and the empty seats seemed a fitting end to the week.

Chapter 26

John whistled to himself as he drove the laden truck over the bleak moorland roads towards the next venue. He remembered this theatre from a few years previously, when he had toured into there with a basic, box set, comedy. He was looking forward to the return to a proper theatre, with adequate facilities and a resident professional crew. He stopped whistling and snorted to himself at the thought of the professional crew. Dour mill town men who made extra money by working the shows that came in. He rather liked their dry humour, their ability to watch the greatest and most lavish show and comment afterwards, 'Ay, it were all reet.' They would not sneer at the minimal scenic offering he was touring, or attempt snobbish analysis of the worthiness of the piece. Indeed it was a racing certainty that they would probably establish the timings on the first night and vanish to the bar whenever they were not required, re-appearing with utter reliability about thirty seconds before they were next needed. He knew these sorts of crews, the mixture of late middle aged or even elderly men who'd been in this one same theatre as casual labour since their youth, interspersed with an occasional youngster, whose future could be seen in the men he was working alongside. These days the casual wages were more valuable than ever, for while once it would have represented a few extra pints in the bar it now probably provided the stage hand's household with a buffer against the steady creep of closing mills and similar manufacturing businesses.

His mind wandered from the venue to his little cast, and particularly to Nicole. He was sure that she had detected his growing fancy for Penelope, and he felt guilty. For the past few nights, since his day away at the offices in fact, there had been a distance between them that he had not quite been able to bridge. Unsure as to how she had discovered his change from near hatred to a fixation on the show's leading lady he had tried several things to reassure the girl, taking Nicole out to meals, and even using the truck for a trip to the countryside. Nicole had been grateful, but even more quiet and withdrawn than usual, and he had the impression that she was endlessly upset. She slept now with her back to him even after they had made love, and when he had kissed her as he left that morning to drive to this venue he'd thought there was an impression of damp saltiness as if she had been crying. Though Penelope and he had done nothing, he worried guiltily at the thought that they had, or both wanted to.

The long miles rolled by as he pondered what to do about the girl. He couldn't push her away, it would, he thought, cause her too much upset. But he became more and more sure that she was not his 'forever' match. Penelope was a different matter. Despite all that had gone between them in the early weeks of the school tour he knew now that he wanted her. Whether she felt the same was a mystery to him. From time to time he had sensed brief flashes of something mutual, but was this enough to let him upset little Nicole on a chance?

The get in and fit up at the theatre went exactly as he had anticipated. He was greeted at the loading doors with bluff friendliness, and a stage manager who said, "Welcome aboard. It's John isn't it?"

The stage door keeper also remembered him. 'All stage door keepers remember everyone', thought John as he allocated dressing rooms ready for the man to dole out keys as the cast arrived.

John's warning about the travelling distance had clearly gone home to the cast, for one by one their cars began to arrive. Bob and Bobbie were first, reporting in before going to the digs to check in not long after John had taken a brief break from the fit up to take his and Nicole's bags to their hotel and register. Laurence's Lancia followed, just in time for him to be standing waiting for Penelope's arrival. Actually he was waiting for Nicole's arrival, but despite opening the door for her to get out and giving her a huge smile of welcome he disguised this by the now regular, in house comments, using the worn 'Lady Penelope' joke and adding, "Is the car blushing, or has it gone pink with the effort of getting here, Penny?"

Penelope used one of her snootier put down looks and refrained from answering. She even failed to correct him with a sharp 'Penelope' as she habitually did. She was still grateful for his efforts on the night of Cynthia's attendance, but she disliked the banter. She noticed that Nicole laughed too much at the quip, and couldn't take her eyes off him. Maybe this week would be the week when she could prise John away from Nicole.

Once the show was lit and ready for the evening performance, and the cast had all stood on stage and admired the ornate auditorium and clapped their hands or uttered sharp vocal yells to appreciate how good the acoustics were, John took Nicole to their hotel. The décor was old, warm and redolent of a high class gentleman's club. It was, Nicole decided, just the sort of place John would have chosen. It somehow matched the Victorian plush and gilt ambience of the theatre and she saw now that his taste in such things was probably older, even more old-fashioned, and in some ways more mature than hers. Another little bit of distancing found its way between them. Politely she made unconvincing suitable admiring comments as they went to their room.

As they arrived at the stage door for the performance the cast felt, for the first time, that they were being properly treated by the venue. The contrast with the past week was marked. From the rather off-hand 'hello' of volunteer box office staff they had moved to a proper doorkeeper who greeted each of them as he handed them their dressing room key.

"Good evening Miss Carson. Settled into your digs all right? Here's your key."

"Mr Drover. Good evening. Your key sir."

Nicole, unused to this level of attention, as her previous experience of real theatres had only seen her as an anonymous member of an ensemble, was almost overwhelmed by, "Good evening Miss Wade..." and wanted to rush off excitedly and tell Laurence. She thought sadly that she had no real wish to rush off and tell John. Earlier in the day he had shown her which of the many dressing rooms he had allocated to her and she had stood at the door studying it, before asking

"Who's 'Max Accom'?"

And John had replied

"Haven't you heard of Max Accom? He was one of the great music hall artists. In those days they painted the artist's name on the door of their dressing room. He used lots of dressing rooms in lots of theatres."

She had looked at him doubtfully, till he had laughed, and admitted the wording stood for 'maximum accommodation'. Their relationship had suffered enough for her to be a little annoyed by his pulling her leg like this at a time when she was worried about what to say to him anyway.

Sales were good, even if they were playing the first half of the week, and over the show relay system the cast could hear the comforting murmur of a house slowly filling. John's backstage calls came through with the clockwork regularity that inspires confidence and the performance was slick and professional, if not inspired like the one in the middle of last week.

From his place in the prompt corner John saw that, now they were back in a 'proper' venue, the cast had returned to watching each other. At least, he told himself, Laurence is watching Nicole when he isn't on, and she is watching him. He assumed she was studying his techniques following their 'lesson' while he had been away, and that Laurence was checking that she'd taken his advice on board. There was no doubt that the girl's performances had been lifted, by something, from the mundane level at the start of the tour.

Meanwhile John watched Penelope from his corner. Was it his imagination, or wishful thinking, that made him believe that she gave a slight exaggeration to the swing of her hips whenever the blocking put her onto his side of the stage and that she seemed to make eye contact whenever she could deliver a line in his direction. He decided it was wishful thinking. There it was though, a hint of the overt sexuality of his ex wife Melanie which he could not ignore.

The performance was followed by one of those tedious social functions that some theatres impose on their visiting companies, at which members of the 'supporters' club', whose annual subscription has gained them discounted tickets for a first night, mingle with any local dignitaries who've attended and expect to be able to meet the performers. In this town there seemed to have been quite a turn out of VIPs, and the clink and glitter of chains of office was keeping pace with the chatter and the clink of the glasses at the function when the cast, having changed into their own clothes and removed make-up, found their way to the circle bar where the party was.

Laurence and Hugh were both centres of small groups of attention due to their past TV work, though Hugh's assembly was noticeably composed of older people. Penelope acquired a little following due to her lead role. Bob, Bobbie and Nicole, all mainly ignored, loitered close to John, nursing their free drinks, and waiting for the moment when they could escape. Since the Mayor seemed in no mood to depart they resigned themselves to a long delay.

Nicole pulled on John's sleeve nervously. She said quietly, almost in a whisper, "I've got to talk to you."

John, who had his gaze fixed on Penelope, and only half heard the girl, completely failed to pick up the urgency in her tone, answering casually, "Oh yes?"

"It's really important."

He looked down at her, clinging to his sleeve, but looking straight at Laurence as she did so. Laurence looked back through the small sea of audience heads and smiled at her. He nodded, encouragingly, as if to say 'Go on', but John didn't see this either.

"I can't tell you here."

"Mmm?" John was still concentrating his attention on Penelope, who seemed to have begun to lose patience with the local 'supporters' and was making obvious, but ignored, efforts to wrap up the stilted conversation. John was half way across the gap between them, intending to rescue her, when his mind slowly registered Nicole's tone of voice. Mid step towards Penelope he suddenly thought 'Oh god, she's pregnant!' and half turned back to her. He heard Penelope say, with relief, to her surrounding captors "Ah, here's John, the company manager." as he stopped, no more than a pace or two away from either of the girls, and looked back and forth, from Nicole to Penelope.

Duty told him to go back to Nicole, particularly given what he feared, but his heart wanted to support Penelope. It was Laurence, his voice carrying through the throng, who inadvertently rescued John by saying to the dignitaries, "... and you should meet Nicole, one of the up and coming actresses we are lucky enough to have in the company." He reached out an encouraging arm to the girl, who instantly stepped toward him and was swallowed by the group.

Relieved of his duty, if not of the worry that had settled on him with a chill of fear, John joined Penelope's group and she quickly pulled him towards her and put an arm round him so they faced her interrogators together.

The function thinned and dispersed as these things do till the house manager and the cast were left alone among tables full of empty glasses and the wreckage of the buffet.

"Thank you," he said briefly. "That went very well. Go out by the stage door please." And he made for his office.

The company trooped wearily backstage and out into the autumn night, handing back dressing room keys to the stage doorkeeper and reforming their groups as they set off for digs. Nicole and Laurence exchanged a look, and she shook her head, saying to him "Tonight, I promise," as she left with John. John, who had been arm in arm with Penelope all the way through the last part of the function and had not let go as they wended their way to the stage door, released her now. She turned to him, and for an instant Hugh thought that the two were going to kiss, right there, in front of Nicole, but they parted and John took Nicole off toward their hotel amid the 'good-night's and 'see you tomorrow's.

They walked silently all the way to their room in the hotel, where she pulled away from him and stood with her back to the room door as if wishing to escape.

"What's the matter then?" he asked her gently.

She began to cry. Just wet tears running down her face silently. He stepped toward her but she turned aside and muttered 'No, No'.

"It will be all right," he tried to reassure her, "we can sort it out. You just decide what you want to do."

"I have decided," she sniffed. "I know what I want to do, but it's not fair on you and I didn't mean to hurt you, and I didn't mean it to happen and I'm so sorry..."

John tried to guess what she had decided. Was she sorry that she wanted to get rid of a child and thought he might have wanted her to keep it? Was she sorry that she was going to keep it and that he would have to pay... Oh hell, how much was she going to try to get from him? Did she want him to marry her, and if so did he really want to marry her under shotgun conditions like these? Or at all? And did this all scupper the fledgling relationship with Penelope? An ice cold fear of all these possibilities made his stomach feel tense. With certainty he knew that the pain he had felt at the parting from Melanie was coming back again, for he was sure that whatever decision Nicole had come to it would part him from Penelope permanently. Why did these angst ridden conversations always take place late at night when everyone involved was tired? He blamed himself for succumbing to the flattering temptation the little actress had offered on that first night. He blamed himself for not insisting on finding her new digs of her own. He mentally cursed the situation.

He sat on the bed and patted a place beside him. Reluctantly she came over to sit next to him and looked pathetically at him with a face wet with tears. It was a familiar situation between them, and he thought how foolish he had been to have slipped into a relationship founded on the 'lost puppy' appeal of the girl's pathetic looks.

"I really am sorry," she said again.

"Tell me what you've decided," he said encouragingly.

"I didn't want to hurt you, you've been so good and kind to me, and I told Laurence so, but he thought it would be best to make a clean break."

John looked confused.

"So I said I'd move to the cast digs with him tomorrow.... But I'll sleep in the chair tonight if you like, and I'll pay my share for the next couple of days till we move on, and I'm so sorry.. "

she gabbled, and for some moments John failed to put the tale together. When he did an intense feeling of relief came over him as he suddenly, and in one moment, was freed from a dread which, although it had only been with him for an hour or so, had frightened him more than anything he could remember. Not only that but now there was the clear prospect of being able to be with Penelope and, if he understood what the girl was saying, a guilt free way of parting from Nicole.

He flung his arms round her in an uncharacteristic way, kissing her tear stained face and reassuring her, or perhaps mostly himself, that everything was all right. Relief and delight on both their parts once it was all sorted out, had them laughing hysterically at the misunderstanding about pregnancy and rekindled some passion that had been on hold for a while, and, both thinking of someone else, they made love for the last time.

* * *

Nearly forty miles away, on the outskirts of the town the show would play next, a teenage youth revved the engine of his elderly Ford Capri in a lock-up garage behind a row of houses. He had bought it cheap in a back street, retuned its old engine, resprayed some of the bodywork and added some stick-on stripes.

A window slid up and a pyjama clad head and shoulders emerged shouting "Shut the f—k up with that bloody car!" before the window slammed again.

Jason shrugged, muttered a curse, turned the ignition off and locked up before going back into the house his father had yelled from. Tomorrow he would fit the extra spotlamps he had bought and then... well the next night he'd go cruising and pick up some girls. He had no doubts about the pulling power of the car with the opposite sex.

* * *

246

In her digs Penelope tossed and turned on her bed. Usually she revelled in first night parties like the one she'd just attended, but this one had merely fed her sexual frustration. John had come to her, and put his arm around her, even if he had dithered over leaving Nicole's side, but the sensation of his closeness had been eradicated by the separation to different digs. Mrs Bray's advice to 'go out there and get him' seemed to be taking a long time to come about. Part of her wanted to get up, march round to his hotel, and confront him with a stark 'me or her' choice. She wouldn't do it, she knew, because there was always the chance that he might yet choose Nicole, despite all the signs she could read.

In the morning she got the landlady to make her a packed lunch, and drove out onto the moors. She'd wanted to take this opportunity to look at the countryside, and she thought that being away and invisible might tease John a little. The little car ground its way up and down the hills till she was miles from the city, from the theatre and from the rest of the cast.

Nicole moved her cases out of the hotel, and Laurence collected them in his car. John lent in to him through the driver's window as Nicole put the last bag in the boot.

"If you muck her about I will hunt you down and make you wish you'd never been born," he whispered in the actor's ear.

"My God, you do really mean that don't you?" said Laurence, completely taken aback by this forcefulness coming from John.

John went round to where Nicole was starting to get into the passenger seat and kissed her gently. Then he shut the car door for her and walked into the hotel without looking back. There was a lump in his throat that he didn't want to admit to.

On the moor Penelope pulled off the minor road she had taken onto a flat patch of grass. She took her sandwiches and climbed to the top of a low bank that allowed her to see over the countryside. There she sat on the grass and scanned the view, quietly eating her lunch and soaking up the autumn sunshine. She was contented for the first time in weeks. If she tried she could be confident and believe that all seemed to be going her way at last. Very occasionally the swish of a car passing on the road reminded her that there were other people about, but for the most part she was alone with her thoughts. And her thoughts were, of course, of John. She hadn't quite hooked him yet, but she knew he was pulling on the line. She smiled to herself at the angling analogy, day-dreaming of the two of them on a riverbank. In the back of her mind she knew that was not likely with John, and changed the mental scenario to theatre settings. Somehow these all seemed to be dusty and dark, and as the sun sank she became chilly, roused herself, and went back to the car.

It stood beside the road like an ice-cream van, all pink and out of place in the countryside. She got in, started the engine and turned the car round on the grass, back towards the industrial town. As she set off there was a sudden clank, an asthmatic wheeze, and the engine cut out completely. Surprised, and very concerned, she tried to start it, but though the engine turned and turned there was no life in it.

Penelope fumbled at the unfamiliar lever under the dashboard and managed to open the bonnet. Standing it on the prop she peered into the engine compartment. There was no point really. Not only did she not have the faintest idea what to do, she also had no tools or spares. She was marooned, miles from civilisation and, she consulted her tiny watch, squinting at it to be sure, due back at the theatre within the next couple of hours.

She stood by the tarmac, now cursing the quiet of the back road she had taken, and waiting for a passing motorist. A few cars passed, but though she waved both arms in the air at them frantically they swept past quickly in a sizzle of tyre noise. It was quite half an hour before a van, travelling away from where she needed to go, screeched to halt and backed up towards her. She was nervous of the stranger, but the driver was a polite, middle aged man, who looked at her car for her, agreed that it had broken down and there was no immediately obvious reason, and took her to the nearest garage about ten miles away.

At the theatre the cast drifted in, piecemeal, as usual. John had been at the venue all afternoon. He had gone looking for Penelope, making quiet enquiries as to where she was when he had chanced to meet Bob and Bobbie in the street, but they only knew that she had driven off on her own somewhere. John was a bit saddened by this news, as he'd been hoping to see her to reassure himself of the exact situation. No, that wasn't right, he thought, he'd been hoping to see her because he fancied her like mad and wanted to be with her, and to tell her so.

Making the best of a bad job he busied himself readying everything for the evening performance, and sorting a backlog of paperwork for the office and making sure the ledger with the cast wages details in was ready for him to fill in when he did the pay for them at the next venue in a couple of days' time. Hugh and John were both old timers enough to use the jargon expression for wages payout, and John smiled to himself anticipating Hugh shouting the news that 'the ghost is walking' to his fellow actors when the time came. He locked the wages cash away in his briefcase in the dressing room that was serving as the company office and tucked the show's petty cash into his inside jacket pocket, before locking the room and wandering front of house for a cup of tea from the foyer bar. The theatre's manager met him there by chance and they chatted, initially about the first night audience's reactions, but eventually about the world of theatre in general, finding acquaintances in common. One cup of tea turned into two, and then three, and the foyer was starting to wake up ready to receive the night's customers and the half was approaching when John made his excuses and returned through the pass door to the backstage world. He checked that the local technicians had everything ready, phoned to the front of house to say 'Your house' so they could start to let the public into the auditorium, and pressed the switch on the stage manager's desk, leaning toward the mic to say, "Ladies and gentlemen this is you half hour call, half an hour please." Tasks completed he strolled to the stage door to chat to the stage door keeper.

"That Miss Carson of yours is cutting it a bit fine tonight," the man said.

"Why, when did she come in?" John asked, surprised.

"Nah, she ain't in yet," the man offered.

John was now worried. Penelope had a long record of late arrival when they had been touring schools, but her arrivals in the proper theatres, even in the arts centres, had been exemplary. He hurried to the dressing rooms, knocking on the various doors, and asking, 'Has anyone seen Penelope?'

No-one had, and no-one knew where she had driven off to earlier. Two immediate concerns worried John, 'had she had an accident?' and 'had she run off for some reason?' He could think of no reason for her to run off, so immediately began to assume the worst. It was a sign of his infatuation that 'what about the show?' came as an unusually low priority in his thoughts.

Back at the stage door he used the payphone to ring the cast's digs' landlords, but they had not seen her either. He went out into the street and looked up and down the road.

Slowly he began to consider the show. The small company had never given any consideration to understudies but now he tried to work out whether there was any way to juggle the parts to do a performance. He thought that both Bobbie and Nicole possibly knew enough of the part to muddle through, Nicole probably more so since she and Laurence had used some of the script as practice pieces, but both of them appeared as so many different characters in so many scenes due to the doubling that he was at a loss to work out the logistics. He was not used to being indecisive, but his mind was full of concern for Penelope.

Time was running out, he would have to make a decision soon. Even now it might be late to get a stand-in into the costume and gear them up to appear, and he didn't want the audience to sit around waiting for a late start if substitutions were to be made. He looked at the road again. Just fifteen minutes to curtain up, and still no sign of her. He headed for the dressing room corridor. Nicole, could she pull it off? It would have to be Nicole.

The stage doorkeeper's shout after him of, "Hold hard Mr Mason, here she is!" stopped him in his tracks. He turned back. And then it was a flurry of breathless greeting, and 'Are you all right' as she ran into the theatre and he grabbed her in his arms and hugged her. He'd been so concerned that there had been an accident that all the relief broke down the barriers and he kissed her urgently and desperately in the little backstage lobby and she kissed him back.

"Can you pay my cab?" she gasped, and, snatching the key the door keeper held out to her, ran for her dressing room.

"Twenty-five quid mate," said the driver, "But she said there might be something in it for me if I managed to get her here on time. Did I?"

John pulled the petty cash from his jacket pocket and peeled off four ten pound notes. It was a lot, but he was enormously relieved and grateful. He pressed the money into the driver's hand, said 'thank you' and headed for the dressing rooms.

"Blimey, thanks mate." The man looked at the door keeper. "Let me know if there's any more jobs like that will yer?"

As he went along the corridor John banged on Bobbie and Nicole's doors, pausing just long enough to poke his head in uninvited and say "Come and help Penelope get changed and made up."

The performance was straightforward after that. He did feel obliged to put a note about the girl's late arrival in the show log, but was pleased to be able to mark the 'time-up' as perfectly normal despite that, even if the first scene did seem a bit breathless.

Scraps of information about the cause of the upset found their way to him during the performance and he gathered that her car had broken down.

After the show he made a point of thanking the other actresses for their help, and then knocked on Penelope's dressing room door.

"Come in."

She had recovered her composure and was sitting in front of the mirror getting rid of make-up.

"I'm sorry I was late," she said a bit formally, as a cast member to a company manager might.

He shut the door and went over and knelt beside her chair.

"I was so worried that something had happened to you."

"Weren't you worried about the show?" she asked, surprised.

"No. Yes. Well not as much," he confessed, unusually confused. "What did happen?"

"Let's go somewhere and I'll tell you all about it," she suggested.

He looked at his watch saying, "I reckon it will have to be Indian or Chinese at this time of night if you want to eat."

Penelope realised how hungry she was. She knew nothing about

Indian restaurant food, but her meal with Hugh gave her confidence to suggest Chinese, so not long after they found a Chinese restaurant that was still serving and were seated opposite each other at a small table while the waiter brought menus, cutlery, no chopsticks she was pleased to see, and glasses. It was smaller and somehow homelier than the restaurant she'd been to with Hugh, though she spotted major similarities. The décor was largely red with gold tassels, and the same litter of spilt rice was evident on tables that people had left, but which had not yet been cleared.

John ignored the menu, reached across the table and took both her hands in his.

"Tell me," he said.

She studied his worried expression. "I'm all right really, but it was a close thing getting back to the theatre... Oh! Did someone pay the taxi driver? He really did his best."

John assured her that he had, and she began to tell him all about her day. They were interrupted by the waiter taking their order, and then further through her tale by the arrival of their food. Penelope had chosen the same as she had had with Hugh, in order to look as though she knew what things were on the menu. John had picked a couple of dishes she had never heard of. They ate for some time in silence before she resumed her account.

"What does the garage think is wrong with it?" he asked when she had explained about having to get the breakdown truck to where she had parked.

"I didn't understand it, he said something about timing belts or chains or something, and that he wouldn't know if it had wrecked anything inside till he took it apart. Anyway he says it will be several days, because of getting the bits." She ate another mouthful. "I don't know if I can afford it. It sounded very expensive. After that I had to call for a cab, he let me borrow the garage phone, and that took ages to arrive. I'm afraid I promised the driver a tip if he got me to the theatre in time, but I didn't actually have enough on me for the fare. The meter kept clicking up and up... Oh I'll have to pay you back, how much did you give him?"

"Don't worry about that. At the moment it's come out of petty cash. I suppose the transport tomorrow for the cast will have to be re-sorted."

She pointed her fork at him. "Trust you. Thinking about the show again."

He grinned. "It might not be so difficult actually. Laurence is obviously going to take Nicole now." She nodded, and tried to detect how he felt about that. He went on, "I guess Hugh might be able to hitch a ride with the florin, I think their car is big enough, and I'm sure Laurence and Nicole won't really want another passenger with them."

She was surprised to see him grin indulgently at this. She'd expected some obvious resentment but saw none. Coyly she said, "And what about me?"

"Unofficially you could come in the truck with me... not that there's any company rule against it but..."

"But you didn't let Nicole, and now you don't really think you should take me?"

"Look, the reason Nicole didn't get a lift in the truck was that it means a lot of waiting around, either while a get-in or get out goes on or while we are rigging, or both. Tomorrow we're all going to be having to get a move on because of the timescale. I'll leave with the truck immediately after the get-out and travel overnight. I've arranged to be let in to my hotel in the middle of the night, but the get in starts at the theatre at half past eight, so it will be a short sleep. You'll remember that we're playing under another show, so we do matinees and they do evenings. I've only really got the morning to rig and so on."

She nodded. She remembered seeing this on the schedule.

"So if you come with me you'll be hanging around waiting..."

"I don't mind hanging around," she said, grabbing his hand across the table. "Please."

"...and I don't expect your digs would let you in in the middle of the night."

There was an shy silence for a minute while they both sat and thought about the alternative, neither daring to believe the possibility that the other might want the same thing.

Penelope remembered bits of Mrs Bray's advice. It was contradictory. She paraphrased it to herself as 'make yourself hard to get', and 'go out there and get him'. She decided to be brave.

"Perhaps I could share with you."

John squeezed her hand tightly, thrilled by the prospect.

"Perhaps you could," he said.

They looked at each other.

"You do know I want to, don't you?" she said after a moment.

"Well that makes two of us then."

"'Us' has a nice sound."

The Chinese waiters were very patient. The other diners had all gone and most of the tables had been reset for the following day before Penelope and John left. Walking to his hotel they held hands, dawdled, and stopped occasionally in doorways, kissing.

Chapter 27

When she woke in the morning Penelope was surprised that John was not there. There was a brief moment of concern, during which she wondered if he had just looked on last night as a one-night-stand, surely not after what had happened, before she found a note from John beside the bed. 'Sorting the truck, meet you in the dining room for breakfast. x'

She made herself a coffee with the small kettle and odd sachets the hotel provided and luxuriated in a shower in the en-suite, thinking how much she preferred this to the hurried washing in shared bathrooms in the digs she and rest of the cast had been inhabiting, where your wash, bath or shower was always punctuated by occasional rattles of the doorknob as others tried the door to see if the room was vacant. She wrapped herself in a towel and sat on the bed looking out of the window as she dried her hair with the room's drier.

It was hardly an attractive view, as the room overlooked the car park, but she could see the flat featureless roof of the hired truck the company's set travelled in, and caught occasional sight of John, apparently checking tyre pressures with a hand held gauge of some sort. After a while she watched as he climbed into the cab and seemed to crank something between the seats, before climbing out and pulling so that the whole cab tipped forward to reveal the engine buried below it. She saw him pour oil from a gallon tin into the engine, stopping every so often to check the level with the dipstick and then adding more. Eventually he seemed to be satisfied with the level and replaced the cap, pushed on the front of the cab, so it tipped back to its normal horizontal position, and wound the hidden handle inside before stowing the oilcan. He wiped his hands on a towel, locked the cab doors and turned back toward the hotel.

Penelope hurried to dress in yesterday's clothes and hastened downstairs, where, by the dining room, she was greeted with "Good morning Mrs Mason. Breakfast? This way," by one of the staff. She thought she could detect a certain amusement in the man's voice, and realised that 'Mrs Mason' was being used to match what was probably on the hotel's register, and more that the man saw straight through it, especially as 'Mrs Mason' was suddenly a different person. Despite this there was something about 'Mrs Mason' that she rather liked, and she was sitting, pensively, day-dreaming about the possibility, when John came in, fresh from scrubbing his hands in one of the cloakrooms.

He pecked her lightly on the lips and sat, saying "Have you ordered yet?"

They ate their breakfasts in near silence. Then Penelope said, "I'll have to go and collect my things from the digs."

"All under control. Hugh's dropping your cases off here in an hour or so."

Penelope felt grateful that she would not have to face the rest of the company too immediately, though she was unsure whether she really wanted Hugh packing her clothes. The close proximity of small scale and theatre in education backstage facilities meant that he'd probably caught a glimpse of her underwear occasionally, but there was something unsettling about the idea of him handling it.

"Bobbie's done your packing for you." John told her, as if he had been reading her mind.

"You really do organise everything don't you?"

"Sorry, force of habit."

"I think it's lovely of you. I'm so ashamed of how I behaved."

He shrugged. "I thought some pretty rude things about you during the schools tour."

"I expect you were entitled think rude things," she laughed and added, "or was it a different sort of rude things you thought about?"

He wagged an admonishing finger at her across the breakfast table.

"What shall we do today, once my cases arrive?" she asked. "No, not that," as she saw his expression. "I want to do something really normal, like...." she thought for a second, "Can we go to the cinema?"

They checked out of the hotel.

Hugh came with Penelope's bags as promised, just as they did so, looking shrewdly at the pair of them as John loaded the cases into the hollow emptiness of the truck alongside his.

"Be good you two," said Hugh as John slammed the roller shutter and motored the tail-gate lift back into place.

"What are you up to today?" John asked him.

"I shall lounge around, conserving my energy to give another one of my scintillating performances tonight," Hugh joked. "I might even read the paper."

They parted, parked the truck by the theatre's loading door, and Penelope and John spent the afternoon in the close, warm darkness of a local cinema.

The evening show, the last performance at this theatre, ran well. The audience was a good one, and the cast seemed to have been reinvigorated after the previous night's worry about Penelope's late arrival. Possibly the news that Nicole had left John and Penny had taken up with him without any obvious animosity had calmed a concern that had been in the background for a while. Hugh certainly felt relief that, so far as he could see, the situation among the cast had resettled amicably. Bob said to Bobbie, "Well, the promised cat fight didn't happen." And she shushed him, looking around to make sure no-one else in the cast had heard the remark.

The 'thank you for the show' conversation between the theatre's manager and John was, as is always the case when the company manager is desperate to start the get-out, a hasty one, but none the less clearly genuine on the part of the local man.

The cast packed their hand props and their costumes and cleared their own personal bags from the dressing rooms before leaving in a succession of 'Good night's' and 'See you tomorrow's' which had John repeating "Don't forget it's a two-thirty show tomorrow, so the half is at one-fifty-five... don't be late," several times.

Penelope was last out of the dressing rooms and he saw her hesitating on the upstage edge of the stage. He went over to her and guided her carefully through the apparent mêlée of scenery being dismantled and flying bars coming in for lighting to be de-rigged to a seat in 'B' row in the auditorium, safely away from the work.

She sat in the stalls and watched as the show came to pieces and was stacked against a wall ready to be loaded. She watched as a bar flew in and John removed the lens, fire effect disc and weighty lantern that were used for the burning house scene, and packed these in a padded case. She watched as the wardrobe skips and rails came through from the dressing rooms and were stood by the dock door. She saw one of the local crew bringing front of house display boards through from the foyer to join the growing piles.

Then, as the last items were being piled up someone opened the dock doors and John went out to unlock the truck and drop the tailgate lift to a point somewhere about halfway between the load bed and the ground to act as a step during loading.

Penelope shivered as the night air came into the theatre, displacing the warm fug of the building's recently departed audience.

The local crew were quick and efficient loading, and John was soon in the back of the truck lashing scenic pieces to the sides. Once it was all done, and he'd made a swift but thorough check of all the areas, "An idiot check," he said..."to make sure we've got all our idiots." And the crew grinned at the well-worn joke.

There was a slightly secretive hand-over of envelopes of cash to the local stage manager to pay the crew, and then he collected Penelope and led her out to the truck.

Goodbyes were shouted, and the local SM told his crew, "Quiet, you'll have the bloody neighbours complaining again." then shook John's hand. "See you again sometime."

"See you again," John answered, and helped Penelope climb up into the cab. She managed it better than Nicole had, but he still made sure she was safely aboard. The dock doors were shut and exterior lights went out before he had walked round to the driver's side and climbed in.

He pulled a new tacho disc from the glove locker and opened the front of the device, rotated the cardboard disc to locate on the lugs and shut the tachograph.

"Belt on?" he asked, pulling at his own over his shoulder.

"Yes," she replied, and the wagon started, and pulled out into the night-time streets.

They wove through a network of roads till John turned them onto a cross country route towards their next theatre.

"I hadn't realised," she said as they drove, "I mean, there's so much happens when we acting types aren't there."

"Ah, the unsung heroes of the industry," he joked.

"No really, I mean it. I just didn't really know. They didn't show us any of the tech side at acting school, and in rep you just go home and leave them to it."

In the town they were heading for, Jason drove along the straight market place for the third time, flinging the Capri around the lamp-post that stood at one end too fast, so the tyres screamed and smoked, and then accelerating to the other end to repeat the reckless manoeuver round the tree that grew from the brick built box at the opposite end.

Two of his passengers squealed as loudly as his tyres. They were short skirted, over made-up, and more than slightly drunk. His friend, Matthew, who everyone called 'MK', was in the back seat with one of the girls, his head bent down slightly from the low roof over the rear of the Capri, encouraging Jason to push the old car harder.

Jason was aware, somewhere in the back of his mind, that three of his tyres were a bit worn, and that the remaining front one was a downright decrepit remould. He could feel a lack of control as he tried to perfect a doughnut around the lamp-post.

Amanda and Ginny shrieked again in the way they would have done on a fairground ride. They had been woozy with drink when they agreed to get into the car when the disco closed and had had several swigs from some vaguely identified bottles that now clinked on the floor as the car swayed about. They had mild worries about being so late home, and what each set of parents might say in the morning, for already it was the early hours, but the drink was subduing that concern.

Distantly, through the trees that bounded the parkland alongside the market place, Jason could see flashing blue lights approaching. He abandoned his doughnuts, and headed out of the town soberly and sedately. The girls' shrieks died down apart from some giggly squeaking from Ginny in the back with Matthew, protesting, not very much, at his hands wandering into her underwear.

Jason took the car onto a road leading out over the moors. As they came to the end of the streetlights he flicked the new switch on the bent metal bracket below the dashboard and the spotlights he had fitted blazed out ahead of them throwing trees and bushes both sides of the road into theatrically highlighted brightness against the black sky. He took his left hand off the steering wheel and put it on Amanda's knee, slowly moving it up her thigh and slipping it under the hem of her skirt. She moved her leg nearer to him till it touched the gear lever.

He felt a bump, which he assumed was a pothole. Thereafter he could feel a slight regular bumping from the steering wheel. It lessened if he drove faster. He wanted to drive fast anyway, that was what this car was for. He sped up.

In the truck John flicked the lights to main beam as they drove along the deserted road. There were narrow verges each side, dotted with bushes and, a little further from the road, beyond a steep sided ditch, occasional trees. The moorland road climbed up, and dipped down from time to time and the countryside was dark and mysterious outside the artificial illumination of the truck's headlights, which showed increasing numbers of stones, and then boulders on the far side of the ditches. Sometimes the boulders had rolled into the ditch and their grey masses gave a momentary wild impression of some creature waiting to jump out onto the road. Mostly the untamed landscape looked as though the glaciers had only just passed by and left these fallen lumps of rock, though they had been deposited millennia earlier.

John shifted gear up and down as the lorry struggled up, and ran more freely down the undulating hilly country road.

The lights showed occasional rabbits, nibbling the short grass on the narrow strip of verge between the road and the ditch, who paid no attention to the truck passing, or perhaps were frozen in fright at its approach.

"Oh look, rabbits!" Penelope exclaimed, when they swept past the first few. "I always wanted a rabbit when I was little."

"Didn't they let you have one?"

"Daddy was very sensible. I think he knew that I would probably lose interest. Anyway, I would have been upset if.. no when, it died, I expect."

"Does the likelihood of its eventual death stop you having a pet?"

"Maybe I don't want to get too close to anything or anyone in case."

"I promise you I'm not going to drop dead."

She reached across the cab to him, and he took his hand from the gear lever knob where it had been resting and held hers.

"I'm pleased about that," she said.

"So am I."

As they went down into one of the valleys the lights lit the road rising ahead of them. At the top of the rise the horizon showed against the black, moonless sky dotted with stars. The truck reached the bottom and began to climb. In the distance behind the crest shafts of light suddenly swept the skies like searchlights. They swung wildly from side to side.

"If they're headlights it must be a very twisty road coming up." said John, puzzled. He took his hand back, to change down, and then held the wheel with both hands as they ground up toward the strange display.

In the Capri Jason's wandering left hand had reached Amanda's knickers. His attention left the road and became fixed on sliding the tips of his fingers under the elastic. The car swerved back and forth from one side of the road to the other. Amanda, torn between drunken excitement and caution, gripped Jason's wrist. For a few moments neither of them was sure whether she intended to pull his hand away, or hold it in place to encourage him to further exploration of her groin.

Tension made Jason's foot press harder on the accelerator so as it crested the brow of the hill the swerving vehicle was speeding flat out and began a headlong plunge, toward the truck coming the other way.

In the Theatre Wagon truck John was blinded by the headlamps and extra spotlights of the zig-zagging Capri as it came over the rise and the angle changed down towards him. Instinctively he slowed slightly, dipped his own headlights and steered nearer to the verge. The car careered downhill towards them, its lights weaving back and forth as Jason failed to straighten it.

Penelope made a frightened noise. The two vehicles rushed at each other. Jason saw the danger too late and with one hand on the wheel swerved, oversteered because of the tiny racing style wheel he had fitted, over-corrected, and lost control as the front remoulded tyre, which had started to strip when Jason had felt the bump, shed the rest of its tread and burst, causing the back of the Capri to swing wildly toward the truck.

Blinded though he was by the lights, John saw the back end of the car coming towards them sideways. He turned more to the left and braked hard. The truck's nearside wheels left the road and began to cross the strip of verge. John and Penelope were bounced about in the cab. The end of the front bumper of the lorry caught the back end of the car. The impact spun the car round so it faced back the way it had come, showering the road with fragments of plastic from the rear light and some shards of metal. The truck's wheels, pushed further to the left by the blow despite its mass, slipped off the edge of the verge into the ditch. Shrubs and weeds lashed at the violently tilting windscreen as the truck which was now leaning into the ditch at forty-five degrees and sliding along it, the off-side two wheels still up on the grass with no real grip so the brakes were having no effect. The boulder that stopped them was one of the larger ones. It demolished the upright of the windscreen... which shattered, and came into the cab on Penelope's side.

In the car there was a fresh, urgent, outbreak of screaming from the girls. Ginny, drunkenly unaware of why, was cursing Matthew, who, reacting to the swerve and the impact had gripped the girl's breast tightly as he was flung forward. Amanda had seen the accident as a confusing swirl of lights, and felt the impact as a frightening change of rotational direction that had twisted her neck. Jason, who was terrified of the possible consequences of the incident realised he was now headed back to town and discovering that the car still ran, floored the accelerator and the Capri left the scene fish-tailing under excess power and a flat front tyre.

John was only slightly dazed from the bang on the head he had received from the driver's window as the truck tipped. He could see blurred impressions of the ditch and the rock through the crazed windscreen lit by the remaining headlight, but it was dark in the cab.

He struggled against the restraining seatbelt which was keeping him dangling on his seat on the uphill side of the cab.

"Penelope! Penelope! Are you all right?"

The silence panicked him. Flailing he managed to reach the switch on the courtesy light above the centre of the windscreen.

The dim light revealed John's worst nightmare. Penelope lay against the passenger side door with her head against the invading boulder. Frightened, he found the seatbelt release and pressed it, falling suddenly across the cab as it freed him. He scrambled about, partly on top of her, calling her.

Penelope was dead.

Epilogue

Bob and Bobbie sat among the other members of the cast in the pub near the stage door of the repertory theatre they were now working at. The lunchtime conversations carried on around them, but through the mêlée they heard someone talking about John.

"He was that bloke who was carrying on with two actresses out of his cast and killed one of them in a crash wasn't he?"

Bob butted in.

"He didn't kill anyone. The drunken lout of a boy racer killed her. And if you don't believe me look at the court case. The yob got sent down for it. And John wasn't two timing anyone either."

A brief lull. Then the first actor said,

"You weren't in that show, were you?"

"Yes, we were," Bob and Bobbie said together.

Bobbie added "And John's the best, the nicest, company manager you'll ever run across."

Bob looked at her, surprised by her vehemence, and had a faint, jealous, dawning of realisation.

"Well he might have been once, but I heard he's company manager on the tour of the revival of 'Chuzzlewit', and he's drinking his way round the circuit."

"I bet he's still the best at the job." Bobbie argued. "Anyway, with what happened I reckon he's got a right to drown his sorrows in a few drinks."